The Shadow Dweller Series
Volume One

J. C. Wilder

LTDBooks

Copyright © 2001 Lisa Hamilton
ISBN 1-55316-490-3
Published by LTDBooks
www.ltdbooks.com

One With the Hunger
Copyright © 1998 Lisa Hamilton

Retribution
Copyright © 1999 Lisa Hamilton

Previously published in electronic format by Dreams Unlimited.

Cover Art copyright © 2001 Emily Black

Published in Canada by LTDBooks, 200 North Service Road West, Unit 1, Suite 301, Oakville, ON L6M 2Y1 [www.ltdbooks.com]

National Library of Canada Cataloguing in Publication Data

Wilder, J. C., 1965-
    The shadow dweller series

ISBN 1-55316-490-3 (v. 1)--ISBN 1-55316-487-3 (v. 2)

    I. Title.

PS3623.I45S432001   813'.6   C2001-902-031-7

Contents

One With the Hunger

Dedication

For those who dare to dream...

Chapter 1

"I think you should take a lover."

Shai paused, her baked potato-filled fork poised in midair. She stared aghast across the table at her friend. "Excuse me?"

"Ohhh, yes," breathed Melanie, "tall, dark and handsome." She twirled a lock of icy blonde hair around her forefinger and fell back against her chair, a smile curving her full mouth. "And rich, of course."

"I think it's a wonderful idea, if I do say so myself." Vivian, the instigator of the conversation, leaned forward, her elbows on the pristine white tablecloth. The stub of a Spanish cigarillo burned between her fingers as she pointed at Shai. "Just what you need to get out of your rut." The rich smoke from the imported cigarette drifted lazily around her head then vanished, vanquished by the efficient air conditioning in the restaurant.

"I wasn't aware I was in a rut," Shai said pointedly.

Vivian rolled her beautiful blue eyes and looked at her as if she were, at the very least, a dimwitted child. "Well, of course you don't see it, dear, that's what your friends are for...to point out these things."

"Even if I don't ask you to," Shai muttered.

Erihn ignored her. "Why do you think we bought that outfit for your birthday?" She waved her speared shrimp in Shai's direction. "Vivian said we had to prime the pump, so to speak."

Shai glanced at the new clothes she wore. Granted, the clothing that had appeared in a beautifully wrapped package on her doorstep earlier in the afternoon weren't her normal cup of tea. The short, black velvet skirt, long-sleeved black silk blouse and brilliant emerald green silk jacket weren't bad. In fact, they looked lovely on her, she admitted shyly.

Before tonight she would never have dreamed of wearing such a revealing ensemble. She had to fight the urge to tug down the skimpy skirt every time she moved. She'd never worn anything in public that only covered her to mid-thigh - it simply wasn't proper. But it wasn't the clothing that worried her; it was the lingerie that had accompanied the gift.

"I'll bet she isn't wearing them," Jennifer, a dark-haired, sloe-eyed woman, speculated.

"Think so?" Vivian stubbed out her cigarette. "Enlighten us, little Shai. Are you wearing the naughty underwear Jen and I picked out?"

"That's rather personal." Shai stalled, setting down her fork with a clang before reaching for her wineglass. Inside the Irish crystal the deep burgundy resembled blood. In the dim lighting of the restaurant, the liquid glowed and shimmered as if lit from within.

She took a hesitant sip, her mind scrambling for an excuse for not wearing the deliciously sexy lingerie. Too small, maybe? No, Jennifer would see right through that one. Damn! She wished they'd not gone shopping together last week. She set her glass down once more.

Maybe she could say a panty raid had occurred while she was in the shower. Or armed guerillas had entered her apartment and stolen them at Uzi-point.

"Looks like you're right. She isn't wearing them." Melanie untangled her hair from her finger and returned her attention to her plate.

"I'm not sure why I put up with you guys," Shai grumbled. She picked up her fork and stuffed the now-cold bite of potato in her mouth, chewing as she glared at her four friends.

"Because we're family in every way that counts," Erihn answered matter-of-factly. "And you love us."

Jennifer grinned like a well-fed Cheshire cat. "That still doesn't answer the question. Are you wearing the naughty bits Viv and I bought for you?"

Shai felt the blush heating her cheeks. While she'd been delighted with the clothing her friends had picked out, the lingerie was intimidating for someone who'd religiously worn plain white cotton all her life.

The black lace demi-bra and matching thong had lain on the bed until the very last minute. As she was getting ready for the evening, she'd kept glancing at the lingerie, torn between her desire to don it and her wish that it would vanish into thin air. In the end, she'd relented.

Sitting in the trendy New York restaurant wearing an outfit and lingerie that would have cost her a week's pay, Shai felt truly free for the first time in her life. She shifted in her seat, her bottom bare against the black silk half-slip. The whisper of black-seamed thigh highs felt foreign and sexy against her skin.

"Yes, I am." She slapped her fork down on the table with a thump. "And I like it."

"Bravo, darling." Viv raised her glass in a mock salute.

"I suspected as much." Jennifer shrugged out of her black velvet bolero-style jacket to reveal gleaming porcelain skin and a tiny black leather bustier. "Maybe I should take another lover," she commented to no one in particular.

"Wore out Marcel already?" Melanie asked. She picked up her glass of wine and finished it off.

"That's the problem with men today," Vivian reached for a new cigarette from Melanie's pack, "no stamina."

Erihn swallowed a gasp as she ducked her head. Her face half-hidden by a wing of rich brown hair, she busied herself with digging a chunk of crabmeat out of a claw. "More ginseng? Powdered deer antler?"

"It would be hard for anyone to keep up with you, Viv dear. How many days a week do you go to the gym?" Melanie asked.

"Three." With a flick of a gold lighter, she lit a fresh cigarette. "I can crush a tin can between these thighs."

"Is *that* why you go through so many men? You crush them to death?" Melanie teased.

Shai glanced at Vivian. "And this is a good thing...how?"

"Maybe Viv is into recycling," chortled Erihn.

Vivian eyed Erihn's Rubenesque figure. "It wouldn't hurt you to go once in a while."

"Oh no, not me." Erihn caught the waitress' attention and waved her hand at the empty wine bottles to show that they needed another one. "What would I do with a man?"

A tender look entered Vivian's eyes. She reached over and brushed Erihn's hair away from her face. Her nimble fingers lightly traced the scar that marred the young woman's cheek.

A madman in Central Park had ended Erihn's budding modeling career seven years ago. In broad daylight, he'd grabbed her as she'd left a photo shoot. He'd kidnapped and terrorized her for three long, agonizing days before the police had caught up with him. She'd escaped with her life and a horrendous scar that would forever mar her face. But it wasn't the exterior scars that concerned her friends; it was the ones hidden deep inside they worried about. To this day, Erihn refused to speak of the incident that had forever changed her life.

"I think you're perfect the way you are," Vivian murmured.

Tears glittered in Erihn's deep brown eyes. "Thanks."

Shai felt the tears stinging her own eyes. This was why she loved these women. Because they were family in the ways that counted the most. They were there when they needed one another and even when they didn't. For the past two years, they'd laughed and cried together, sharing their lives as only they could with other women. In a silent toast to her friends, she picked up her glass and drank.

"Well, I for one have no desire to crush anything between these thighs," Jennifer spoke. "Anything that gets between these legs will sigh with pleasure...not pain." Shai choked on her wine. Without missing a beat, Jennifer pounded her on the back as she continued. "I haven't had any complaints yet."

"Nor will you ever, dear," Melanie said. She grinned as the waitress appeared with another bottle of burgundy. "Can you grab some of these here?" She waved her hand at the empty wine bottles that littered the table before returning her attention to her friends. "Of course, that doesn't fix the matter at hand."

"Which is?" Erihn asked.

"Finding a lover for Shai," Vivian frowned at the young woman. "Weren't you paying attention at all?

"Well, of course I was. I'm sitting right here."

Shai leaned back, the base of her wineglass hitting the plate with a chime of fine china. "How in the world did we get on this topic? Who says I need a lover anyway?"

"I did, dear." Vivian captured the bottle of burgundy before Melanie could help herself. She leaned around Erihn to fill Shai's glass and then her own. "It's your thirty-first birthday today and, in the two years I've known you, you've never mentioned a man once."

"So?"

"This needs to stop." Melanie liberated the bottle from Viv and filled her own glass. "Come to think about it, I've never heard you speak about any men. What's up with that?"

Shai picked up her glass and took a quick swallow. How in the world was she going to get out of this one gracefully? She set the glass on the table before she spoke. "Just because I don't need a man to make my life complete, does this make me a freak?"

"Yes," they all spoke in unison.

Shai rolled her eyes. "So much for woman's lib. It's lost on you guys. I don't see anything wrong with being alone."

"I do. It simply isn't natural." Jennifer leaned forward to pick up her case and extract a cigarette. "Take me, for example. I'm a very successful journalist and I'm not in a relationship. However," she dropped the case on the table, "I do have several gentlemen I can call to entertain me and take the edge off."

Shai blinked. "Take the edge off what?"

"Sex, dear." Vivian snared a crab claw off the platter in the center of the table and set to freeing the succulent white meat. "You know, to get your rocks off?"

"To get nailed," Jennifer returned, her tone wry.

"To poke the hole in the doughnut," Melanie chimed in.

"You *ladies* are so vulgar," Erihn spoke without heat.

Vivian grinned, "Thank you, little mouse." She popped the chunk of crab, dripping with butter, into her mouth.

"Oh, brother." Shai rolled her eyes again.

"You're a virgin," Melanie announced.

Silence reigned at the table as Shai found her friends hushed for the first time that evening. They watched her, their expressions ranging from doubt to wonder as they pondered this idea. She squirmed in her seat, uncomfortable with their questioning stares.

She wasn't a virgin...but she wasn't far from the mark either. In fact, Melanie's off-hand statement was a little too close for comfort. Hasty fumblings in college with a nearsighted computer major didn't make for a satisfied woman. After her somewhat anti-climactic experience, she'd decided that sex wasn't all it was cracked up to be, so she hadn't pursued it further. However, technically, she wasn't a virgin.

"I am not," she protested. "Just because I don't sleep with half of the New York Yankees..."

"I object." Vivian dipped another bit of crab into her container of drawn butter. "It was only the first baseman and the shortstop." A sensual throaty laugh escaped her. "And let me say, my dears, he was *anything* but short."

"Really?" exclaimed Melanie. "Do tell."

Vivian shifted in her seat. A soft smile played about her thin, red-painted lips. "He had this thing about biting my toes as he came." She shook her head. "Very strange, as I'd never seen that particular trick before. But he did have this amazing maneuver with..."

"Stop!" Erihn's hand came up to halt any further revelations, her cheeks crimson.

Jennifer reached for the wine. "That's a word that's never passed Vivian's lips."

"Oh, I don't know, the word *don't* might have been in front of that." Melanie cracked a lobster tail with a practiced flick of her wrist as the ladies dissolved into laughter.

Shai drained her wineglass. Her cheeks were hot and she just knew she was blushing to the roots of her already-red hair. She'd never understood how all of them had become friends over the years. They were all so different with very little in common.

She glanced at Vivian, stunning in her blue silk jacket and black leather pants. Her clothing, cultured accent and mannerisms screamed money. Divorced several times, Vivian was known for her outlandish lovers, her flouting of society's mores and her family's seemingly limitless supply of cash. She was lesser known for her charitable works with the homeless within New York City, but that was something she rarely spoke about. A stunning brunette with a wicked sense of humor, she moved in circles that Shai could only dream of.

Jennifer, physically, was almost Vivian's twin. Both had black hair, Jen's long and straight while Viv's was short and curly. Distinguished and elegant, Jennifer was one of the nations' top print journalists and Shai's co-worker at the *New York Times*. Jennifer was also one of the lucky three percent who made the big money at it. After writing a piece on a little known war in South America and winning a Pulitzer, the sky was the limit for her and she wrote her own ticket. Shai knew little about her background and Jennifer volunteered very little personal information.

Melanie was the vivacious one of the group. Blonde and a bit ditzy, she'd worked for a late night television talk show as the cue card girl. Her many appearances on television when the show's flamboyant host had picked on her during the show had given her entrée to commercials and soon she was headed to Hollywood to make her first movie. She dreamed of making it big in the movies and marrying Mel Gibson. While the Mel Gibson part was out, they all wished her well and supported her at every turn.

And then there was Erihn who was like none of them. She was a romance writer and a long-time friend of Jennifer's. Erihn and Shai had met when Shai, on her first assignment as a reporter, had been sent to interview her on the changing face of romance novels. Both women were almost painfully shy, but they'd hit if off immediately, becoming the best of friends.

But someone was missing.

"Where's Evie?" Shai asked.

Vivian shrugged and reached for a roll. "Maybe she got tied up?"

Melanie sighed. "Only if she's lucky."

"No. Don't tell me that white-bread man you're engaged to ties you up?" Jennifer drawled.

Erihn leaned forward; the candlelight flickered over the scar, making it softer, less apparent. Shai could practically see her jotting mental notes for yet another book.

"Only once." Melanie's creamy skin grew flushed and Shai couldn't tell if it was from the alcohol, conversation, or the memories of the event in question. "It was wonderful. Liberating, actually."

Vivian licked butter off her fingers and grinned at her blonde friend. "Isn't it just?"

Shai blinked. After all the years of outrageous conversations, she should be used to this kind of talk by now. But she wasn't and it made her uneasy. Sex was foreign to her and, in her mind, overrated. She picked up her wineglass and drained it yet again. She'd already had much more than she was used to drinking and tomorrow she'd pay the price.

"So, what's your ultimate sexual fantasy, Jennifer?" Erihn asked, her eyes bright with curiosity and far too much wine.

"Mmm," Jennifer paused, her lips screwed up in concentration. "I don't know." A wicked gleam entered her eyes. "How about handcuffed in the back of a police car? Cuffed to the dividing cage while Joe Police-guy frisks me with his really hard...baton."

Erihn and Melanie dissolved into laughter as Vivian smiled. "Been there, done that. His last name was Mathison from the Thirteenth precinct here in New York." She sighed and picked up her wineglass, her eyes growing dreamy. "And, oh my, what a baton he had."

"Okay." Jennifer stubbed out her cigarette, her tone challenging. "What's your ultimate fantasy, Viv dear, and don't be shy."

"Yet another word that's never been associated with Viv," Melanie laughed.

Vivian paused, her glass halfway to her mouth. Her expression turned whimsical. "Well, I can't honestly think of many things I fantasize about when, let's face it, I've lived most of them. I suppose, if I really had to come up with one, there is the bar wench fantasy, the Madame and slave fantasy, and the bad cop fantasy is *always* a good one..."

"Just one, Viv. You needn't recite your entire repertoire of tricks," grumbled Jennifer. She picked up the now-empty bottle of wine and waved it in the direction of the waitress.

"Hmm...Probably the saloon girl fantasy." Vivian shifted in her chair. "I'm working in a saloon in the old west as some trail riders come in. Three of them, I think. They order a drink as they eye me in my revealing peasant blouse." She traced her fingertips lightly over the suntanned skin showing between the lapels of her jacket. A sensual smile curved her lips as she began to lose herself in the fantasy.

"The tallest man's name is Stud Lonewolf and he's a sight for sore eyes. With long blond hair, dark blue eyes and pecs that would make a romance cover model cry with shame. As I set his drink in front of him, he grabs my wrist and pulls me into his lap." She shifted in her seat once more before crossing and re-crossing her legs. "I can tell it's been a long time since he's seen a real woman. He whispers in my ear all the wicked things he wants to do to me. As I lean back against his chest, he reaches up to untie my blouse and my breasts fall free. Callused fingers tease my nipples as his knee parts my thighs.

"His teeth nip my neck as one hand traces down my side, across my thighs to the bottom of my skirt. His hand on my skin causes goosebumps to break out. His fingers tear into my pantaloons to plunder my waiting flesh. Growing impatient, he reaches down with his free hand to unleash himself before lifting me to rub against his stiff rod. My eyes fly open at the sensation to realize that his two friends are watching me. As their eyes grow dark with lust, Stud impales me on his manhood."

Her voice changed pitch as she continued. "Soft groans escape my lips as his blond friend comes forward. His greedy lips suckle my breast as I twine my fingers in his hair. The third man comes over to take my other breast into his mouth as Stud forces me up and down...up and down. It's relentless. Just as I begin to reach my peak, he comes with a growl, deep inside of me.

"For a second, I'm disappointed. But, before I can draw breath, the blond cowboy grabs me around the waist and tosses me on the table, thighs spread. Releasing a cock that would do a horse proud, he shoves inside and begins thrusting. Pumping, pumping until screams claw my throat and I shatter into a million pieces in his arms."

Vivian slumped in her chair and fell silent. Her cheeks were flushed, a look of near satisfaction on her face.

Shai swallowed hard and reached for her wineglass. *Goodness...*

"What about the third guy?" Melanie asked, entranced.

Leave it to Melanie. Shai struggled not to choke on her wine.

Vivian picked up her napkin to fan her rosy cheeks. "Oh, him. I wait and nail him later."

Jennifer burst into laughter and slapped her palm on the table. "Bravo, dearest!"

Vivian grinned. "Too bad I only have a vibrator to go home to tonight. I'm feeling a bit frisky right now." She cast an appraising look around the restaurant as if to spy a willing victim.

"Amen, sister," Erihn whispered. She picked up her wine and gulped the remains.

Jennifer turned her dark eyes on Shai. "So tell us - what gets your panties in a bunch, my dear?"

Shai blinked. "My fantasies?"

Vivian gave a throaty laugh. "Why, of course. I have a feeling you aren't as pristine as you pretend to be." Her flashing blue eyes dared Shai to step up to the plate.

"Whoever said I was pristine?" Shai squeaked.

"No one, dear." Erihn patted her hand as if to soothe ruffled feathers.

Shai stared at her neglected dinner while four pairs of expectant eyes watched her. What did she do now?

She cleared her throat. "Well..." She hesitated before letting her eyes drift closed. "I'm lying in my bed. It's a hot summer night, like tonight. The drapes are moving in a faint breeze, but it's not strong enough to relieve the humidity that has me trapped in my bed. Restless, I kick at my covers as a shadow appears in the window. It's a man."

"*Who are you?*" *she whispered.*

"*You know who I am.*" *His voice was deep, sensual like the purr of a giant jungle cat. Ripples of awareness moved across her skin. Her nipples tightened beneath her simple cotton nightgown.*

"*Yes, I know who you are.*" *She sat upright in her bed and held out her hand in silent invitation to the dark figure in the window.*

"*What do you want from me?*" *he asked.*

"*Come to me.*"

"*You're inviting me in?*"

"*Yes,*" *she replied.*

"*Once I cross the threshold, there is no going back. Is this what you really want?*"

She rose to her knees, her gown clinging to her overheated skin. "*Yes, I want you, all of you.*"

His teeth gleamed in the darkness when he smiled. He stepped in through the window, onto her window seat, scattering soft pillows with his booted feet. He was very tall, much taller than her five foot four. He was dressed in all black - black jeans and a black T-shirt that stretched across his broad chest and shoulders. Black hair brushed his shoulders in a tumble of riotous curls.

Feverish blue eyes gleamed beneath heavy brows. His full sensual mouth curved in pleasure. "*I've come to give you your ultimate fantasy.*"

She gave a faint nod.

He held out his hand, tempting her to reach for the ecstasy he offered. Hesitant, she reached for him, and her breath caught as his warm fingers closed around hers. With a gentle tug, he urged her to her feet. Her gown swirled around her thighs as she moved toward him. A strong arm slipped around her waist as he gathered her close, his arousal evident against her lower stomach.

"*Tell me what you want,*" *he whispered against her skin. His lips moved over her neck, taking a nibble here, a taste there.*

"*Everything. Anything. I want every woman's fantasy.*" *She sighed as his mouth touched her ear, teasing the delicate lobe.*

His husky chuckle raised gooseflesh on her skin, "*I did your laundry and balanced your checkbook.*"

Shai opened her eyes to find her friends staring at her, their expressions ranging from wonder to outright amusement. Suddenly, Melanie and Erihn broke into shrieks of laughter.

Viv lifted her cigarette case, a soft smile tugging at her mouth. "Well, that's definitely a fantasy we know will never happen. Brava, my friend."

Jennifer shrugged. "Not true, Viv. It could happen with some men." She turned toward Shai. "Is that your fantasy? A tall dark stranger entering your bedroom in the dark of night? To make love to you until you can't think? To fulfill your darkest fantasies?"

"Sounds good to me." Erihn reached for her glass of water. Tears of mirth streaked her cheeks.

"I don't know." Shai shrugged. "If I knew I was perfectly safe?" She took another drink of wine. She knew she was half-past drunk now and careening her way into dangerous territory. For her to discuss her sexual fantasies was something she would never think of doing, ever. But here she was, sitting in a public restaurant drinking loads of wine and discussing intimacies with her friends.

A sudden streak of boldness shot through her and she sat forward, slamming her glass onto the table. "Sure? Why not? Who wouldn't want to have a dark handsome stranger take control of them, body and soul? To make love until they merge as one? To be worshipped with his body till the end of time?"

Jennifer nodded, a speculative gleam in her eyes. "Another one of my favorite fantasies."

Vivian nodded slowly. "As is mine." She raised her wineglass in Shai's direction. "Happy birthday, my friend. I think you just revealed more about yourself than you'll ever know."

Jennifer raised her glass. "And may your darkest fantasies come true, my dear Shai."

Shai laughed and raised her glass as Erihn followed suit.

"To fantasies," chimed in Melanie as they clinked their glasses and the occupants dissolved into laughter.

Shai raised her glass to her lips and the laughter caught in her throat when a shifting in the shadows snared her attention. She glanced over Melanie's head to stare into the darkest blue eyes she'd ever seen.

Prickles of awareness raced across her skin and her nipples tightened against the soft lace of her bra. Her mouth went dry. Surely he was a figment of her imagination. No mortal man could have eyes so dark, so ageless. So haunted.

He was, without a doubt, the most beautiful man she'd ever seen.

Piercing blue eyes shadowed by winged black brows. Black hair swept away from his high forehead to fall an inch below his shoulders in soft waves that her fingers ached to explore. Sharp features, high cheekbones and a patrician nose, saved from austere by his mouth. Full and sensual, it screamed of long, hot nights, rumpled silk sheets and musky sex.

It was the face of a fallen angel.

He was definitely not of this earthly plane.

Images came unbidden of the two of them in her wrought iron canopy bed. Sweat gleamed on skin as his hands stroked her overheated flesh seemingly everywhere at once. Her heart thundered in her chest as she imagined his lips on her stomach, leaving a damp trail as he moved toward her breast. His mouth closed over its aching tip and he suckled deeply as she arched off the bed toward him, wanting more of his dark magic. Her hands clinging to broad shoulders, her thighs opening to him, permitting access to the apex that wept only for this man. For his touch alone.

A whimper broke from her lips as sensation poured through her body. She jerked in her chair, her wineglass clattering against her plate as she bobbled it and blindly set it down. Her breath came in gasps, the unexpected arousal leaving her unsatisfied body throbbing in places she barely acknowledged even existed.

Erihn turned and frowned at her as Jennifer gave a delighted laugh and held her hands toward the stranger in greeting. "Are you okay?" Erihn whispered.

Shai was shaken as he broke eye contact, looking away from her to speak with Jennifer. She nodded, wondering if she really was okay.

What on earth was wrong with her? She'd never reacted like that to another human being in her life. She moved the wine out of reach and picked up her glass of water. No more alcohol for her, that was for sure.

The stranger's voice interrupted her musings. It was deep and resonant with a faint accent she couldn't place. A shiver zipped across her skin. Rich, like dark chocolate, fine aged brandy or velvet, it was a voice she could listen to for an eternity. She resisted the peculiar urge to swoon.

"I had business with Jacques, the owner here." He moved with the lethal grace of a big cat. He was unconsciously sexy. No mortal man should be able to move like that. It had to be illegal somewhere.

Pleasure curled in her stomach, sending waves of desire racing through her blood. Stop that. Time to sober up. Coffee, maybe? Yes, coffee, that would surely do the trick. She glanced around for their waitress who was nowhere in sight. Damn!

The stranger laughed and her toes curled with pleasure as her gaze was dragged back against her will.

He held Jennifer's hand and Shai struggled to quell the rush of jealousy as he brought it to his mouth. His smile was intimate, his gaze knowing as he brushed his mouth over her skin.

Jennifer laughed and pulled her hand away. "Quit trying to impress me, Val. You forget yourself."

He smiled easily, unabashed by Jennifer's rejection and Shai's heart gave a little flutter. This man was dangerous to her well-being and she knew, in that instant, nothing would ever be the same again.

He glanced around the table, his gaze coming to rest on her. His eyes glittered with a dark heat. "Indeed, I do. It's hard to remember myself when I am surrounded by such beauty." He tipped his head in her direction. The dim lights gleamed in his thick glossy black hair, giving it a bluish sheen.

Melanie gave an awkward twitter as Shai forced herself to look away.

"Is it?" quipped Vivian. Her eyes were fastened to the front of the stranger's pants. "Doesn't look like it to me, but give it some time." A catlike smile curved her mouth as she licked her lips.

He chuckled as he moved around the table to take Vivian's hand and kiss it also. He crouched beside her to murmur something into her ear as Viv pressed her ample breast against his chest and circled an arm around his shoulders, tangling those obscene red nails in his hair.

Shai's cheeks heated in the face of such a blatant attempt at seduction. She shifted her gaze, staring down at her plate while trying to ignore Vivian. She'd never been the kind of woman who attracted men easily. There were times when simply conversing with a man could bring on hives. She wished she could slip under the table and vanish in the face of her friend's easy sensuality.

The soft caress of a fingertip touched her cheek, bringing her head up. She glanced around. No one was even looking in her direction, let alone close enough to touch her.

"Shai." Jennifer's voice brought her attention back to the table. "I'd love for you to meet someone. This is Valentin and he's a very old and dear friend of mine." She waved her hand in his general direction. "Val, this is Shai Jordan, a much newer friend of mine."

Shai caught the amusement in Jennifer's voice and flushed. She tensed as the dark man untangled himself from Viv and moved toward her with his lazy grace. A richly embroidered vest hung open, displaying laces on his flowing white shirt. Open at the throat, it revealed the strong column of his throat melding into broad muscular shoulders. Black jeans clung to taut muscular thighs. A black belt with a plain gold buckle circled his waist and black boots encased his feet.

He captured her hand within his much larger one. Warmth surrounded before invading her chilled flesh. Strong fingers, artist's fingers, encircled hers as he slowly raised her hand toward his mouth. "*Enchanté.*" His breath teased the sensitized skin of her knuckles.

His lips were warm and dry, eliciting a shiver as his tongue touched the back of her hand. Carnal images crowded her mind as desire burned her like a wildfire. Before her eyes flashed images of this man in her bed, buried deep within her, burrowing into her very soul.

Val pulled away, his teeth shutting with a sharp click and Shai caught a glimpse of an emotion akin to shock racing across his face. Was he in pain?

"Are you okay?" she asked, startled when her voice came out husky.

He flashed her a picture perfect smile. "Better than I was before meeting you." He straightened smoothly, never releasing her hand. "Ladies, it has been a great pleasure seeing you, but I am afraid I have to run." He glanced down at Shai, his gaze capturing and holding hers easily. "Business does not await my personal pleasures." He gave her hand a gentle squeeze.

Vivian fairly purred her displeasure. "That's too bad, Val. It's been such a *long* time since we've seen each other. We're headed to the Pyramid after dinner. Maybe you can join us there?"

"Indeed, it has been a long time. If I can get away, it would be an honor to join you ladies this evening." His gaze never left Shai's as he raised her hand to his lips once again. "Until next we meet, little one." He kissed her hand a second time, his teeth brushing her skin before he released her. Turning, he headed toward the door, every woman's eye on him as he exited.

"Now *that* is a fantasy," Erihn announced into the silence.

"It seems our little Shai caught Val's eye," Jennifer commented.

"Lucky girl. I've been after him since he first appeared in New York about a year ago." Vivian's tone was sour. "Never even looked twice at me."

"I certainly wouldn't kick him out of bed," Melanie said.

"I wouldn't either," Shai, still feeling dazed, spoke through numb lips.

Vivian laughed, her pique apparently forgotten. "It's about damned time. A man to turn Shai's head. And what a man he is." She leaned closer to Shai. "Watch out, little one. Val is one of the sharks in the ocean of life," she paused. "Of course, that makes him all the more desirable." She raised her wineglass. "Here's to Shai and her deepest, darkest fantasies. Long may Val fill them...and a few other things."

"I don't..." Shai began, only to realize they were no longer listening to her. Shivers danced along her spine as she recalled his deep blue eyes and sinfully sexy mouth.

"Oh, what the hell...Here's to fantasies."

Chapter 2

Shai tumbled headfirst through her apartment door. Clinging to the doorknob, she skidded to a stop as her oversized purse banged into the coat tree, sending it crashing to the floor. She straightened and stared at it, her vision distorted as if she were underwater.

"Bummer."

Her voice sounded slurred and she giggled as she kicked the door shut with one foot. She started across the wood floor toward the darkness of her bedroom door. As she walked, she discarded her clothing in an uneven trail, marking her progress through the apartment. Her silk jacket landed on the arm of a chair, her purse a hill of soft leather in the middle of her living room. Next came her black skirt, a puddle of velvet in the hall.

As she neared the doorway, she noticed with alarm that the room was tilting. She reached out a hand to brace herself against the wall and keep herself upright.

"What the..." She glanced down at her feet. One high-heeled shoe was missing. She turned too fast only to send her head spinning and she staggered into the wall with a thud. "Oooof..." She squinted toward the hall, looking for the missing footwear. Her errant shoe lay tangled in her skirt.

"Too much effort." Turning, she stumbled through the door, losing her other shoe in the process. Her shirt slithered to the floor.

Her four-poster bed lay bathed in a pool of brilliant moonlight. The windows were wide open and a soft, humid breeze tugged at the heavy blue drapes. With a sigh of delight, Shai fell onto the bed, her body numb with drink and sensual intoxication. Her fingers curled into the crisp white sheets. Oh, how she loved her bed. It was the best bed in the world. Unbidden, an image of Val entered her mind. She groaned.

Val in her room.

In her bed.

In her.

She closed her eyes and grabbed a pillow to cradle it against her overheated body. Enough of that. Fantasies were one thing, but her reality was that a man like Val would never be interested in a boring, white-cotton woman like her.

She sighed into her pillow and scrunched her face deeper into the pristine cotton, willing her body to relax. Within seconds, she gave in to the demands too much alcohol had placed on her, and she fell asleep.

She looked like a whore.

The vampire settled on the windowsill, mere feet from the woman's sleeping form. A derisive smile curled his lips. Whore or not, she was even more exquisite than he'd ever imagined.

Thick red hair lay tumbled across her pillow in a river of curls. Dark lashes shadowed her cheeks, hiding eyes he knew were a brilliant green. A small, delicately shaped nose with a slight bump at the bridge as if it had been broken at one time. Her mouth was generous with a full lower lip and slightly thinner upper one. Her skin was the creamy delight of a redhead. Her throat was slender, marred only by a small scar at the base on the right side.

Perfection.

A black lace bra barely covered her breasts, full and round. He ached to touch them, to taste them. Her belly looked soft and inviting while her hips and upper thighs were covered by a silk half-slip. Naughty black nylons encased her thighs and lovely calves down to slender ankles and feet. A delicate gold ankle bracelet glittered in the moonlight.

He certainly appreciated her choice in underclothing. But he was surprised that a woman as conservative as Shai would dress like a seasoned harlot beneath her street clothes.

It would be so easy to kill her, he thought dispassionately. He knew exactly where to touch her slender throat and, in mere seconds, she'd be one of the dearly departed. Just another victim found dead in their bed in the city called New York.

He looked at his hands, his pale skin gleaming white in the moonlight. They didn't look like they were over nine hundred years old. Nine hundred years of murder, mayhem and blood. He stroked his chin. For Shai's sake, it would be more humane for her if he did kill her with his hands. Quick and efficient, no fuss no muss. No mortal would want to live through what he'd planned for her. But even when he'd been human, he hadn't been humane.

A mirthless smile curved his mouth.

Oh, how he wanted her. More now than the first time he'd laid eyes on her. Every year, the desire had grown stronger until he'd reached this breaking point. Sitting outside of her bedroom window watching her sleep, lusting after her yet unwilling to touch her.

Yet. Soon her time would come.

A faint, self-deprecating laugh escaped him.

She stirred in sleep, a frown marring the perfection of her face. As if she knew he was there, she turned her face and twisted her body away from his gaze as if to avoid him. The silk half-slip tightened, sliding up to reveal the tops of her stockings and the tiny black thong panties she wore.

The vampire's breath caught in his throat and a faint hiss of air escaped him. Her panties left nothing to the imagination. Moonlight gilded the perfection of her skin, the smooth slopes and tantalizing indentations.

Her backside was larger than considered fashionable by today's standards. But it was perfectly round and taut. He preferred his women to be shaped like women, not sticks with boobs. This beauty had something to hang onto, a backside that would fill his ample hands admirably.

He longed to slip in her window and grab her, pulling her against his raging erection. To bury himself in her softness until she cried. He pictured himself in bed with her, her body moving against him, her eyes sleepy with lust.

A growl escaped his throat.

With one last look at the sleeping woman, he turned away. Mortal women. They were the downfall of many a vampire. To meld with living flesh, breathing and crying out beneath him, on top of him, it didn't matter. It was an addiction and he was in serious need of a fix.

Weakness was weakness and it had to be either destroyed or appeased. He glanced back at her. It was rare that a mortal had reached him the way she did, the way she always had.

Just as her mother had many years before.

He bared his teeth. The moonlight seemed even more brilliant than it had been before. It was time to feed and feed he must. Clicking his jaw in frustration, the vampire caressed her one last time with his gaze. Moving with the near silence of one of the very old, he leapt from the window to the alley thirty feet below.

He landed with a gentle thud and straightened, checking to ensure his clothing was in perfect order before moving toward the mouth of the alley and the darkened streets beyond.

Shai's time would come, as would her companions. He knew that for a certainty. Unfortunately her friends were average, not exceptional like her. If they'd been exceptional, he might have spared them. The only possible exception was Jennifer. She could be a problem. But the rest of them would serve their purpose and serve it well.

First things first, though. There was a merry game to be played. The players in this drama were in place and act one had already commenced.

Laughter filled the night as the vampire faded into the shadows.

"So who's the woman?"

Val started, the forgotten book falling from his fingertips to land on the pine floor with a hollow thump. He looked up to see his unexpected visitor standing near the fireplace, a bemused expression on her face. "Miranda, what a lovely surprise. I didn't hear you pop in."

A silvery laugh echoed in the expanse of the library. "That's a new one." Miranda shed her black velvet cape and draped it over the back of the chair across from him. She stooped to rescue the leather-bound book from the floor. "*Wuthering Heights*," she read, carefully closing the cover. Her crimson fingernails gleamed in the subdued lighting as she stroked the priceless binding. "First edition, even. Dreaming of unrequited love, my friend?" A smile danced across her face as she perched on the arm of the opposite chair.

"Just enjoying a classic, my dear." Val rose from the chair to reclaim his book from her.

She didn't release it. "What's her name?"

"And why do you think a woman is on my mind?" he asked, careful to keep his tone light.

Her smile turned sad, almost disappointed. "And who knows you better than I? You can fool others, but you can never fool me."

He brushed his finger down her cold cheek. The first time he'd laid eyes on her, he'd thought Miranda was the most beautiful creature he'd ever seen. Hair as black as night fell in thick luscious waves to her tiny waist. Skin the color of clotted cream; by contrast her lips were full and red. Deep blue eyes framed in sooty lashes stared, unflinching in their regard of him. Tall and built like a Rubenesque statue, she was perfection wrapped in a rich, black velvet dress. She was a woman many men would desire.

Miranda was his dark angel, his savior. She'd saved him from himself many times through the years they'd been friends and confidants. But he also knew she wanted more, much more than he could give. It pained him to hurt her so. When he'd met the red-haired angel last night, he'd known it was inevitable that someone would be hurt. Unfortunately, it would be Miranda.

"Never you, Miranda," he whispered.

She released her grip on the book; her gaze unwavering as she folded her hands in her lap like a prim spinster at an afternoon tea. "She's mortal?"

"Yes." His tone was resigned. Didn't she see that he didn't want to hurt her with this?

"Do you love her?"

Anger surged to life. How could he dare love any mortal woman? Their relationship would always be doomed to failure and loss. A vampire would always outlive a mortal, many lifetimes over. "How can I love her?" he bit out. "How can I love anyone?"

"The same way any of us can love." Her tone was soft, her voice musical, sensual. It was that voice which had pulled him back from the edge many times. He felt the lure of it even now.

"I've only met her once."

"She must be quite the woman to have captured your attention."

"It's only lust." He said the words, but they rang hollow to his ears.

"If you believe it's only lust, then you're a bigger fool than I ever knew you were." She looked down to pick at imaginary lint on her skirt. "You realize that mortals can be our downfall?"

"Yes."

She abandoned her task, raising her gaze to meet his. "Do you want to die that badly?" she whispered.

"No, not anymore. I have you to thank for that." He moved away from her and toward the floor-to-ceiling windows. "I don't know how to explain it." Burgundy velvet drapes were pulled back to reveal the clear, starry night. The shadows beyond the glass beckoned his soul and, for the first time in many years, he wanted to curse the night that enshrouded him.

"You don't have to explain, Val," Miranda spoke softly. "You owe me nothing."

"No, you're wrong," he said, his voice harsh. "I owe you everything." He turned to the beauty who stared at him with the face of love. Love that would ease the crushing loneliness of his life. Love he could never return. "Everything."

"You owe me nothing you will not give willingly." Her tone was pained as she rose from her perch. "I'll take nothing you do not offer of yourself." She picked up her cape and moved to stand before him, her cool fingers caressing his face as if committing it to memory. She dropped her hand as tears filled her eyes. "I take my leave of you with a heart filled with love for the boy you once were, and the man you've become."

She vanished, leaving the faint scent of jasmine and a delicate tingling on his skin. His heart heavy, Val turned, his eyes once again searching the darkness of a New York night. How had his life come to this?

Chapter 3

Shai frowned at the gorgeous roses on her desk. One dozen long-stemmed, blood red roses in a black glass vase sat near the edge of her scribbled-on blotter. They'd been waiting for her when she'd returned from lunch and now, three and a half hours later, she was no closer to determining who'd sent them. There'd been no card with the gift.

She drew her fingertip over one of the half-opened buds. Their sweet scent surrounded her, invoking a longing she'd never dreamed even existed.

Over the years she'd worked at the *Times*, she'd seen her co-workers receive beautiful bouquets for birthdays and anniversaries or for no reason at all. Something to tell them they were loved. How many times had she watched them being delivered, all the while knowing it would never happen to her.

She'd dreamt for years of her Knight In Shining Armor only to realize she was allergic to horses.

A bitter smile touched her lips as she caressed the fragile petals of a delicate bloom. Soft as a lover's kiss. Unbidden, images of the man she'd met the night before entered her mind. He'd occupied her thoughts ever since she'd risen early that afternoon to get ready for work.

Valentin.

Even his name wrought faint shivers of awareness over her skin. He was, without a doubt, the handsomest man she'd ever seen. And she'd certainly never had a reaction like that to another living soul.

Her cheeks colored at the thought of her sudden arousal when she'd laid eyes on him. Normally she avoided men like the plague. They made her feel nervous, anxious and lacking. But Val drew her like a moth to the flame. She frowned. That was a bad analogy. Was she trying to warn herself that she'd get burned?

A sigh escaped her. What did it matter anyhow? She'd likely never see him again anyway. He wouldn't recognize the frumpy woman who sat behind her desk tonight. She was nothing compared to the woman in the naughty lingerie sitting in a restaurant while laughing and talking with her friends.

"They found another one."

Shai jumped, gasping as her finger caught on a thorn, tearing the unsuspecting flesh. Blood welled through the cut in a brilliant red bead. She reached for a tissue, watching the droplet shiver with her movements.

"Found another what?" Shai wrapped the tissue around her finger before looking at her boss.

The night editor of the *Times*, Mariah White strolled into the tiny office Shai shared with three other junior employees. In one hand, she carried a sheet of fax paper and in the other, a well-chewed pencil. She planted her generous backside on the corner of Shai's desk and dropped the paper in front of her.

Weary, Shai leaned back in her chair and rubbed her forehead with her undamaged hand. She wished she knew what the heck was wrong with her. She'd met a handsome man last night and now, twenty-four hours later, she was all maudlin and acting silly. This wasn't like the normally stoic, unemotional woman she was comfortable with.

"Hello?" Mariah waved her pencil in the air. "I'm not talking for my health here. Wake up."

A yawn escaped before Shai could stop it. "I'm sorry. What were you saying?"

"Body. Another woman, same MO as the others." Mariah snatched a chocolate drop from a jar on the desk and popped it into her mouth. "Found behind the old Festival Garden Theater on Forty-Second. Just came across the fax not five minutes ago."

"Sounds like the place to be." She yawned again, reaching for her ever-present notepad and tape recorder.

Mariah helped herself to another candy. "I knew you'd say that." She slipped off the desk and headed for the office door. Pausing in the doorway, she turned back. "I am curious, though. Why are you taking such a personal interest in these murders? Brett Springer is writing them for the paper and murder isn't usually your beat."

Shai pushed herself out of her chair and stifled a groan. "Everyone has to have a hobby," she said dryly. She pulled the tissue off her finger to inspect her wound. The bleeding had stopped, leaving a tiny red scratch. She dropped the tissue in the trash.

"Maybe you need to get out more."

No, I got out too much last night.

She forced a smile, hoping it didn't look as fake at it felt. "Maybe you're right."

"Of course I am. That's why I make the big bucks." Laughing at her own joke, Mariah vanished out the door.

Shai stuffed the tools of her trade into her large handbag and tried to gather her strength for the coming ordeal. To think, ten more minutes and she would have escaped for the evening. Home to her quiet apartment. Home to a good book, some canned soup and a good night's sleep.

Boy, she had rotten luck.

The cab ride to the old theater was quick. The streets of New York City were relatively quiet at 2:30 A.M. and the traffic was light. A large crowd was gathered at the end of the alley behind the theater when Shai's cab pulled to the curb.

The muggy August air smacked her in the face as she opened the door. She'd lived in New York for most of her life, but tonight the scents in the air were alien. The smell of too much garbage, too many people, of human waste and dirt. And the underlying scent of fear and violent death.

Not again...

"Hey lady, youse gonna shut da door or just stand aroun' all night?"

The cab driver's strident voice interrupted her musing. "Oh, sorry." She shoved a five-dollar bill into his hand then slammed the door.

"Youse wants me to wait?"

"No, no thank you."

He gave an abrupt nod and sped away from the curb, leaving her fervently wishing she'd gone with him.

She shouldered her bag and turned to scan the crowd, trying to ignore the churning in her gut. Why would people stand around a desolate street in the middle of the night at a murder scene? What drove someone to do that? Didn't they realize that someone had died violently and it wasn't a joke? It wasn't television. It was real life and it was painful and ugly.

Relief washed over her as she spied a familiar face.

Detective J. B. Henry stood just beyond the bright yellow police line. Henry and Shai had first met when he'd arrested her for stealing food.

She'd been eight years old and slowly starving to death on the streets of New York. He'd taken her to Children's Services, who'd found her a place to stay and helped her get a good education. If it weren't for him, Shai was pretty sure she wouldn't have been alive today.

After she'd graduated from SUNY with a degree in journalism, her first job had been writing the Police Beat section of the *Village Investigator* newspaper. She'd always made sure to mention the cases he worked on. Keeping him in the public eye had helped him to move up the ranks of the NYPD quickly. In return, he could always be counted on for accurate information and a good exclusive.

Shai shoved her hair off her sticky forehead, squaring her shoulders for the oncoming ordeal. She clipped her plastic PRESS badge onto the collar of her cotton blouse as she slipped along the edge of the crowd. She ducked under the tape while the harried patrol officers fended off curious onlookers. She sauntered up to Detective Henry.

"Lots of lookie-loos for this early in the morning."

Reminding Shai of Albert Einstein with his wild hair and droopy mustache, Henry looked around, a scowl on his face when he spotted her. "What are you doing here? You know better than to cross the police line."

"And you know me, Henry, just like a bad penny. One never knows where I might turn up." She grinned.

"Boy, isn't that the truth." His cop eyes took in her rumpled tan slacks and white cotton blouse. "Long hours again?"

"When aren't they?" She glanced at the sheet-draped figure surrounded by a knot of cigarette-smoking detectives. "I went out to dinner with friends last night. It turned into a late evening." She nodded toward the victim. "And now this."

"What's his name?"

Confused, she looked at him. "Whose name?"

"The fella..."

"What fellow?"

"The ones you went out with last night?"

"Now, who said it was a man?" she asked, exasperated. First her friends, now Henry. Did everyone think she needed a date?

"I can only hope," he grumbled.

"Keep trying, Henry." She smothered a grin and waved a hand toward the body on the ground. "What's the story?"

"Shai," he said sternly.

She shook her head. "Just between you and me, Henry. I'm not writing this one."

He gave her a doubtful look, then shook his head as if to indicate she was crazy. "Same as the other three. Prostitute accompanies a john into an alley, nails him and then her throat gets ripped out." Henry shrugged. "Nothing new with this one."

"I heard from someone at the coroner's office that there was no sign of semen with the other three. No sign of latex residue either," she mused, hoping he'd add more information.

"It is a puzzling one, all right. One would think that girls like them would use condoms, for heaven's sake. However, this one isn't like the others." Henry started walking toward the corpse, leaving Shai to follow.

"What's different?"

"She's not your average good-time girl. She's an expensive piece from an escort service."

Shai dogged his steps. "Why would an expensive woman like that do her business in an alley in the middle of the night?"

"That's the question of the hour." Henry shook his head. "What is this world coming to?" He waved the junior investigators away from the corpse.

"No good, that's for certain." She was disappointed that he didn't add more to her statement, but she didn't let that deter her. Henry could be a fount of knowledge when properly persuaded.

She tried to brace herself to look death in the face. It was never pretty, and she was sure this one would be worse than most. So far, all of the victims had been young and beautiful and this one would probably be the same. So many lives ruined, such a waste.

Henry motioned to a uniformed officer to pull back the bloodstained sheet. "She was a looker all right," he commented.

Shai caught her breath and struggled to control her rebelling stomach while keeping her expression impassive.

In a brief glimpse, she noted the wild mane of expertly dyed red hair tumbled across the victim's shoulders, and her skin was clear. Dull, emerald-green eyes stared at the black sky, horror reflected in their depths. Before she turned away, Shai caught a glimpse of the corpse's torn red evening gown hiked to her waist to reveal a black garter belt and stockings.

She swallowed hard as she looked away. The woman's head had almost been torn off.

"Pity, isn't it? Why such a beautiful woman would turn to whoring is beyond me." Henry reached inside his jacket for a cigarette. A faint tremor marred his movements.

"Who knows why anyone does anything?" Shai mumbled more to herself than in response to his words. Those dull green eyes would haunt her until the killer was caught. She shook herself. There was nothing she could do about it, though. Not yet, anyway. All she could do was continue to gather facts and file them away for future reference.

"Who knows why anyone does anything, Henry?" Shai repeated, suddenly weary to the bone. She wanted to get this over with as quickly as possible so she forced herself to look back at the corpse. Trying to remain objective, she viewed the victim's nearly nude body as impersonally as possible.

Outwardly, she didn't see anything different from the other three victims found in various locations in the past two weeks. Beautiful, prostitute, dark brown or red hair, well-dressed, had sex before dying, was left to die in an undignified position in a very public place.

She motioned to the uniformed officer to replace the sheet. "One would assume that, with a wound this large, there'd be more blood than this."

Henry nodded. "Another one of the mysteries in this case."

"You'll let me have a copy of the coroner's report?" Shai asked him, walking toward the entrance to the alley.

He fell in step beside her. "Sure thing. You've taken a mighty big interest in these killings. Why?"

She glanced at the star-speckled sky visible between the buildings. "Maybe I'm tired of seeing this happen day in and day out."

Dozens of images crowded her mind. Images of slain women, brutalized bodies. Like that of her mother, dead at twenty-seven-years-old. Murdered after turning a trick in their ramshackle apartment. Several years later, the building had burned to the ground under mysterious circumstances and she'd been glad. No one had been charged with arson.

"You and me both," Henry said in a sad voice. He held up the police tape while Shai escaped under it. "I'll be in touch."

She nodded and walked to the edge of the curb to hail a cab that was cruising down the street toward her. A prickling at the nape of her neck caused her to pause, her hand half-raised.

Someone was watching her.

She scanned the crowd and the open windows in the buildings surrounding them before turning to see a man across the street. He was little more than a shadow against the brownstone building. A shiver rippled over her skin as he smiled, his teeth flashing white against the darkness.

She knew him...didn't she?

The arrival of the coroner's wagon interrupted her thought. The vehicle rumbled down the street, its damaged muffler shattering the early morning stillness. It rumbled past, hiding the man for a few seconds as it pulled to the curb next to her. The engine was cut and the sudden silence was eerie, pregnant with tension. It felt as if something awaited her in the darkness, untouched by the scant lighting from the streetlights.

She glanced across the street. He was gone. She frowned. Had she imagined him? Maybe her tired eyes were playing tricks on her. It was definitely time to head home and get some sleep.

Shai stepped into the street to hail the cab.

She'd seen him. The vampire watched the redheaded journalist ride away in her cab. She was a wily one and he was enjoying the chase. Nothing got his blood going like the anticipation of an intelligent adversary, but this one was special. He'd been waiting for her for many years and now she was ripe for the taking. She'd grown beautiful and he wanted her more than anything in the world. She was to be his greatest achievement. He relished the familiar stirring of his loins.

He wanted her beneath him, hot and panting, crying out for him. He would have her, too, when he tired of the chase. It was rare that a mortal woman managed to capture his attention, but Shai Jordan was different. He didn't want to end this game too soon.

He sighed in anticipation. The things they would do together...What fun they'd have. A smile curled his lips.

Chapter 4

He came to her that night.

Shai went from a deep, dreamless sleep into full wakefulness within seconds. She glanced at the clock next to her bed. It was only four A.M., for heaven's sake! No one in his or her right mind should be awake at that time.

She glanced around her small bedroom, her gaze bleary, wondering what had awakened her, when she noticed the soft golden glow in the room. Candles flickered in various holders scattered about the bedroom and she frowned. She certainly hadn't lit them. What the devil was going on?

She sat up. Her breath caught in her throat as a sultry finger of breeze parted her curtains and she caught sight of a figure crouched on the fire escape outside her window. Her heart gave a shudder and she drew in breath to scream when he leaned into the flickering golden light.

In an instant, she knew it was him. Val. The man from the restaurant.

"Invite me in," he ordered.

Pleasure curled her toes as his low voice sounded in the night. A ripple of anticipation skittered down her spine. Her mind screamed, *"Is he crazy?"* even as her body longed to invite him in.

Her lips parted to order him away from her window and she was stunned as the exact opposite escaped from her mouth.

"You're welcome here."

He stretched one leg through the open window and climbed into her room, his booted feet scattering the throw pillows on her window seat. His movements easy, graceful, he advanced to her bed, a predatory gleam in his eyes.

Her breathing deepened. This had to be a dream, of course. This couldn't happen in real life. But what a lovely dream it was! He was much taller than she'd originally thought, well above her own five-foot-four. His shoulder-length black hair hung loose around his sharply chiseled features, and his black eyes gleamed against the paleness of his skin.

His clothing was simple. Tight-fitting black jeans, a loose-flowing white shirt and black leather boots. A jeweled dagger was tucked into the black leather belt that encircled his waist. Shai thought he looked like a pirate.

"You know who I am?" His voice was deep and resonant, causing flames of awareness to lick her heightened senses. Her cotton sleep shirt felt heavy and stifling against her skin. More than anything, she wanted this man to remove it from her overheated body.

"Yes." Her voice sounded odd to her ears, slow, as if she were drugged.

"And you know what I want from you?"

Her throat dry, she could only nod in response.

A smile of pure male satisfaction curved his sensuous lips. He held out his hand. "Come with me, my love."

She could no more stop herself from taking his hand than she could have stopped time from marching forward. Covered in thin leather gloves, his hand gripped her heated flesh in a strong, sure grip. Wicked thoughts of that brawny hand against other parts of her body, stroking, caressing, brought a rush of heat to her face.

What a vivid dream.

His brow arched and he smiled as if he could read her naughty thoughts. Raising her hand to his lips, he kissed it, flicking her skin with his tongue. "Tell me what you desire," he murmured against her knuckles.

Raw lust hit her like a tidal wave, rendering her dizzy. She'd never felt anything like this before. My word, but those romance novels were right! She sucked in a noisy breath. She longed to lean into him and allow him frightful liberties, while her rationale screamed for her to run away. This *was* a dream...wasn't it? Surely it was...

What would it hurt to give in to her base instincts?

"You, I want you," she whispered.

His eyes gleamed with satisfaction as he pulled her to her feet. Keeping hold of her hand, he turned and led her into the tiny dining room. With a swipe of his powerful arm, he cleared the table. An overripe peach hit the floor with a dull splat as he reached for a fat pillar candle located in a wall sconce. He set the candle on the table and lit it with a lighter he'd produced from his pocket. She barely had time to appreciate the golden glow when he swept her up and deposited her on the edge of the table. Spreading her thighs, he moved between her legs. The ridge of his erection pressed against her cotton panties and the delicate folds hidden beneath.

Startled, she whimpered and tried to push him away, to close her legs against his invasion. "I don't want..." she stopped, confused.

"This is your fantasy," he whispered. "This is what you asked for. A dark lover seducing you, forcing you to yield to your body's demands. Taking you to heights you have never dared before."

His leather-clad hands lightly caressed the sensitive undersides of her breasts through her shirt. Her nipples tightened and she leaned toward him, her breath quickening as an involuntary sound broke from her lips.

Her rational mind might be telling her to object, but her body was leading her elsewhere.

He chuckled. "I thought so." He captured her wrists, one in each hand, and reached to arrange her palms flat on the table behind her back. The position forced her body to arch like a bow towards him. "Do not remove your hands from the table," he warned in his whiskey-rough voice. "If you do, I will stop touching you."

Shai nodded. Though she was afraid, she'd never felt more alive in her life. Her skin tingled with anticipation.

His dark eyes glittered with heated desire as he traced a path of sensation along her jaw with a fingertip. "You're very obedient and shall be amply rewarded..."

He dipped his dark head, his lips tracing a path of fire along her jaw, down her throat to where her pulse beat frantically. A lazy fingertip brushed the tip of her breast and she shuddered as pure sensation poured through her body.

Dipping low, he took her erect nipple into his mouth, dampening the thin cotton. A cry wrenched from her lips as a surge of primal lust raced in her veins. Her nether regions begin to moisten and swell as he suckled. She arched against him, wanting him to take more of her into his mouth. Tipping her head back, she was helpless against him and the raging desire he aroused in her.

His hand traced a line of fire down her ribcage as he pulled back and blew on the moist cotton, torturing her aroused flesh. A sob escaped her lips and she struggled to keep her hands on the table. A leather-clad hand brushed her thigh as he reached for the hem of the shirt to draw it over her head. He raised her hands from the tabletop long enough to pull the shirt free and toss it over a chair. He replaced her hands on the table, then stepped back.

Sluggish with desire, she raised her head, her breasts heaving as she gulped for air. A smile curved the corners of his mouth as he drew the dagger from his belt. Shai tensed as candlelight gleamed on the wicked steel blade. He pressed the cold flat of it against her soft belly and she whimpered, raising her hands, trying to move away.

"No, little one."

He shook his head as he forced her hands back on the table. This time, he positioned them closer to her buttocks, pushing her breasts forward, allowing him better access. He drew the flat of the blade slowly over one nipple, teasing, tempting, before giving the other the same attention.

He moved it down over her stomach, tracing a line of anticipation toward her white panties. His eyes sharp on her face, he slipped the blade under the strap at her hip and cut them away from her body, first one side then the other. Urging her hips up, he slipped them from beneath her and dropped them to the floor.

She met his gaze as his gloved fingers broached her damp curls to slip into her warmth. Shai sighed as he found the seat of her nerves and she hesitantly moved against his hand, her body overruling her mind. He watched her closely with a gentle, encouraging smile. Under the subtle ministrations of his hand, moisture spread as his pace increased.

He tangled the fingers of his other hand in her long hair, forcing her head back so she could no longer watch him. She moaned in protest. As his hands continued to work their magic, her groans grew louder as the pace increased. Her eyes closed and she struggled to draw enough air into her starved lungs.

Brilliant light flashed beneath her closed eyelids as she came. Spasms of ecstasy rocked her body and her arms threatened to collapse and drop her to the table. Her breath came in shuddering gasps as a strong arm slipped around her shoulders and pulled her against him.

Head sagging against the expanse of his chest, her mind swirled as her heart slowed. His hand traced a comforting path up and down her spine as she quieted against him and awareness returned.

She stirred, his leather-clad fingers still buried within her. Now what did she do? He hadn't reached his satisfaction yet. What would Emily Post say about this situation?

"Better?" he rumbled.

"Mmm," she sighed and nodded.

He leaned forward, pushing her back into her prior position on the table. She tensed as his fingers brushed her engorged flesh and desire reawakened within her. His eyes were dark as he gave her a gentle rub. Her hips arched to follow his movement to its delicious completion.

"You like that?"

Her eyes slitted as he took up a slow, figure eight dance centered directly on the seat of her power. Wordless, she nodded as her hips took up the lazy rhythm, her thighs parting once more to allow him better access. Their gazes clashed as his breathing deepened and grew harsher, his eyes more feverish.

A low growl erupted from his throat and he pulled his hand away. She moaned in protest as his free hand tangled in her hair once more and he pulled her head back. She heard the rasp of the zipper on his pants, the sound mingling with his out-of-control breathing.

A soft glow of wonder rose within her chest as she heard him curse lightly. She'd driven him to this edge. She. Plain, little Shai.

All coherent thought fled as she felt the hard tip of his erection against her thigh. She moaned in torment, spreading her legs farther and lifting her hips, offering herself to him.

At once he was inside her. She sighed as he filled her, stretching her, completing her. He released his grip on her hair to grasp her waist as he thrust deep. His hands worked her hips, back and forth over his thrusting manhood, harder and harder as her cries broke the silence of the room. Unable to remain still, she grabbed his arms and moved against him, taking everything he offered and giving back as good as she got.

Sensation tightened her muscles and within a few thrusts she came, hard. Sobbing, she clung to him as her orgasm claimed her body and soul. Gulping for air, her muscles refused to heed her commands and she released her grip on him. Dimly, she was aware of him still inside her, hard as a rock. Her arms trembled and she almost fell to the table. He pulled her back into his arms, cradling her against his chest as he brushed her hair from her damp skin.

His lips were cool against her throat. "You're mine, now." He sounded breathless.

She nodded as he raised her arms, urging her to wrap them around his neck and shoulders. Secure, he swung her off the table. She gave an inarticulate grunt as his cock rubbed her sensitized flesh once more.

She rocked against him in response as he turned and braced her back against the wall. Cool against her heated skin, he pressed into her. Slowly he rolled his hips and began to thrust again.

"Say it," he gasped against her throat as he pounded into her. "You're mine."

"Yes..." She groaned as sparks flashed and danced against her eyelids once more. She was so close...

"I am your master." He increased his thrusts.

Her grip tightened as ecstasy beckoned, so close yet so far away. "Yes, you are my master."

He pulled her higher, changing his angle ever so subtly, his grip bruising on her waist as he picked up the pace. Within seconds he brought her to the precipice and tumbled her over the edge. As her body exploded into a million shining pieces, she felt a faint stinging at her throat, then a warm open-mouthed kiss. He sucked her flesh. Her body tingled as if on fire, the intense ecstasy seeming to increase as he consumed her.

Seconds later, he drove his own climax deep into her body.

The shrill ringing of the telephone brought her straight up in her bed. Disoriented, she glanced around her bedroom and noted that everything was in place. She ran a hand through her tumbled hair. "Wow...what a dream." She turned to scowl at the offending phone by her bed as it continued to ring. She reached for it.

"Hello," she grunted.

"Shai, where are you?" Mariah's voice barked in her ear.

"What do you mean, I should think it's obvious where I am." She glanced at her clock. "It's only seven-thirty. What's the big deal? I just went to bed a few hours ago"

"Shai...it's seven-thirty at night."

She blinked and looked at her window. Sure enough, the sun was riding low in the sky. "I slept seventeen hours? How is that possible?"

"I don't know, but you did it! You missed the city council meeting you were supposed to write up. I had Jenny take care of it. I don't know what's up with you lately, but you're blowing it. You used to be one of our most reliable reporters and now I can't count on you for anything."

Mind scrambling, Shai straightened, her heart thudding in her chest. "Mariah, I'm really sorry..."

"So am I, kid." Resignation weighed heavily in Mariah's voice. "I know these murders have you on edge - "

"This has nothing to do with the murders," she cut in. "I've been working hard lately and I just had my birthday and I had some late nights..."

"It's more than that and you know it. These murders are messing with everyone, but you seem obsessed by them."

"But - "

"I want you to take the night off and reevaluate your career here at the *Times*. You're a great reporter but I need you *here* in body as well as spirit, Shai. Not half-assed and half-hearted."

"Mariah - "

"Do it and I'll see you tomorrow night."

She slumped as the receiver was dropped on the other end and the dial tone filled her ears. Tears stung her eyes as she, too, dropped the receiver into the cradle. She wasn't obsessed with the murders - she *wasn't*. She had a professional curiosity that had nothing to do with her mother being killed in a similar manner many years before. It had nothing to do with this.

Nothing.

As she stumbled to her feet, the phone rang again. Thinking it was Mariah, she snatched it up and headed toward the dining room with the cordless in hand.

"I really don't need..." Shai began.

"I know who killed them," a low, masculine voice purred in her ear.

Ripples of shock filtered through her body. She blindly pulled out a chair and sank into it. "W-w-what?" she stammered. On the floor next to the chair, she found a scrap of lace, lace from the panties she'd worn to bed last night. Perplexed, she ran a finger over her shirt-covered hip. She blanched. Panties she wasn't wearing now. Her hand clenched in a fist around the material as her mind scrabbled for a reasonable explanation for them being on the floor.

"You know who I am," he spoke again.

"Yes." Her throat felt suddenly dry and she concentrated on drawing deep, even breaths. It was *him*.

"I know the identity of the killer of these soiled doves. Meet me this evening at ten P.M. at Lindy's on Broadway and please come alone."

Alone? Is he nuts...

"I..."

His voice turned coaxing. "I have information you need to solve these crimes. Think of the lives that you alone can save...so unlike the last time."

Her blood turned to ice in her veins and she strove to remain calm. Did he know about her mother? Who was this man? She opened her palm to see the lace lying there as if to mock her. Was this man her dark lover, Val? She had to know.

"I'll be there," she murmured.

He chuckled. "I knew you would be."

Chapter 5

Shai dug through the bottom drawer of her desk at the newspaper office. Where in the devil was her spare tape recorder? She pulled out a crumpled bag of a once-popular snack. Heavens - how long had that been there? Didn't they quit making those about five years ago? It hit the trash with a dull thud.

She located the errant recorder under a stack of yellowed newspapers and a brittle package of chewing gum. She retrieved the recorder and replaced the batteries as she told herself for the hundredth time that she was a complete fool to meet this man alone, but a multitude of questions ran through her brain. The first one was how had he gotten into her apartment last night? Secondly, what, if anything, did he know about the murder of her mother?

She didn't talk about her mother, not even to her best friends. In her mind, her mother was sacred emotional territory and her rocky childhood was a stone better left unturned.

"Shai." Leonard, one of the senior reporters, popped his head into her office and broke her train of thought. He tossed a manila envelope onto her desk. "This came for you this afternoon. It's the preliminary report from the coroner on the autopsy of one Regina Williams, the woman found outside the theater last night."

"Did you read it?" She snatched up the envelope and opened it.

"Of course." He moved into the office, his near-skeletal body swamped by jeans and a button-down oxford shirt. He'd been the original reporter when the first body was found several weeks before and had lots of good insider information. He took a huge bite from a shiny red apple and continued speaking around it, spewing tiny bits of apple and spit. "Cause of death is massive blood loss, not to mention the fact that most of her throat was missing. She was literally drained dry. Of course, now the question of the hour is: where did all that blood go?"

Shai frowned and flipped through the papers. "That's a good question," she said, not looking up from the report. She'd noticed the lack of blood last night and still no one seemed to have any answers. All of the victims had been literally drained of blood yet none of the coroner's reports could shed any light on why. The bodies had shown no evidence of being moved. Many reports indicated the victims had been killed where they'd been found, yet the blood had been missing from the scene.

"According to that, it certainly wasn't at the scene." Leonard chomped noisily on the near-decimated fruit. "There were spots, but none of them were big enough to equal the amount drained. It'll take days until the results from the lab come back which will determine if the blood found all belonged to the victim."

Shai met his gaze, dropping the pages on her desk. "So, no one has any clue? No scuttlebutt, no nothing?"

He shook his head. "Nothing. The police are stumped, the detectives are stumped and there are rumors of calling in the Feds."

She bit her lip. Now *that* was news. No one hated calling the Feds more than New York's finest. If they were contemplating such a step, it had to be because they were out of leads. In all of the murders combined, little forensic evidence had been left at the scene.

From what she could gather, the authorities had only one leather glove and a single spot of blood from the second murder. That one spot had had some peculiar characteristics and they were still trying to determine if it was human or animal. So far, the theory was that it was human and very old, possibly from another unreported crime in the alley from years before. All in all, it was a perplexing series of crimes.

"The police mentioned something about the possibility of a satanic cult or some such silliness." Leonard took another huge bite, spewing almost as much as he swallowed as he spoke.

"What?"

"The killings are almost ritualistic in nature." He tossed the decimated core into the trashcan. "We definitely have a new breed of serial killer on the prowl in lovely New York. Quicker, more efficient and fastidious, this person is the cream of the crop. Not that most serial killers aren't tidy because they are. However, it's nearly impossible to commit the perfect crime, yet, after several killings, this one is coming as close to the perfect crime as I've ever seen. They're leaving nothing of themselves behind. That doesn't happen every day."

She gave a slow nod, her mind whirling with possibilities. "Who or what do you think is doing this, Leonard?"

"If you ask me, I think it was vampires." He left her office, his laughter echoing in the hall.

The small scratch on the side of Shai's neck began to tingle and she rubbed it absently. Despite his laughter, Leonard was probably serious about the vampire nonsense.

Lindy's was a trendy restaurant in Manhattan, right off Broadway. When she arrived a few minutes early, it was packed from wall to wall with people. After telling the waiter she was expecting someone, he led her to a tiny table in the back of the long, narrow room and sat her facing the wall, away from the other patrons.

Uneasy, she glanced around the room. Large crowds made her uncomfortable even though her job required a lot of social interaction in all sorts of situations. This was an especially well-dressed crowd, which made it worse.

She tugged self-consciously at her worn blazer then patted her pocket reassuringly. Her tape recorder was in place and ready to go. Now, if she could just survive the confrontation.

Please, please don't let it be *him*.

She pulled out a pack of cigarettes and dropped them onto the table. She didn't smoke much, but now seemed like a good time to renew her acquaintance with Mr. Marlboro.

Strong hands clamped her shoulders as a voice whispered into her ear. "Missing me?"

Shai almost jumped out of her chair as cool lips brushed her ear, sending chills rocketing down neck. He released her then moved quickly around to the empty chair on the opposite side of the table.

Her eyes widened as the newcomer relaxed into an elegant sprawl. The man last night didn't have blond hair nor were his eyes so icy. This definitely wasn't Val. Who the devil was this stranger?

Whoever he was, he was quite handsome. Thick blond hair brushed his shoulders and he wore a black turtleneck teamed with immaculate cream-colored trousers with knife-sharp pleats. His features were fine, almost feminine, and his eyes were a hypnotic, icy blue. A smile curved his finely sculpted mouth, but it wasn't a friendly smile.

"Who are you?" she blurted.

He shook his head, his expression turned mocking. "If I told you that, it would spoil the game, wouldn't it?"

His gaze was disconcerting in its directness, leaving Shai feeling naked, vulnerable. She forced her gaze from his and pulled a cigarette from the pack. Reaching into her pocket, she turned on the tape recorder.

"Who are you and what did you want to talk to me about?" She withdrew a slim silver lighter and prayed the stranger didn't notice the trembling of her fingers.

His smile grew. "I wish to talk to you about a great many things and I can't decide where to be begin. Let's keep things simple, shall we? We're going to play a game. A very special game called 'Catch Me If You Can'."

Nutcase.

"And why would I want to play this game? I don't know who you are or what you know. How do I know you aren't some fruitcake who got my name from the newspaper?"

A dangerous glint entered his eye to let her know that her words weren't pleasing him. His smile faded.

"Many years ago, I had a pet like you. A she-wolf who'd been hunted for killing livestock." His voice almost crooned. "She needed to be... broken. After many weeks, she learned to take food from my hand only. Subservient and beautiful, and that was exactly how I wanted her to behave."

A trickle of fear eased along Shai's spine at the menace lacing his words. "Lovely story, but what does that have to do with the murders?" She fought for a note of disdain in her voice.

He visibly shook himself, and the smile returned. "There are certain aspects that haven't been released to the press."

"Such as?"

"The lack of blood from the victim and the scarcity of forensic evidence left behind." He leaned back, his expression self-satisfied.

It was true that this information hadn't been released to the press. Only the killer or someone who'd been to the crime scene would have known any of what he'd just given her. Her eyes narrowed. It wouldn't be wise to let him know what she was thinking. She had a feeling he knew too much already.

"Are you trying to tell me that *you're* the killer?"

He held out his hands in a placating gesture, and she noticed that they seemed exceptionally pale. "But, of course, why else would I be here?"

"For coffee?" She struggled to control her fear. If he really was the murderer, she could be in serious danger. Even after the call, she'd been skeptical. But it only took one look into his eyes to see the truth. She was sitting across from a madman.

He snorted and waved a hand at the elegant patrons and masterpieces of food spread before them. "I can assure you there's nothing here that I want." He impaled her with his cold gaze. "Except you, of course."

"Why me?"

His expression turned dreamy. "You have the look of your mother about you."

Panic lanced her heart as his eyes moved about her face as if to memorize every feature. "What do you know about my mother?" Her voice dropped to a whisper.

He blinked and the faraway look left his eyes. "Tell me what you know about serial killers," he commanded, ignoring her question.

She sat back, surprised. Two could play this game and she wasn't intimidated yet. Frightened, yes. Unnerved, yes. Intimidated, no. As long as she was in a crowd, she should be safe enough. "You keep hinting that you're the killer. You tell me."

He slammed his hand on the table and it wobbled precariously. "That isn't how the game is played!" he snarled.

The hum of activity died as some of the patrons glanced at them curiously before resuming their conversations. Great - only in New York could a madman threaten her in a crowd and have no one pay the slightest bit of attention.

Shai leaned forward. "Maybe you should let me know the rules," she hissed.

"I ask the questions and you answer them," he snapped.

She leaned back in her chair, grateful for the small table between them. Inadequate it might be, but she was grateful nonetheless. "Well, they usually kill within their own ethnic groups," she began.

"No, no, no! I want to know why they kill." His eyes glittered feverishly and a trickle of fear ran down her spine.

She glanced around the room. Even though the room was crowded, no one seemed to be aware they were even there. New Yorkers were notorious for not wanting to "get involved." Maybe she wasn't as safe as she'd thought?

"They usually kill because they covet or..." she began.

He shook his head. "Wrong again." He leaned forward and caught her hand. Icy fingers dug into her wrist, pulling her closer until they were nose to nose. The table dug into her stomach and she grunted in surprise. He was quick.

"It's the hunger." His breath licked her mouth and she recoiled at the damp, almost coppery scent. "If you find another way to appease the hunger," his lips brushed hers, "the killing will stop."

She recoiled from the feel of his cool lips. She wanted to cry out, but she was afraid once she started she wouldn't be able to stop. Instead, she concentrated on breathing evenly to control the rising panic. Without warning, he let go of her hand and she fell back against her chair. She rubbed her abused wrist.

His smile was cruel as he licked his lips. Revulsion curled in her stomach. "The hunger drives us and there's no end to it. You, too, will soon know the hunger. It will consume your entire life and you'll spend all your time finding ways to appease it. Until you become one with the hunger..."

She stared at him, her mind scrambling for a point of reference in this obscure conversation. She could find nothing.

"You know exactly what I'm referring to." He reached across the table and captured her face with one cool hand before she could evade him. He held her captive as he drew a strong finger along her full lower lip, his gaze fixed on it.

"To feel the burning, the eternal burning. The rush of desire that threatens to devour you. It, too, will possess you, body and soul, and you'll kill to feel it again and again."

His chilling gaze flicked up to meet hers. Shai recognized the look that burned in the depths of his eyes. Lust. Her insides turned to ice.

"The question is, who will be the winner and will you choose that winner wisely?" He chuckled. "'Tis a merry game we play."

He released her and she jerked back in her chair. She closed her eyes, thankful for the tape recorder whirring in her pocket because no one was going to believe this conversation. She wasn't even sure that she did and she was a participant.

"I'm afraid you..." She faltered when she opened her eyes and the chair before her was empty.

The sudden silence in the restaurant caused her to look around. Nearby patrons were staring at her as if she'd lost her mind. A creeping feeling of unreality washed over her. What had just happened?

Her cheeks flushed as she snatched up her cigarettes and rose from her seat. Turning, she walked to the door, the pinprick of dozens of gazes tickling her back. Her heart pounded as she dodged spectators, tables and serving people. She had the killer on tape and she'd seen him up close. It was time to go to the police.

"Shai." Detective Henry placed his hands on the scarred wooden conference table and leaned across it to where she huddled in the chair. "I'm telling you, the only thing on that tape is your own voice. It sounded like you were having a one-sided conversation with yourself."

"And I'm telling you I spoke to him." She gripped the chipped gray coffee mug and wondered if she was going insane.

"And I'm telling you, there's nothing on that tape, and no one at the restaurant saw anyone with you. However, they do tell an interesting story of a young redhead talking to herself."

How can this be?

She bit her lip and stared sullenly at the tape recorder sitting on the table, her mind whirling madly in an attempt to find an answer. She jumped when Henry laid a hand on her shoulder. She hadn't heard him walk around the table.

"Shai - "

She knew what he was going to say and cut him off by pulling away and getting to her feet.

"I'm not surprised you're having trouble with the murders. Your mother..." he began again.

"She has nothing to do with this." Shai grabbed the offending recorder and shoved it into her bag. "I knew it was a mistake to tell you about her. This is a different matter altogether, and it's become personal. It's between him and me now. If you won't listen to me and use the information I have to stop him, then, by heaven, I will!"

"Don't do anything rash," he cautioned.

"'Rash'?" She glanced back over her shoulder as she wrenched open the door to the interview room. "You haven't seen anything yet." Detectives in the office fell silent, watching her surreptitiously over their paperwork. Mindless of the people staring at her, she stomped through the room, heading for the hall that led to the outside and freedom.

"Don't make me lock you up, Shai," Henry bellowed after her.

She gave a short bark of laughter. "Catch me if you can."

Chapter 6

Shai swirled the scotch in her ancient Flintstones jelly glass, the golden liquid catching the light from a single candle, turning it to amber fire. A Christmas gift from several years before, the small bottle of scotch had rarely seen the light of day. She tugged at the dusty red ribbon around its neck.

"Some of the Highlands' finest." She giggled, her voice sounded slurred. Raising the glass, she downed the liquid. The afterburn brought tears to her eyes and she blinked them away.

She'd drunk enough in the last hour that she shouldn't be feeling anything. But she was. She was feeling too much. And remembering even more.

She had few memories of her father, but one was crystal clear. A vision of him sitting at a lopsided kitchen table in the middle of the night after a fight with her mother. He was wearing a T-shirt and grimy jeans and sat swilling the cheapest whiskey he could afford that week. She'd seen him do this many times in the few short years he'd remained with them. It was shortly after one of their horrendous fights that he'd abandoned them, and her mother had turned to prostitution to support her drug habit and the daughter she'd never wanted.

Her mother.

Now there was a tangled mess. When not on dope, Sarah Jordan had been a lovely woman. She'd had a quick wit and a soft heart, too soft to withstand the rigors of raising a child alone. Always in pursuit of happiness and someone to look after her, more men than Shai could remember had paraded through their home and their lives. None of them had amounted to anything, though a few had been nice to the shy daughter Sarah had kept hidden away most of the time. It was her own father who'd led Sarah down the path of alcoholism, then drugs. A veteran alcoholic, Jared Jordan had tried to keep it together and, for a short time, he'd succeeded.

Then it had all come apart.

Just after her fourth birthday, he'd left them on a cold winter's night. Haunted by unnamed demons in his past, he'd succumbed to the darkness and allowed himself to be consumed by cheap whiskey and heroin.

So long, Dad...

As she refilled her glass with a shaky hand, she wondered if her father was still alive. If he were, she doubted he could have afforded scotch of this caliber. She raised the glass in a mock salute. "Here's to you, Dad."

As she swallowed, she wondered how many more drinks it would take until she passed out. It was a time-honored tradition in the Jordan family to drink until passing out. Hell, her mother had turned it into an art form, pretty much her life's mission. Shai couldn't argue. Anything was better than this endless torment she was enduring. Had she finally followed in her mother's footsteps and gone around the bend? How long until she took strangers to bed for money?

She set down the glass and stared at the tape recorder on the coffee table. It hadn't been a hallucination, had it? She reached over and flipped it on. Her voice drifted out from the tiny speaker and she could hear the noises of the restaurant in between her words. The clinking of glass, the scrape of silverware on china, then dead silence. After a few seconds of silence, the sounds resumed. It was almost as if his words had been erased with the rest of the tape intact.

She frowned. Complete silence. Even the background noises were missing. Had the killer known about the recorder? Was he a magician? Had he somehow fixed it so his voice wasn't recorded?

Turning off the recorder, Shai settled back on the couch. There was no doubt about it, she was nuts. "Certifiable" was what they'd called her mother. "Like mother, like daughter." She reached for the glass once more and downed the contents.

"Finally! That one didn't burn all the way down." She raised the bottle and noticed that it was almost empty. She cursed as she emptied the remains into her glass. An errant spring from the worn couch dug into her lower back, but she paid it no mind. A warm lethargy stole over her as she settled into a comfortable position to nurse the rest of her drink.

Within minutes, her glass slid to the gray carpeting and the scotch spilled. Shai closed her eyes and reveled in a rare feeling of peace and well being as she drifted to sleep.

The scent of roses slowly woke her. She blinked and stretched, feeling better than she had in years. Something sinfully soft caressed her skin as she moved, causing her eyes to fly open. Looking down, she was startled to see white silk sheets and hundreds of rose petals had replaced her usual cotton linens.

What the devil...

She caught a movement in the corner of her eye and her gaze was drawn to the man sitting in her rocking chair. It was him. Her dream lover, Val. A chorus of words clamored in her mind, begging to be set free. She wanted to tell him everything that had happened to her in the restaurant. Most of all she wanted to say that she was deliriously happy he wasn't the killer.

Who was the killer? How had Val gotten into her bedroom?

Bewildered, she sat up in bed. The evening air was warm on her skin and she felt curiously exposed. She looked down to see a royal blue silk chemise had replaced her customary sleep shirt. Someone had unbraided her hair and the liberated locks tumbled about her shoulders.

"You..." She didn't know how to finish her thought.

He rose from the chair and crossed the room to sit on the edge of her bed. He gently laid a warm finger over her mouth and shook his head. "Not tonight, my love," he murmured. "Tonight is for you."

"But - "

"Shh - Only you."

He drew back the sheet and captured her hand before helping her to her feet. More rose petals littered the floor. They felt wonderfully sexy against her bare feet as she allowed him to lead her to the full-length cheval mirror tucked into a corner of the room. He positioned her in front of him and placed his hands on her shoulders.

"I want you to watch, my love."

A tremor of desire shot through her limbs, far more potent then any alcohol on earth. Shai felt weak, her limbs jellylike as he drew her back to rest against him. He towered behind her and his hands looked shockingly erotic against the blue silk as he traced the curves of her body. A rush of desire raced through her limbs, so strong it threatened to knock her to her knees.

Reaching her shoulders, he drew his hands down her arms and

captured her slender wrists. His fingers locked around them as he drew her arms up, guiding her fingers to lace behind his neck. The silk of her chemise drew taut across her full breasts and a soft entreaty broke from her lips as her nipples tightened against the gentle friction.

"You remember last night, do you not?" he murmured against her shoulder, his lips brushing her sensitized flesh.

"Yes." Her voice quivered.

"Don't remove your hands or I'll stop touching you. Do you understand?"

Throat dry, she nodded as he slid his hands down the curve of her arms before stopping at the tops of her breasts.

"I want you to watch as I love you. If you close your eyes, I'll stop until you open them again." He nipped her neck, his teeth blazing a trail of fire over her skin, before raising his dark head to meet her heated gaze in the mirror.

She nodded once more, not trusting herself to speak.

He smiled. "Good." His fingertips lightly outlined her breasts, the sensitive outside curve and the vulnerable underside. Back and forth. Back and forth. "Tell me what you want me to do, Shai."

"Touch me." Her voice came out as a sigh, long and drawn.

"Where do you want me to touch you?"

"Everywhere." In the mirror, she watched as he stroked her aroused flesh through thin silk. The feel of his hands against her chemise and exposed skin was shocking, erotic.

He chuckled. "That's not specific enough."

"Touch my breasts."

He cupped their full weight, gently plumping and squeezing while making no attempt to caress their aching tips.

"Please," she panted, torn between pulling away from his tormenting touch and leaning into him for more.

"Please what? Tell me what you desire, Shai."

"I..." Her cheeks colored at the thought of whispering such explicit requests.

"Come now." His tone was gently chiding. "Don't be embarrassed with me, my love. There's no room for modesty in the bedroom."

"Touch my nipples," she whispered. He complied by caressing them into full arousal, gently pinching and teasing until she bucked against his increasing erection. "I want you to use your mouth," she gasped. "Suckle me."

He chuckled. "I thought you would never ask."

He unlaced her hands from behind his neck and moved. Placing her hands on his shoulders, he lifted her into his arms until her breasts were level with his mouth. Slowly, he drew one silk-covered nipple into his mouth and rolled it with his tongue.

She cried out at the sensations he was creating through the delicate silk. Warmth rushed to her vagina, raising her temperature to a fevered pitch. She wrapped her legs tightly around his waist, her fingers tangling in his hair, urging him closer as he transferred his mouth to her other breast. He nipped, sensations of pleasure and pain mingling to bring her to mindlessness.

He released his grip on her, allowing her to slide down his body, then resumed his former position behind her, replacing her hands behind his neck. He withdrew the jewel-handled dagger from his waist.

He held the knife in full view and the candlelight gleamed brilliantly on its colored stones and wicked blade. Her breath caught. He moved the dagger and gently pressed the flat of it against her silk-covered stomach, then slowly began to draw it upward.

Shai couldn't tear her gaze from the blade. Half of her was afraid he'd cut her while her other half was turned on beyond belief. Jewels glistened and she ached to feel them against her skin.

As if reading her thoughts, he removed the blade to slip it inside the low neck of her chemise.

"Is this what you want, my love?" He nipped her earlobe before catching it, tugging on her trapped flesh. The blade dipped lower and sliced through the silk. "I won't let it score your skin. It's only here to tempt and tease, not maim."

The knife continued its path, separating the delicate silk to her belly button. Shai quivered, her breath catching as it reached the top of her panties. He didn't stop until he reached the hem and her chemise hung limply on her body, the front sliced neatly in two. He raised the blade to the delicate shoulder straps. Dipping the blade under the first, his eyes met hers in the mirror.

Should she want this? Was she being incredibly brazen?

Holding her breath, Shai nodded and he cut first one, then the other.

The chemise fell in a silken swoosh, leaving her bare except for the matching panties.

He slipped his hand over her stomach, his fingers lightly brushing the top of her panties. "Shall I?"

"Please." She arched against him, his erection pressing into her lower back. If she didn't get him inside her quickly, she'd explode.

He brought the knife around and cut the panties away, allowing them to drop to the floor.

She quelled the urge to cover herself. In the mirror, reflected in the golden candlelight, her skin looked creamy pale. For the first time in her life, wrapped in this man's arms, she almost felt beautiful.

"Spread your legs for me."

She hastened to comply, spreading her legs ever so slightly. The air felt warm and alien against her damp, exposed flesh.

"More."

She took a shaky breath and parted her legs further. Her gaze met his in the mirror and he smiled.

"Watch closely, my angel. I want to see you come apart for me." He dipped his fingers inside her warmth and a cry wrenched from her as he touched the center of her desire. "Does this please you?"

She nodded, not trusting herself to speak coherently. She arched as his strokes increased. Her breathing grew labored and her legs wobblier as he quickly brought her to the edge and tumbled her over. She fell back fully against him and he effortlessly swept her off her feet and carried her across the room.

He dropped her onto the bed in a flurry of petals and stood over her, his breathing ragged, eyes dark with desire. He dropped to his knees and pressed her thighs apart, skimming his hands upward until he reached her apex. He delved into her damp folds, seeking the aching bud at the center of her desire.

He stroked with a slow figure eight motion and Shai arched against his masterful touch. Her gaze never left his as he moved the blade into view.

Surely he wouldn't...

"Is this what you want?" He lowered the dagger and teased her damp opening with the cool metal of the handle. She quivered, horribly afraid, yet wanting it inside her all the more.

Breathless, she nodded and he smiled in satisfaction. Gently, he inserted the handle until the hilt was firmly pressed against her clitoris, the cool metal stretching her, filling her. He pressed her knees upright and together, then rocked her back and forth as he retained a grip on the blade.

The friction was incredible. As her body moved against the tenderly caressing hilt, the large jewels created delicious friction in her vagina. Shai cried out, barely able to draw oxygen into her lungs. Wild pulses of rapture ripped through her body, her senses concentrated on that magical jeweled handle and the man who controlled it.

A low moan signaled the first spasm as her peak loomed before her. She writhed off the bed and her hands knotted in the silk sheets, crushing the fragile petals. Her cries escalated into a shriek as the power of her orgasm ripped through her.

She lay limp and breathless as Val parted her thighs and removed her metal lover. She heard the rasp of a zipper and sighed when his weight settled between her thighs. With a smooth thrust, he embedded himself deep within her. His worn black jeans were soft against her calves and she raised her hands to clutch the front of his shirt. She shifted, taking him deeper and he bit back a groan as his hips gave an involuntary thrust.

She forced her eyes open and met his heated black gaze. He held himself completely still within her and she drew her legs against his hips to urge him on.

He caught her face between his hands. "You're mine," he whispered urgently as he began to stroke.

She groaned, wrapping her arms around his broad shoulders, and met him motion for motion. "Yes," she breathed as that awful, terrible tension began to build once more. "I'm yours."

"Forever," he whispered.

"Forever," she sobbed as she reached her peak once more.

With one final thrust, he dipped his head to her exposed throat. He peaked just as his teeth broke her skin and he began to drink.

She was perfection. The vampire fondled her full white breasts and the redhead squealed in delight. She was giving him the king of all blow jobs and he was loving life. Maybe he would let her keep this up for hours. Little did she know that he wouldn't allow himself to reach release until he drank her blood.

He sighed and tangled his hands in her brilliant red hair, forcing her head to bob faster and faster on his aching rod. She could easily wear herself out doing this and he could take her without much fuss. But did he want that?

Usually he enjoyed the battle more than the victory. Too bad mortals didn't have more stamina. He grinned as he imagined another redhead whom he'd just left with her dark lover only an hour before. Now there was a woman with stamina! Watching his old nemesis Valentin fuck her with the dagger had almost been his undoing. How he wished he'd been the one wielding that blade.

Soon enough, though, she would be his. Shai would be dangling from his rod and his alone. Maybe he'd let her suck him like an all day sucker and, if she didn't please, then he'd bind and whip her like a dog. He'd really enjoy that and he'd bet she would also.

The image of her bound and waiting for the caress of his whip brought the vampire to a level of desire he'd attained only once before. His teeth snapped together as the delirious rush of lust and hunger made him dizzy with its virulence. Roughly, he wrenched the woman's head upward and tossed her back on the bed. She squealed in delight as he pushed her thighs apart and impaled her.

He slipped his hands around her throat and slowly began to squeeze as his thrusts increased. Her cries changed to pleas as she began fighting and clawing at his ice-cold hands. Strangled sounds emerged from her throat as she struggled to escape him.

The vampire was imagining another redhead beneath him. Wild and willing as she'd been for Val, crying out in ecstasy, only it was his name that she sobbed. "Shai, Shai," he screamed as his desire reached a fevered pitch.

He wrenched his hands from the struggling woman's throat and dropped full length upon her. Enjoying the feel of her full breasts as she struggled to breathe, he caressed her cheek tenderly then dipped his head to her throat.

Her screams filled the night.

Chapter 7

Shai awoke with a groan. The late afternoon sun poured through the half-opened drapes and hit her eyes with the delicacy of a truck through whipped cream. She clambered to her feet, staggered drunkenly to the window and clawed at the fabric until they shut out the blinding rays. She leaned weakly against the wall.

Why in heaven's name did she feel like this? She ran a shaky hand through her tangled hair. Her mouth felt like cotton. How had someone gotten all these tiny fuzzy socks on each individual tooth? She grimaced.

Maybe breakfast would help. The thought of food sent her stomach rolling and elicited another groan. No! What did she do last night? She frowned as bits and pieces of her evening and her fractured dreams began reasserting themselves.

She remembered sitting on the couch with a bottle of scotch, polishing it off, and she must have fallen asleep. Then he'd arrived.

Or had he?

She frowned, her head pounding. Was he real? A flash of red caught her eye and she reached down to pluck a single red rose petal from her carpet.

Nah...he couldn't be...

She lifted the petal to her nose and the fragile scent of roses teased her senses, evoking images from her dreams of last night. A slow itch began between her thighs and her breasts ached. The small scratches on the base of her neck where he'd bitten her tingled.

What was going on?

She shoved her tangled hair out of her face with a weary hand. Whatever had happened or hadn't, she needed a shower and a cup of coffee right now. She dropped the petal on the dresser and walked toward the bathroom. The ringing of the phone stopped her progress. She grabbed the phone and groaned a greeting into it.

"How soon can you be at the Celebrity Deli on Forty-Second?" Mariah barked into her ear.

"Fifteen minutes. Why?" Shai stifled a yawn. The only thing she really wanted was to climb back into bed. Why was she sleeping so much all of a sudden? It was unusual for her to sleep more than seven hours a day. Was she coming down with something?

"They found another one. Detective Henry is waiting for you on scene. He said you need to see this one in particular."

She frowned, trying to ignore the sudden tightening of her stomach muscles and the churning in her gut that had nothing to do with the scotch from last night. "Why?" she asked.

"How would I know? Get your behind down there ASAP." With that, Mariah hung up the phone.

She dropped the phone into the cradle and hurled herself to the closet. She had a feeling this wasn't going to be pretty. But horrible things like this were best taken like medicine - quickly.

The requisite crowd was crammed around the police barricade when she arrived a half-hour later. She approached the nearest police officer and asked that he direct her to Detective Henry.

Henry waved her over as Shai started down the dim alley, skirting piles of rotting garbage. She noted with amusement that his hair was more rumpled than ever. That and the rings under his eyes told the story and she knew this case was wearing him out. He wasn't the only one.

"Another one?" she asked without preamble.

He nodded slowly. "Sure is. Another beautiful girl, slain and thrown aside like yesterday's rubbish."

"Why did you call me down here, Henry?"

"I think you can help me on this one, Shai." He was watching her carefully. "I want you to take a look at this young woman and tell me what you see."

Sweat broke across her brow and her palms went clammy. She rubbed her hands against her worn jeans. "Okay."

He led her to where a small knot of police detectives stood. She caught a glimpse of bright red hair between their suit-clad legs and polished shoes. A wave of dizziness hit her and she paused, placing her hand on the damp brick wall to get her bearings. Henry ushered the men away and waved her closer.

One look told her more than she wanted to know about this victim.

The corpse's hair was tangled about her head and trailed into a puddle. Her vivid green eyes stared accusingly into Shai's and she had the feeling she was found guilty. Her eyes closed as she tried to block out the merciless vision of death that danced against her eyelids.

Why is this happening?

She forced her eyes open, fixing her gaze on the woman who lay before her. This beautiful woman was dead because she'd failed her and the killer was still on the loose gathering more victims each day. She blinked her tears away and swallowed the lump in her throat. She wouldn't make that mistake again. Bracing herself, she avoided the woman's face and tried to view the scene impartially.

Perfect pale skin and full red lips were parted in a death grimace to reveal even white teeth. Diamond earrings glinted in her ears and a heavy gold chain remained on what was left of her throat. Her nails were long, painted pale pink, and her toenails matched.

Her breath locked in her throat. The world spun wildly and she wondered why she didn't fall to the ground. Henry continued to speak, but she could make no sense of his words. It wasn't the woman that shook her - it was her clothing.

She was wearing the blue silk chemise that had been cut off of Shai's oh-so-willing body not twelve hours ago by a man she barely knew.

She turned away as tears burned her eyes and bile churned in her throat. Henry caught her arm and led her away from the body to settle her on a battered fruit crate. She caught her breath as he moved in front of her, watching with a concerned expression on his face.

"What did you see?"

"Umm..." Shai frantically scrambled for something. Anything. "She isn't like the others, is she?"

"No, she's not. What's different about her?"

Her hands shook as she rummaged in her bag for a mint, anything to quell her restless stomach. "You're the cop here. Don't you know?"

He snorted. "Of course I do. I want to know what *you* really know about this."

Defeated, she gave up her search and pulled her cotton jacket closer around her. "I tried to tell you what I knew but you wouldn't listen to me," she shot back.

"Shai - "

She was suddenly freezing cold. So cold that nothing would ever warm her again. "She has good teeth," she mumbled into her jacket collar. "Diamond earrings, gold chain. She isn't a prostitute." She raised her head to look at Henry. "That's it, isn't it? She wasn't a prostitute at all."

"Exactly. This young woman was a SUNY student by the name of Rebecca Leigh. She and her sister, Maeve, were reported missing early yesterday evening. Since rigor mortis hasn't set in, she's been dead less than a few hours. What could have happened in that twenty-four-hour period?"

Shai stood and looked him straight in the eye. "I have no idea, Detective."

"You told me yesterday that you'd met the killer of these young women last night, and this was hours after she was reported missing. What did you do after you left the police station?"

She sucked in a startled breath. "You don't think I..."

Henry held up his hand, stopping her flow of words. "I'm not accusing you of anything, Shai. I've known you for many years and I know better than that. I'm simply saying, if you did indeed speak to the killer last night, why would he single you out?"

She didn't answer, her gaze remained fixed with his.

He remained silent for a few seconds. "Do you realize that this young woman resembles you? Is the killer obsessed with you? Why did he suddenly change his MO after all this time? Before, it was prostitutes only, now he's reached into mid-suburbia."

She scowled. "Does this make it an even more hateful crime since it's no longer prostitutes? Once it hits the lily-white public, they'll go ballistic. Is this what you're saying?"

"That's not what I said at all. The bottom line is that I want some answers and I think you're the only one who can give them to me."

"I don't happen to agree." She turned away and walked toward the end of the alley to make her escape. Frustration and anger rolled in her gut, tears stung her eyes. She needed to get away from the police, from the stench of death. The cops had felt the same way about her mother. She was just a whore, they'd said. Did it really matter? Yes. It mattered then and it mattered now.

Henry grabbed her arm and forced her around to face him once again. "Talk to me, Shai. Talk to me now or I'll have you hauled in."

She pulled away from him. "Henry, we've known each other for years, so please trust me now. If I knew what was going on, don't you think I'd tell you? Believe me when I say that I have no more of a clue than you do."

Henry looked doubtful. "Then why did this guy meet you last night?"

"I don't know why this psycho singled me out. All I know is that he did and now I have to deal with his actions. I swear to you that I'll call you immediately if he attempts to contact me again. I honestly think he's a crackpot and he won't." Shai turned and walked away from him once more.

"I'm assigning you twenty-four-hour protection," he bellowed after her.

She shot a smile over her shoulder and continued walking. "It won't help, Henry," she whispered under her breath. "Not this time."

He'd come for her tonight, and this time she was ready for him.

Stretched out on her battered couch, she was dressed in worn sweats and a long-sleeved flannel shirt. She sighed. Even in the height of August, she was freezing. In one pocket, she had a small silver cross. She'd tucked a two-foot sharpened stake under the front of the couch. In her right hand, she clutched a vial of holy water.

Maybe she was going insane, she mused as the clock struck midnight. If she were truly insane, she'd commit herself to Bellevue Hospital. But tonight she wanted answers and there was only one place to get them.

A slight shifting in the shadows drew her attention. The figure of a man took shape in the window, then her lover materialized.

He stepped through the window and Shai struggled to control her breathing as she followed Val's movement toward her with her eyes. She felt an almost irresistible pull towards him, and it was a physical struggle to remain on the couch and lay perfectly still. Her grip tightened on the vial of water.

As he reached the foot of the couch, she swung her leg out and hooked him behind the knee. With a quick jerk, she knocked him off balance. She rolled off the couch and, using his momentum against him, knocked him to the floor. She landed on top, her elbow digging into his diaphragm.

He was much bigger than she'd remembered, she thought wildly as she struggled to pin him and uncork the tiny bottle. Maybe she should have taken some self-defense courses before trying this. She managed to get it open and spilled a few drops on her stunned lover. He hissed. With shaking hands, she dribbled a few drops on her fingertips and began to chant a traditional Catholic blessing while she drew a cross on his forehead with the liquid.

"In the name of the mother," she gasped.

He laughed and shoved her off him and onto the floor next to him. She landed with a thud. "You have that backward. It starts 'In the name of the Father...'"

She whipped the small silver cross out of her pocket and held it before her like a shield. "Stay back."

Val burst into laughter and the sound of it sent shivers of desire down her spine. Until she noted that he was rolling on the floor like a child, clutching his sides.

"You're supposed to be reeling in horror," she snapped.

He shook his dark head and reached over, plucking the cross from her numb fingers. "I wasn't a Christian when I lived on this earth as a mortal. It certainly has no power against me now. You watch too many movies." He tossed the cross over his shoulder and it landed somewhere in the darkened corner of the room.

She pulled the stake out from under the couch and pointed it at him. "Come any closer and I'll stake you," her voice wobbled.

He grinned, his mirth subsiding as he easily pulled the stake from her hands. "I don't eat meat," he quipped.

She glared and began moving away in an awkward crab walk. Within seconds, he caught her and forced her flat to the floor, his body imprisoning her. "No!" She protested as his lips trailed fire down her throat.

He pulled back and stared down at her. "Why the resistance now, angel?" he purred. "You weren't fighting me last night. In fact, I thought you were going to tear me apart to get me inside of you." He nipped her earlobe, wrenching a moan from her.

"I didn't know what you were last night." She struggled to free her arms.

"And this matters?" He bit the top button off her blouse and spit it carelessly across the room.

"Of course it matters." She jerked to the left, trying to avoid his oh-so-talented mouth as it descended once more.

"It won't matter once I've buried myself in you." He licked the vulnerable skin between her breasts before zeroing in on the next button. It bounced off the end table when he spit it to the side.

Shai groaned. Already her body betrayed her. Her breasts ached and she squirmed against the wonderful yet terrible hardness in his pants. "I don't want you," she protested as her desire grew to an almost unbearable level. "I can't want you." She moved restlessly beneath him.

He chuckled against her plump breast. "You lie to me, beautiful. Your body tells me the truth." He nipped the rosy peak of her breast. "Tell me why you're trying to lie to me." He noisily suckled her.

She could barely think, let alone speak coherently. "Let me up. I can't breathe." He let go of her nipple reluctantly and gave a devilish smile that curled her toes. He moved off her body and allowed her room to rise. She struggled to pull her rumpled self back together, but it was difficult when most of her shirt buttons had been bitten off. She settled for pulling the two halves together, then crossing her arms under her breasts.

She looked down at the vampire who still sat on her floor. "I have some questions for you," she announced, then settled on the edge of the couch. She regretted her move when he rose from the floor and sat next to her.

"I am an open book." He reached out, captured a bright red curl and twirled it about his finger.

Shai started to rise, but he refused to relinquish her lock of hair. Instead, she scooted herself into a corner of the couch and tried to sit as far away from him as possible. "W-w-who are you?" Her voice trembled.

He grinned. "It is a bit late for that, isn't it? I think you know me very well by now...Better than most..."

"Did I have a choice?" she snapped.

He looked surprised. "A choice? From what I understand, you never wanted a choice. If I remember correctly, your exact words were that you wanted 'a dark, mysterious lover to ravish you long into the night. A man who would force you to give into your body's demands.'"

She frowned. The statement niggled her brain. Then it hit her. "That night at the Casa Roma. You weren't there when we were talking about that - "

"I heard you nonetheless. You were with your friends and the pretty blonde asked you what your secret fantasy was. You said you wanted someone to enter your room by the bedroom window and ravish you until dawn. To give yourself completely to him and your desires, I believe." He dropped her curl and captured her hand. "Did I not do this?"

"I was drunk and you were eavesdropping," she stated baldly. "You can't just break into people's houses..."

He shook his head as he turned her hand and traced the delicate lines of her palm. "You invited me in. You knew I was there that night and you knew who I was and exactly what I wanted." He kissed her palm.

Shai tried to ignore the current that tingled up her arm. Oh, how she wanted to give in to him. "No! I didn't know, I thought you were a dream, a figment of my imagination."

He dropped her hand and sat back with a pained expression on his handsome face. "I've been friends with Jennifer for many years. Surely this will go a long way to reassure you as to my character."

"She's never mentioned you before."

"Do all of your friends know all of your other friends?"

"Well, not really - "

"Is there anything else?" He captured her ankle and tugged her toward him. "I'd really like to move on to more important matters."

"What could be more important than a dead woman wearing the nightgown you cut off of me?"

Val stopped and stared at her, his expression annoyed. "What are you speaking of?"

"Have you been reading about the serial killer here in New York?"

He nodded, his expression guarded.

"The police found another body in an alley tonight. She looked like me and she wore the chemise that you cut off me last night." Shai watched his expression turn stony. She was hoping he'd show some kind of emotion that would tell her one way or the other if she were off base. She was sorely disappointed. "What can you tell me of this?"

"What would I know of dead women and torn lingerie?" His tone was remote.

"You tell me." She wrenched her foot from his grasp and stood. "You know a hell of a lot more than you let on."

Val ran his fingers through his hair, causing it to tumble onto his forehead. His expression was exasperated.

Damn, but he's gorgeous.

"He will not hurt you, Shai. I swear it."

She tensed. *Now* she was getting somewhere. "You know who he is?"

"Yes, but..."

"Give me his name," she demanded.

"No. You cannot stop him. No one can."

"Is he blond with icy blue eyes? Stands about six feet and built like a wall?" she snarled. "I already know his physical description. I met him last night. All I need is a name and I can get him put away for good."

His expression turned dark. "You met him? Where?"

"He called and asked me to meet him - "

"You actually went to meet him?" he roared as he came up off the couch. His eyes glittered with a strange black light and she wondered if she'd been unwise in letting that piece of information slip.

"It was in a restaurant and it was crowded. He couldn't have hurt me in public - "

"You're a fool! He could have killed you and left you to bleed to death in your soup and none would have been the wiser." He paced the floor like a caged animal and she couldn't help but admire the ripple of sleek muscles under his black cotton shirt and black jeans. "You'd have been a number like the rest of them - "

"I don't think he wants to hurt me. It appears he's playing a game with me," Shai interrupted. "He said he enjoyed the chase and that I was to catch him."

Val whirled to face her and gripped her upper arms. "You'll go nowhere near him," he hissed.

"Indeed!" She tried to pull away, but he didn't release his hold. "Who do you think you are?"

"Your master, little one. You gave yourself to me, don't you remember?" He smiled. "If you do not have the sense to keep yourself safe, it looks like I'll have to do it for you."

With a wave of his hand, she felt a prickle of energy race along her skin before surrounding her, scooping her off the floor as if it were a large invisible hand. She gave a stifled shriek as she floated across the room and into the bedroom to land none too gently on the bed. "What the hell..." she squealed and tried to escape as the energy subsided.

He appeared in the doorway and, with another wave of his hand, white silk ties appeared at the bedposts and tied themselves around her arms and legs, securing her spread-eagled to the bed. Panic fluttered in her chest as she tugged against her bonds to no avail. "Let me go."

Val entered the room and approached the bed, a warm smile curving his lips. "Not until much later, my love. When I'm sure you will be safe." He settled himself on the edge of the bed and leaned against the footboard. "What do you suppose we should do until then, my angel?"

Shai struggled, tears of frustration burning in her eyes. She didn't want to give in to him, but already her body was betraying her. An ancient voice from her soul seemed to be calling for her to give herself to him. She was helpless to resist.

"No," she whispered.

He shook his dark head. "Give in, my love. You know you will in the end. You cannot resist me any more than I can resist you. We're both helpless against our desires. This is your fantasy, is it not?"

She squeezed her eyes shut as his familiar touch moved over her, efficiently removing her clothing. Nimble fingers worked their way over her body until they lightly caressed her breasts. Slowly, they parted the buttonless shirt and her eyes flew open when humid night air touched her breasts.

Val sat unmoving at the end of the bed, his eyes dark with untamed desire, his arms crossing his chest. He smiled as she arched under his invisible caresses. "Do you like that? I can watch you be pleasured by an invisible lover, all the while knowing that I am the only one."

Invisible lips settled over the rosy crest of her breast and began to suckle while she twisted and whimpered on the bed. Already, he knew where to touch, to caress, to arouse cries from her soul. Fingertips traced a trail of fire to the tops of her sweats. With a flick of his finger, all of her clothing disappeared and she lay naked and vulnerable on the bed before him.

"Just wait till you see the things I can do for you, my love. I can give you the world," he crooned as her invisible lover took her to the heights of pleasure.

She strained toward mystical hands as they plundered her body. No part was left untouched, unkissed. She didn't want him this way. She wanted him, the man, not the magic.

"I want to feel you against me," she gasped out. "Your flesh against mine." She looked deep into his black eyes. "Please."

Val looked startled, yet absurdly pleased. Suddenly the invisible hands on her body were gone and there was only the two of them. "Your wish is my command, angel," he breathed.

He slipped the dagger from the top of his pants and dropped it soundlessly to the rag rug beside the bed. She held her breath as he reached for her. Long-fingered and lightly callused, he had capable hands, sensual hands.

He moved between her thighs to stroke her warm, sensitive flesh. She shivered as his strong fingers pressed into her skin. Lightly, he skimmed upward, parting her delicate folds.

"I saved the best for myself, of course." He dipped his head.

Shocked, she tried to twist away from him, "Val!"

He kissed the inside of her thigh. "Do not be so shy, angel. We have shared much more than this simple kiss."

He dipped his head and touched his tongue to her innermost core, and she cried out at the exquisite sensations he aroused. She tried to get away from his tormenting kisses, but he held her firmly against his mouth by gripping her hips and holding her still. Ripples of ecstasy began deep inside and radiated out as whimpers broke from her lips. Soft breathy cries filled the room as Val brought her desire to full flame.

He kissed a path up her body, pausing to suckle here and nibble there as Shai lay sated in his arms. He gave her a knowing smile, then took her lips in a kiss that was earthy and powerful. He tasted of dark, carnal desire and her sex. Her hands and legs were released all at once and she wrapped her legs around his jeans-clad waist and tangled her fingers in his hair.

She clung to him as his tongue thrust deep into her mouth in an erotic imitation of the ecstasy that was to come. She wanted him against her, not hidden by the barrier of Levi Strauss. She reluctantly let go of his hair and skimmed her hands down to liberate the buttons on his jeans, sighing as the heavy length of him sprang free. He was magnificently made. She broke their kiss as she slipped her hand around his erection and began stroking him in a lazy fashion.

"For me?" she purred.

Val grinned. "But of course, madam." He gripped her by the waist and rolled over until she was sprawled across him. He laced his fingers behind his head. "To do with as you wish."

She put her hand on his chest to catch her balance. A feeling of power surged through her and she knew exactly what she wanted. She wanted to impale herself on his flesh and remain there the rest of her life. She arched backward. Her long hair brushed her backside and she shivered. His erection jumped and throbbed, pressing tightly against her damp folds.

She rose on her knees and poised over him. Gaze intent upon his face, she impaled herself on his willing flesh. He filled her so perfectly, like they were made for each other. She raised her arms behind her head, thrusting her breasts outward. She tipped her head forward, shifting her hips slightly as she adjusted her position. She looked down at him through a thick curtain of hair. "I'm perfectly content now. How about you?"

His grin was wicked. Suddenly, he shifted his legs up and she tumbled forward onto his chest. Before she knew what was happening, he'd turned her onto her back and she lay pinned beneath him.

"Minx," he whispered between thrusts.

Shai cried out as he nipped her shoulder. She clutched him tightly as his thrusts grew deeper, wilder. Her release was approaching rapidly and it was going to tear her apart.

"Who started this?" she gasped, clutching his backside with damp hands and urging him deeper, harder.

"Does it really matter?" he growled into her ear. "I'm looking forward to the end."

Her release broke over her like a summer storm. Wild and powerful, it seemed to last forever. Tilting her head back, she offered her throat to him for his dark kiss. As his needle sharp teeth broke her skin, she was besieged with a feeling of rightness that she'd never known before.

Chapter 8

Shai adjusted her sunglasses against the late afternoon glare. She wasn't feeling well and she wanted nothing more than to curl up in her bed and remain there until nightfall. Until he came again. Tingles of awareness raced across her body and her knees wobbled. She stifled a grin. She was becoming insatiable.

The sunlight burned her eyes and she felt like she hadn't slept in weeks. She couldn't seem to keep food down either. Everything she ate came back up within minutes. Maybe she was catching the summer flu. There was a particularly virulent strain going around this year.

She scanned the steps of the coroner's office for any familiar faces and saw a few fellow reporters from various newspapers around the city. She nodded in their direction but made no attempt to speak to them. The steps and sidewalk were crammed with reporters from the local press and some from as far away as Maine. They were all waiting for David Worth, the head coroner, to release information about the young woman found last night.

The polished glass door swung open as several men in suits exited and headed for the small bank of microphones. Most of them wore neatly pressed suits and serious expressions. Detective Henry brought up the rear. Henry was dressed as usual, Shai noted with amusement, in rumpled clothing and sporting an ugly brown stain (that looked suspiciously like gravy) on his tie.

"They don't have a clue," a voice whispered in her ear. Cool lips brushed her skin, causing Shai to jump. She spun to face her visitor.

The man from the restaurant stood behind her. His light blond hair was swept back from his forehead and dark glasses hid his eyes. He was dressed simply in blue jeans, a white silk shirt and a lightweight black blazer. He smiled rakishly and grabbed her by the shoulders, forcing her to face the crowd again.

A scream lodged in her throat as he spoke again.

"Don't bother calling, my dear," he breathed. "No one can see me but you."

"Aren't I lucky?" she hissed, forcing her gaze back to the podium.

He chuckled and brushed a cold finger down her cheek. Funny, when Val touched her he didn't feel particularly cold.

"Indeed you are, dearest."

"How did you get the clothing out of my apartment?"

"Who said I did?" he chuckled. "What about your lover? Is Valentin really so innocent? Are you so willing to believe in someone because they fuck you well?"

Shai froze. Was Val as innocent as he appeared? It was glaringly obvious from last night that he knew much more than he'd revealed. She'd even confronted him with this very sentiment and he hadn't bothered to answer her. In fact, he'd done everything he could to distract her.

"Tell me, Shai, how does it feel when he's buried deep inside you? Does he make you all hot and bothered? Does he make you go out of your mind?" He teased her ear.

Revolted, she tried to move away from him, but he yanked her back in place before him. "Shouldn't you be inside or something?" She poked him with her elbow, once again trying to put distance between them. He hauled her back against his chest.

"Sunlight has no effect on me," he laughed.

"That isn't what they say in the movies," she snapped. Several people close to her gave her an odd look. Shai smiled benignly.

"You watch too many movies," he shot back.

"So I've heard," she grumbled.

"Ah yes, very touching, that scene between you and your dark lover. Too bad the stake didn't work or we both might have been rid of him."

She froze, horror trickled down her spine like ice water. "You - "

"Yes, I did. I saw every sordid second of your little interlude. My word, but you are a screamer, aren't you? I would bet that I can make you scream even louder than he. I can't wait to get you underneath me and begging for it."

"Not on your life." She gritted her teeth as he drew her deeper into his steely embrace. She could feel his growing erection against her lower back as he pressed against her.

"No, dear, not on yours." He drew a hand slowly up her thigh and

Shai struggled to remain still. He cupped the apex of her thighs roughly, eliciting a grunt of pain from her.

Damn him...

Desperate to get away, she wrenched herself away from his icy grip and threw herself down the stone steps. She fell down the four steps to land in an undignified heap. Startled gasps were elicited from the crowd as people moved to see if she was okay. Hands reached down to help her to her feet. As her Samaritans stepped away, she swayed on wobbly legs. She locked her knees and looked up the steps to see the killer standing at the top, laughing at her.

"Good move, Shai. You took me by surprise with that one. You may have won this round, but the next one will be mine. Figure out who the killer is and catch him if you can. If you fail, you'll be next."

She turned and shoved her way through the hovering throng and ran toward the street, her heart pounding. She was so confused. Who was telling the truth? She didn't know Val from anyone. Was he lying to her? Was the stranger really the killer or was it her lover all along?

The sun had barely set when he arrived at her apartment. Shai sat at her dining room table, a fragile bone china cup of Darjeeling tea set before her. She glanced briefly at him then back at the wilting flowers on the table. "I saw him again today," she said tonelessly.

He moved closer and she held up her hand to stop him. "No. Please sit down." She waved at the chair facing hers. "I want to know what's going on here, and I mean all of it."

Val hesitated before he sat and Shai felt his black gaze impaling her, staring hard at the purple bruises on her temple and cheek. "Did he do that to you?" He spoke in a deathly calm voice.

She shook her head in denial. "It was an accident."

"Why do I not believe you?" When she failed to respond, he spoke quietly. "What do you want to know?"

"Who is he?"

"His name is Mikhail. He was born in Kiev about nine hundred years ago," he stated simply. "He was a Viking slaver."

"What about you? Who are you?"

"I am Valentin, the son of Merrick from what is now known as England. I am twelve-hundred years old."

"How do you know Mikhail and what is he doing here?"

He hesitated and Shai glanced away from the limp flowers to meet his disturbed gaze. A part of her wanted to soothe his wrinkled brow while a larger part of her wanted to rail at him for hiding things from her.

"I created him," he said in a quiet voice.

Disbelief formed in the pit of her stomach. "You did what?"

"I made him into a vampire. Accidentally."

"How does one do this *accidentally*?" She struggled to control her voice. Her head was aching horribly and all she wanted was to lie down. Her body was a mass of bruises and there wasn't anything on her that didn't hurt. Funny, she didn't remember hitting that many steps when she'd fallen.

"It isn't very easy," he admitted. "In order to turn someone into a vampire, you must either drink from them three times and force them to drink the blood of a vampire, or drain them completely and force them to drink."

"Three times?" she asked faintly, and grabbed her throat.

"You're perfectly safe unless you drink from me."

"That's so reassuring." Shivers ran down her back at the thought of actually drinking blood. More disturbing was that her stomach didn't rebel as much as it would at the thought of a sandwich.

He frowned. "You doubt me."

"What do you expect? I don't know you!"

He shook his head, his expression sad. "You're so wrong, Shai. You know everything about me that is important. Mortals place such emphasis on knowing someone for a long period of time before trusting them. Little do they realize how limited their time on this earth is."

She felt like a crumb. But how could she trust a man who crept around in the dark of night? He held too many secrets and made no attempt to share any part of himself. Now some madman was stalking her and Val expected blind faith. She couldn't do that. Too many times she'd been let down with disastrous results. She knew without a doubt that failure now would spell her death.

"I can't," she whispered brokenly. Already, she felt the distance growing between them at her words. It was that couldn't be breached, and that would surely break her heart.

Val nodded and rose from his chair, his expression closed. He moved to the window. "Let me know when you are ready to trust in me. It is this that will set you free." He faded into the shadows leaving her alone in the darkness.

Chapter 9

The vampire settled on the truck ramp to wait. Midnight approached and soon his little angel would, also. Too late for this one, of course, but he considered her a mere appetizer. He smiled and absently fondled the woman's breast. She wasn't nearly as well-endowed as Shai, but he would have to make do with what he had.

Shai would be his ultimate triumph. He'd wanted her since the first time he'd seen her, many years before when he'd visited her mother on that fatal night. An image of rich mahogany hair and milky white thighs came to mind. Now she'd been a talented woman. She'd given a blow job that had left mortal men reeling for days.

The vampire smiled fondly. And then there'd been her little daughter, Shai. She'd hidden in the living room behind an old armchair while her mother entertained various men. No doubt she'd heard her mother's cries of pleasure when he had paid her a visit. He reached inside his unzipped pants and roughly fondled his stiffening member.

He'd carried a constant hard-on since he'd had Shai in his arms earlier that day. How he loved being a vampire. Hard-ons at the drop of a hat and he could perform anytime, anywhere he wanted and for as long as he wanted. Immortality was the gift that most people associated with being a vampire, but there was so much more than that to enjoy.

Of course, this little woman beside him would take care of that. Not that he needed much time with her. He chuckled and glanced at the sleeping redhead. She was a sure thing.

The woman moaned and tossed her head restlessly as she began to wake. With a flick of his wrist, her clothing was removed and replaced with the cotton sleep shirt that Shai usually wore to bed. Another flick of his wrist produced the black silk ties that he so adored, and the young woman was bound and helpless. He moved over her and, when her drugged green eyes opened, he smiled.

"Who are you?" she asked faintly.

"Maeve Leigh, I'm your local priest and I'm going to help save your immortal soul," he laughed.

She frowned, confusion etched on her picture-perfect face. "What?"

"I call this baptism by fire." He reached down and released his engorged flesh. The confusion left her eyes and her expression turned horrified.

"No," she cried, struggling against her silken bonds.

The vampire grabbed her thighs, roughly forced them apart, and entered her with one swift thrust. As he bent his head to her exposed throat, her screams filled the empty warehouse.

The building was silent and Shai shivered in her lightweight summer jacket. Her hands were clenched in her pockets as her heart pounded. She was on her own this time. Val wasn't going to rescue her, the girls didn't know anything about what was going on, and the police had turned their backs on her. Survival depended completely upon her own actions. She clutched the handle of Val's jeweled dagger secreted in her pocket. It was cold against her damp palm.

She'd never felt more alone in her life.

Her boot heels made hollow thumps on the floor as she walked into the main section of the empty warehouse. Every atom in her being screamed at her to run from this dark place, but her conscience wouldn't let her.

There was an unpleasant odor in the air: mildew, rotting cardboard and the slight underlying scent of death. Something had definitely died in here. Now, if she could just keep herself from being next, she thought with a bitter smile.

Mikhail materialized before her, wearing a tuxedo and a welcoming smile. "I didn't think you would show, my love." He gave a courtly bow.

"How could I refuse such a charming..." She swallowed hard. "...invitation?" Mikhail had called her house just minutes after Val had left. With the screams of a terrified woman in the background, he'd requested her presence. "Where is she?"

"She's here and completely unharmed. A little worse for the wear, of course." He laughed. With a flick of his hand, the shadows behind him shifted and a slight figure walked toward them.

Shai swallowed a cry as the woman stepped into the light. She was an exact replica of her twin found in the alley only the night before. Rich red hair was tangled about her face. Her pale flesh was bruised and she was covered in drying blood from a cut high on her neck. She was dressed simply in a T-shirt and her feet were bare. Shai noted the blank look in her green eyes.

"What did you do to her?" she asked coldly.

"I merely claimed her for myself," he said simply. "Meet Maeve, my latest revenant. All too soon she, too, will become one of the damned. All it takes is one drop, you know!" he laughed gleefully. "Once I have you, I will let the twit go, of course."

"Are you really so sure that you'll have me?"

"Of course I'm sure. I may be many things, lovely Shai, but I am never wrong. You are a moral, upstanding young woman." He waved a hand toward the battered woman. "You would never allow someone to suffer when there is something you could do to prevent it."

He moved forward and she stopped him by shaking her head. "Not so fast, please. May I ask one question first? Why me? Why me out of all the women in this city?"

Mikhail looked surprised. "You don't remember? Don't I look familiar?"

She shook her head once more.

"Of course, you were very young at that time. A child, really. With your mother having so many men in and out of your dingy hovel, why would I have stood out from the herd?"

It was as if ice water were dumped over her head. Dozens of shattered images replayed through her mind like a scratched record. The pattern of the musty old armchair where she'd hidden when her mother "entertained." The strange grunts and cries that had come from behind the closed door. All of her "uncles" wanting to hold her and fondle her. A teddy bear missing one arm. A tall blond man with cold skin and icy eyes.

It was that last night, a handsome blond man with a present for a small child. It had been a glorious china doll, the likes of which a little white trash girl had never seen. She remembered the familiar sounds of sex, the rattling bedsprings and the screams afterward. But these screams had been different, more terrifying. Still, she'd remained behind the chair, too frightened to come out. When the door had opened, Shai remembered feeling so relieved that everything was just as it had always been.

Only it wasn't her mother who emerged from the room, it had been Mikhail. He'd ripped her mother's throat out and drained her like the others. What he hadn't taken, he'd left to soak the bed and the floor around it.

She remembered being picked up and hugged by Mikhail, looking over his shoulder to see her mother lying in a pool of blood, her limbs bound with black silk scarves and her eyes staring accusingly at the young daughter she'd never wanted.

"I see you remember," he commented.

"Why? Why did you kill her?" Shai whispered. "She was all I had."

"Time makes your memory fuzzy, my love. She was but a whore, one of the countless in the world. She beat you, she starved you and she allowed men to pay her to fuck her. How long would it have been until she'd forced you to whore for her? How long would it have been before her customers began to look at you, paw you?" he roared. "She deserved to die!"

Her vision wavered and she felt the world threatening to recede as she struggled to remain upright. To faint now would certainly spell her death. Her only chance was to enrage him enough to forget himself, let his guard down and let her near enough to destroy him.

"You were too late, Mikhail." She feigned nonchalance. "You were years too late. I don't believe you killed her for any altruistic reason. No matter what she did to me or anyone else, no one deserved to die like that."

"I was not too late!" he snarled. "I saved you, damn it!" He began to walk around her in a slow circle like an animal stalking its prey. "Did you know your mother liked kinky things in bed? She loved to be tied up and whipped like a dog."

Shai clamped her lips shut to keep from screaming. Nothing he said mattered to her, she wouldn't let it. Her mother was dead and there was nothing she could do to rectify the past. All she could do now was save herself.

"You killed her to hide the fact that you couldn't satisfy a woman in bed," she taunted.

His face twisted with rage. "You fucking bitch."

She knew she had to push him over the edge. There was a slim possibility she could survive in hand-to-hand combat. If not, hopefully he was so angry he'd destroy her quickly. "I heard her laughing while you were with her. I never heard her laugh at the other men, only you. Why is that? Are you defective below the waist? Can you get it up at all?" She gave him a scathing look. "I don't think so."

A cry of rage ripped from his mouth and he lunged at her. She braced herself and pulled the dagger from her pocket and aimed for his throat. With a snarl, Mikhail impaled himself upon the razor sharp tip. An almost comical look of disbelief crossed his face as blood squirted like a geyser, dousing Shai and the floor around her. She staggered back, scrubbing furiously at her eyes and sliding on the slick floor. The taste of blood filled her mouth while a dull roar filled her ears.

The world tilted wildly and she fell to the cement. She struggled to open her eyes only to see Maeve move toward her, as if to help, but Mikhail backhanded the young woman, knocking her to the ground where she lay still.

He loomed over Shai, calmly pulling the knife out of his throat. He smiled a feral smile. "You lose." His voice was raspy from his damaged vocal chords. "Don't you know you cannot kill a vampire? I told you before you watched too many movies."

"Bastard," she croaked. She watched in disbelief as the gaping wound closed itself, but she noticed he was much paler than before.

He began to remove his tie and unbutton his once-elegant shirt. "And to the victor, the spoils."

Her head throbbed and she was having trouble breathing. Everything seemed to move in slow motion around her. Grayness beckoned at the edge of her vision and she longed to give in to it. Curling onto her side, she clutched her legs, drawing them up into a fetal position.

"This is no time to play the innocent angel," he crooned, tossing his shirt aside. With a wave of his hand, she was stripped naked and clothed in a white silk nightgown. From the hard cement beneath her, a bed materialized, cushioning her battered body. Blood-red sheets adorned the bed and soon she was bound to the brass head- and footboard with black silk ties.

"Time to accept your new lover."

She wheezed painfully. Her ribs creaked, as if they were under a great deal of pressure. The pain was excruciating; yet nothing was touching her. She was freezing cold and her teeth chattered uncontrollably. She tried to move away as he settled on the edge of the bed, but her limbs wouldn't cooperate.

He roughly cupped one breast, but she could barely feel his hand. He was speaking to her, but she couldn't understand his words. It was like someone had turned down the volume on the television and all she heard was white noise.

A sudden movement swung her attention from Mikhail and toward an approaching shadow. All of a sudden, the sound was back with the bang of a gunshot.

Val stepped into the pool of light, anger flashing in his black eyes as he looked at the two of them on the bed. "Enough!" he roared.

Mikhail jumped up from the bed, his expression feral. "You? What are you doing here?"

"Stopping you," Val shot back. "I should have killed you years ago."

Mikhail laughed - a bitter, harsh sound. "Who are you kidding?" he sneered. "It was your mistake that made me into the monster I am."

"You're correct. I did create you and I will destroy you. It's my duty. You've wrought enough havoc in this world. It is over."

He withdrew a gleaming-edged sword from the scabbard at his waist and moved gracefully towards Mikhail, each movement deliberate, deadly. "You cannot escape. Give in to me and I'll show mercy." He spared a glance at Maeve, lying still on the cold cement floor. "Which is more than I can say for you."

"You won't get away with this, Val. You cannot kill another vampire. The Council will not allow this."

"Says who? I'm one of the oldest on this earth. I make my own laws."

A sword materialized in Mikhail's hand. He waved it at his adversary. "So be it. To the victor, the young woman." He slashed the air, not even close to the other man's sword. "Just think of me between those beautiful thighs." He nodded at Shai. "She won't even remember your name."

She raised her head weakly at the crash of swords. Val had Mikhail on the run. His movements were graceful, efficient, while Mikhail flailed wildly like a fish out of water. The blond vampire struggled to keep his footing as Val relentlessly backed him toward the wall.

Her head fell back to the bed as the sounds of battle grew muted and began to fade in and out. Snatches of their angry words washed over her.

"First blood to me," Mikhail chortled.

Shai turned to watch, her heart in her throat as her vision dimmed.

"Merely a scratch, 'twill be healed in moments." Val lunged and slashed at Mikhail's sword arm, nearly severing the appendage. "And the last will be to me," he growled. "Now you die."

A wave of pain crashed over her and she gave an agonized groan. Her stomach rolled. She hurt so badly. How could she stand it much longer? She was dying. She had to be. She couldn't feel anything from the waist down and she was so damnably cold. Mikhail's furious screams broke into her thoughts.

"This is not over," he snarled. "I'll destroy you and your rabid bitch!"

For a blissful moment, there was silence, then the crash of a sword striking cement. Val appeared next to the bed, his sword in one hand, his dagger in the other, and blood soaking his shirt. Shai forced her eyes to remain open as he leaned over her.

"My love," he whispered.

She blinked as she caught his worried expression and tried to reassure him with a smile. "What happened?" she groaned as more chills wracked her body.

He dropped the sword to the floor and cut away her bonds with the dagger. He pulled out a handkerchief and began to wipe the blood from her face. "He's gone, Shai. You did it."

She shook her head, stopping when the movement caused the pain to increase. "No, my love, you did," she panted.

"Did you make the right decision?" he asked. His voice was low, urgent. "You do believe I had nothing to do with these murders?"

"I was foolish. I was so afraid of trusting you. I've been hurt so many times. But that girl is gone now."

His eyes glinted devilishly. "I hope some of her remains with you."

"She does." Her eyelids drooped.

His hand stilled. "Shai, did you drink any of his blood?"

"N-n-no," she chattered as a violent icy chill shook her body.

He pulled the blankets around her in a vain attempt to warm her. "It splattered all over your face. Not even a drop entered your mouth?"

Shai frowned. She remembered stabbing Mikhail and his blood erupting from the wound. It had struck her in the face and mouth. It was possible that she'd swallowed some of it.

She nodded. "Yes, it's possible, but it was only a little. I'm just so glad that t-t-this is over," she chattered. Why was she so terribly cold? She forced her eyes open once more, looked up into his eyes and saw something had disturbed him. She tried to push away and he refused to let her go. She frowned. "What..."

"My angel. You're dying," he whispered.

She stared at him, uncomprehending. He looked about to cry. Was it because of her? "I can't be dying," she whispered. Tears filled her eyes as she became aware of the breath-stealing pain, spreading through her body as her organs ceased functioning. She raised a trembling hand to his cheek, shocked to see purple veins showing through her pale skin. "I can't... I just can't leave you," she cried softly.

"Do you want to stay with me?"

"More than life itself," she whispered as her eyes began to close. She felt so terribly weary. It was too much of an effort to keep her eyes open.

"You have chosen...wisely." His voice was whisper soft as he lowered his head to her throat and his teeth plunged into her neck. Her screams filled the storeroom.

The transformation began...

Retribution

Dedication

*If you are truly blessed, someone will enter your life
and demonstrate that courage, strength and dignity are
more than just words in the dictionary.*

This one's for you, Daddy.

Acknowledgements

I would like to thank the following people, without whose support there would be no J. C. Wilder.

Carol - Your friendship and wisdom mean more to me than you will ever know.

Julia - For saying, "You can" every time I say, "I can't."

Debbie - For listening to me blather about vampires, were-cats and witches...oh my!

To the Ladies of the Keep - may the Moet always be chilled, may the bonbons always be Godiva, and may the DB's always dance in your honor.

Chapter 1

Current day - London, England

Conor MacNaughten gripped his partner's generous hips as he thrust into her. Her magnificent breasts, highlighted by the harsh noonday sun, jiggled with his movements and with each thrust an excited cry broke from her lips. Damp blonde hair obscured her features as she dug at the tangled sheets with red-tipped claws. The scent of sex filled the air.

Catherine had the best breasts he'd seen in years, at least for breasts that were organically grown. Large and pert with coral shaded aureoles and distended nipples, these beauties were a feast for a starving man. And Conor MacNaughten considered himself a starving man. His hips never slowing, he leaned forward, took a firm nipple into his mouth and suckled deeply.

A hoarse cry emerged from Catherine's mouth as she bucked wildly beneath him. She reached for him and fisted her hands in his hair. He nipped at her breast, leaving a tiny love bite before lavishing attention on the other as he continued his slow thrusts. Rolling his hips easily as he slipped into her moist heat, he felt the faint tingling in the back of his calves that signaled his approaching orgasm.

"Conor..."

Mac paused, stifling a groan. While her body was any seventeen-year-old's wet dream, her voice was a definite problem. Shrill and somewhat whiny, it was the voice of a petulant five-year-old, not a mature, sexually adventurous woman. And he definitely was not in the mood to listen to it now. It had been over three weeks since he last had sex and he had some lost time to make up.

Without as so much as a "by your leave," he withdrew from her damp heat, and gathered the scattered pillows from the floor. As he bent over, his medallion swung forward on its fine gold chain and hit him on the nose. Impatiently, he tossed it over his shoulder and continued his task, piling the pillows on the bed. Grabbing her by her waist, he then rolled her over onto the pyramid of silk so that her generous backside now pointed upward.

"What are yo..."

He cut her off by gently pushing her face down into the sheets, angling her backside even higher and exposing her glistening inner flesh. He thrust deep inside her once again and her muffled squeal of delight emanated from the bedcovers. Taking a firm grip on her hips, Mac settled himself in for a leisurely ride.

Current Day - South of Manchester, England

Terror and rage warred within Jennifer Beaumont's soul as she entered the sprawling house. Rage was winning the battle.

The massive front door slammed with a heavy thud as she kicked it shut. Her Italian leather pumps clicked sharply on the marble floor as she barreled toward the double doors of the library. She tossed her purse in the direction of the glass-topped table in the center of the foyer, where it glanced off the towering vase of pink and white gladioli. The arrangement tottered dangerously before righting itself.

"Damn his miserable hide," she swore as she wrenched the brass doorknob downward. She hit the oak door with the palm of her hand, slamming it backward into the wall with a crash, destroying the cozy scene inside.

The vampire Mikhail stood before the fireplace watching her entrance with an indulgent smile. Hundreds of years ago, she'd thought Mikhail a handsome man. At six feet in height, every inch of it lean-muscled, he cut a striking figure. His pale gold hair was shorn just beneath his ears and neatly combed back to reveal a narrow face with exquisite cheekbones, sharp nose and a full mouth. With his impeccably cut black leather pants that accentuated his strong runner's legs and his flowing white silk shirt, he resembled a golden pirate of old. It was only when she looked into his eyes that she could see his one flaw.

He had no soul. His icy blue eyes reflected only emptiness.

"Damn your black heart, Mikhail," Jennifer ground out. "You've gone too far this time."

He laughed gently and held his arms out as if he expected a welcoming hug. "Darling Jennifer, is this anyway to greet your master?"

Jennifer could barely control the rage that flared as he spoke. She wanted to scream until the fine crystal of the chandelier shattered, raining down on them in piercing shards. She wished to tear him limb from limb, scattering the pieces to the ends of the earth. She wanted to personally escort his black soul to the very gates of hell.

Calling upon her infamous iron will, she restrained herself. Throwing a fit in front of Mikhail would accomplish very little. Indeed, it would only give him the upper hand.

"What have you done?" she bit out.

Mikhail's smiled smoothly, his movements fluid as he picked up a squat Baccarat crystal glass filled with a thick red liquid. Jennifer caught the scent of chilled blood, like cold wet pennies, as he slowly swirled the glass.

"I have no idea what you are speaking of, Jennifer," he purred. Never taking his eyes from hers, he took a sip of the liquid. Jennifer masked her revulsion as he swallowed.

Mikhail's smile broadened as he licked his lips and tipped his head slightly in her direction. "Is this an example of your legendary manners, Jennifer? You storm into my home, damage my library wall and so rudely ignore my guest." With one slim, pale hand, he gestured to the woman seated on the couch. "Your mother would be ashamed of you."

Ignoring his jibe, Jennifer's lip curled as she turned to see Gabrielle DesNoir. Gabrielle's brilliant blue eyes gleamed in stark contrast to the whiteness of her long hair and pale skin. Her full lips were painted a shiny blood red. Her finely honed body was clad in a white leather bustier dress, with matching silk stockings and four-inch pumps.

All in all, she was a perfect advertisement for an ice princess from hell. Gabrielle was well known and not particularly well liked in most vampire circles. Her appeal lay in the fact that her lover, Mikhail, was one of the most powerful vampires on the planet. Very few immortals dared to say no to him. Gabrielle was a young vampire, only about a hundred years old and still learning. With Mikhail as her mentor, she was far more advanced than the average century-old vampire. She was also known for her lack of scruples, which made her the perfect partner for him.

Jennifer inclined her head in Gabrielle's direction. "Gaby," she acknowledged, knowing how the other woman detested the shortening of her name.

"*Chère* Jennifer, so lovely to see you again." Gabrielle's voice was thick with a French accent that Jennifer knew to be as false as her current hair color.

Jennifer turned back to Mikhail. "Where is she?"

"I have no idea what you are talking about." He braced his shoulder against the ornate fireplace mantel. His eyes gleamed with the golden glow from the leaping fire. He reminded her of a sleek jungle cat readying to pounce on its unsuspecting prey. While he might decide to make her his next victim, she wouldn't go down without a fight.

"Who's missing?" His expression was bemused.

"Miranda of Glencoe."

Jennifer didn't miss the spark of satisfaction that flared in his eyes before he feigned surprise. "Really? Miranda is missing? How dreadful. My love," he addressed Gabrielle, "when was the last time we saw Miranda?"

Gabrielle rose from the couch with her unearthly grace and moved toward her lover. "Well, I think it may have been a few years, at least. Maybe it was at Kitty Von Helgen's birthday party? She'd just turned 371 though she doesn't look a day over 40." She reached Mikhail's side and took the glass from him, then turned to Jennifer. "I don't remember seeing you at that party. Weren't you invited?" She took a drink, her sharp eyes watching Jennifer over the rim of the glass.

Jennifer struggled keep her expression impassive. "I hope the next time I see Kitty Von Helgen it will be to spit upon her rotting corpse," she spoke evenly. Ignoring Gabrielle's start of surprise, she turned her attention back to Mikhail. His icy eyes were amused. "You've gone too far this time, Mikhail," she warned.

"Dearest Jennifer, you wound me." He placed a slim hand over his heart as if her words had dealt him a mortal blow.

"How can I wound someone who is not human?" She glanced from Mikhail's amused gaze to Gabrielle's self-satisfied one. They were presenting a united front. Maybe now was a good time to put a crease into it. A little dissension in the enemy's ranks was a good thing when faced with open warfare.

"Both you and I know that I could never actually hurt you, Mikhail." Jennifer moved over to a navy leather wing chair and settled herself on the arm. She carefully arranged her burgundy skirt, allowing Mikhail a flash of thigh. She swallowed her revulsion as she felt his interested gaze sweep her flesh. "However," she leaned against the back of the chair, her posture deceptively casual. The V-neck of her blouse gaped slightly, allowing Mikhail an unobstructed view of her black lace bra. "We both know that would be a waste of time and energy."

Mikhail smiled faintly. Gabrielle hissed her displeasure as her lover's gaze lingered on Jennifer's exposed flesh. Mikhail ignored her. "What do you want from me, little Jennifer?"

"The truth." Jennifer shifted so her blouse once again obstructed his personal peep show. "Renault found evidence of drugs and he saw you and this she-cat steal Miranda away. I want to know why you have done this. As you know, Miranda is an old and dear friend of mine and quite naturally I am concerned for her welfare."

Mikhail's smile faltered and then returned in full force. "So much for stealth, my dear," he said to the bristling Gabrielle. He looked again at Jennifer, "And here I thought I was being so clever."

Jennifer wasn't fooled. Mikhail was not a stupid man. Unbalanced and reckless yes, but never stupid. He'd wanted Renault to see him and Gabrielle take Miranda. She was as certain as she knew her own name that this little "slip" was a part of his plan. Now she just had to figure out the purpose of his actions and how to get Miranda out of the middle of it. "What have you done with her?"

"I have her hidden away, somewhere safe."

"I want to see her."

"No," Gabrielle snarled. "You cannot see her. Now you toddle off and tell Val..."

Jennifer glanced at Gabrielle, concentrating briefly on the crystal glass in the other woman's hand. A second later it exploded, raining blood and crystal over both Mikhail and Gabrielle, who erupted into shrieks while Mikhail looked pained.

"Really Jennifer, Baccarat crystal. Was that necessary?" He retrieved a snowy white handkerchief from his pants pocket and dabbed at the front of his ruined silk shirt. "I think you have damaged enough of my possessions for one day. First you damage the wall by throwing the door open, now this."

"You fucking bitch," Gabrielle snarled, her accent changed from stilted

French to harsh Brooklyn tones.

Jennifer noted with some satisfaction that the exquisite crystal had cut deeply into the woman's hand. Blood flowed from the wound and if it was possible, she looked even paler than before.

Jennifer laughed shortly, "It isn't as if you won't heal." She rose from the arm of the chair, fixing Mikhail with her stare. "I meant what I said, Mikhail, I want to see Miranda before this goes on any longer."

Mikhail tossed the blood-soaked cloth into the fire with a hiss. "Fine. I will..."

"You cannot take her to..." Gabrielle interrupted.

"Silence," Mikhail ordered. He glanced down at the slowly expanding pool of blood at her feet. "You are ruining my Aubusson. Get a towel and go drip somewhere else."

Gabrielle cradled her injured hand to her chest as she started toward the door and threw a venomous glare at Jennifer. "I will get you for this, you bitch," she snarled. "You are only a revenant, a servant of the Master, and you can be killed."

"And you are a woman of your word, aren't you, Gaby?" Jennifer's smile was thin. "Go do your roots, they need attending." As the female vampire stormed from the room, Jennifer knew she would regret her words sooner or later. Her smile faded. Gabrielle would not soon forget this slight and she just might end up paying dearly for having the last word. Jennifer could only hope that she would not end up paying with her life.

Mikhail chuckled, causing chills to roll down her spine. "And you thought that I was bad."

Jennifer forced a mocking smile. "You, sir, are not a very attentive lover."

He rolled his eyes theatrically. "If my dearest Gaby were in true mortal danger, as it were, I would leap to the ends of the earth to save her, or at least into town to get her some bandages. But we both know she will heal within moments and be back to prick your side with yet another thorn."

"Which we know will do very little if no lasting damage to me as well," Jennifer said lightly.

"Touché." Mikhail smiled as he moved across the room to take her arm. "You asked to see Miranda. She is this way."

She took a deep breath, steeling herself for his touch. As his cold hand clasped her arm, the chill sank instantly through the silk of her shirt and fear once again reasserted itself. The first thing she was going to do when she got back to the house was burn her clothing and take a searing hot bath. Yet she nodded serenely and allowed him to lead her from the room. Mikhail escorted her out into the foyer and toward the back of the house.

"You have heard the old adage, 'Be careful what you wish for because you soon might get it'?" he asked.

Jennifer ignored her growing sense of unease. "What do you hope to accomplish?"

He laughed and shivers rippled across her skin. "Even you should know the answer to that one, Jennifer. I want retribution from Val." He shrugged easily as he opened a small door tucked beneath the mammoth staircase. He gestured for her to go first. "He owes me."

She glanced uneasily down the narrow, twisting staircase. The scent of mildew, rotting cardboard and something not easily defined reached her nose. She didn't think Mikhail would play foul with her; he needed her too much to accomplish the next step in this deadly game he played. But she still wasn't one hundred percent sure. Besides, she'd never liked small, dark places.

"Scared?" Mikhail's smooth voice taunted.

Jennifer squared her shoulders and stepped through the door into the stench, stopping at the small landing at the top of the steps that descended into her own personal version of hell. "What does Val owe you for?" she asked, desperate to keep her mind off the numbing darkness that awaited her on those narrow steps.

"Where shall I begin? Stealing my women, for one. Shai was mine as her mother was before her. Maeve was also a chosen one as was her sister Rebecca. And let's not forget you, dearest Jennifer. You were to be my greatest triumph until *he* ruined it. Val had no right to interfere in my plans."

He shut the door with a soft click and the darkness was complete. She pressed her back against the wall as he maneuvered past, and her hand curled convulsively around the wrought iron banister. He took the opportunity to press tightly against her, and she felt the iron of his arousal. Biting her lip until she tasted blood, she held herself stiff,

97

unyielding as he reached around her, his breath caressing her unprotected throat.

"Do you remember that night?" Cool fingertips caressed the exposed skin. "The night I made you immortal?"

"Made me a monster, you mean?" Jennifer choked, unable to hide the bitterness in her tone.

"You aren't a monster, darling, and you know it. You will live forever, just like me." His voice trailed off as he pressed a tiny kiss against the base of her throat. "Just like me..."

"I am nothing like you," she ground out. She raised her hands to his chest and pushed, but he didn't give an inch. Panic blossomed in her chest as the twin devils of the darkness and the vampire began to claw at her soul.

"Ah, darling, you are exactly like me. More like me than you will ever know. That is why I chose you. I would have loved you forever, Jennifer. I would have put you above all others, even Shai. But then you left me." His tone was mockingly sorrowful as his hands skimmed down her back to grab at her backside, and he thrust himself against her even tighter.

"Escaped is what you mean. Are you angry with Val for taking away Shai and rescuing Maeve or because he, too, escaped you? Is it because he beat you at your own game? He's one of the few vampires that doesn't cower before you, and that bothers you doesn't it?" She concentrated on her words rather than the man who was pressed so tightly against her. Panic threatened to strangle her as a scream built in her chest.

He shoved her, knocking her head into the wall with a sharp rap. "He did not beat me and neither did you. You came back to me not long ago, and you will again," he growled. His hands slid up her back to grip her shoulders, his breath, stale with old blood, on her cheek. "You betrayed me. But then again you betray all the men in your life don't you, my dearest?"

Jennifer stiffened at his verbal jab. "I was taught by the master. Aren't we a little old for groping in a closet?" she snapped, struggling for a tone of disdain.

Mikhail laughed and then released her abruptly. He flicked a wall switch and the narrow staircase was flooded with light. "If you prefer a bed, I can accommodate you." He moved away, gesturing for her to begin the journey down the twisting steps.

"Not on your life." She started down the circular staircase, ducking her head to avoid hitting it on the steps above.

"I wouldn't bet on that if I were you." His hand slipped neatly beneath the weight of her long hair, finding the sensitive nape of her neck. She stumbled and had to put her hands on the rough wall to avoid plunging down the remaining steps. "Whose life will you bet on it? Miranda's?"

"Stop that," she snapped.

Mikhail laughed again and withdrew his hand. "The gods hate cowards."

"I would hardly call it cowardice. I would call it good taste," she replied, starting down the steps again, this time keeping herself at least three steps in front of him.

"Still mourning for Conor MacNaughten, my dear? Or shall I call him The One Who Got Away? How about your Knight in Tarnished Silver?" he taunted. "He left and never looked back, did he? Called you a few choice names if I remember correctly. Of course your name was Lilith then, wasn't it? Was betrayal your middle name then too, darling Lilith?"

Jennifer clutched at the narrow banister, grateful that Mikhail could not see her stricken expression. She'd driven Mac away for his own good, not that he would have seen it that way had he known the circumstances for her defection. Both of their lives had been damaged, hers irrevocably, by her actions. On that night, over a century ago, she'd been left no choice. But not this time. The vampire wouldn't win this game and she would gladly forfeit her life in an effort to stop him from destroying the lives of others.

She forced a carefree laugh from her tight throat. "We parted amicably enough over a century ago, Mikhail. Everyone knows that. Why bring up ancient history?"

"Is that all it is? Has the love of your life been relegated to 'ancient history' in your mind?" He chuckled and Jennifer dearly wanted to drive a rusty nail into his heart. "Somehow I don't think so. I think he mattered very much and he still does, much more than you are letting on. Of course, I alone know that he really wasn't the man for you."

"Then once again, Mikhail, you are wrong as you were then. I never thought he was the man for me."

Engrossed in conversation, Jennifer missed the bottom step. She staggered through the doorway, clutching the doorframe to regain her balance. It opened into a cramped, dank hallway lined with three black doors, each with heavy padlocks.

She glanced back at Mikhail. "Is this *Let's Make A Deal* and I get to pick a door?"

He shook his head, his blond hair gleaming in the subdued lighting. "No, I would say it is more like my own personal chamber of delights." He moved around her easily and strode to the middle door. He unlocked the padlock and opened the door with a flourish. He stepped back, allowing her to once again lead the way.

Jennifer saw with a start that the walls of the small room were covered in a shiny reflective material. Candlelight glowed on the walls, giving it an odd golden gleam. She felt like she'd been wrapped in tinfoil. On closer inspection, she noted that thin sheets of beaten sterling silver had been affixed to the walls, floor and ceiling so not a crack of plaster or wood was visible. No vampire or revenant alive would be able to telepathically link to someone on the outside and call for help.

Including her.

The door closed with a soft snick and she struggled to quell her burgeoning panic. She swallowed, forcing herself to focus on the problem at hand. Now was not the time for hysterics. Miranda needed her calm and focused. Her friend's life depended on the outcome of the next few minutes. In control, she turned toward the narrow bed and the battered woman who lay imprisoned upon it.

Under normal circumstances, Miranda of Glencoe was a strikingly beautiful woman. Almost six feet in height, she was built like a Rubenesque statue. Now she lay on the bed, emaciated and pale. Her long black hair was dirty and tangled, her wrists raw from the silver chains that kept her immobilized. Jennifer noted the tattered clothing and the partially healed bite marks on the woman's throat.

"What have you done to her?" she whispered, unable to hide her horror.

Mikhail tittered. "Only what I knew would bring Val running."

Jennifer swallowed the bile that burned at the back of her throat. Rage clawed at her heart. If it took everything she had for the rest of her days on earth, she would see to it that Mikhail paid for the ill he had perpetrated on Miranda. Even if he killed her in the process, it was a small price to pay for a woman who had been one of her only friends so long ago.

She forced herself to move toward the bed, her usually graceful movements jerky. She seated herself on the edge of the bed before her knees collapsed beneath her. Hesitantly, she touched the woman's hand, where a golden Celtic knot ring gleamed. Jennifer drew her fingers over the familiar pattern that matched the silver ring on her own right hand. A ring of eternity given a lifetime ago from an old vampire to a young and frightened revenant.

A low moan escaped Miranda. From the pale hue of her skin and her apparent weakness, she surmised it had been some time since the vampire had fed. Luckily, Miranda was an Elder and could go for a long period of time without feeding and she wouldn't sustain any lasting damage.

"Miranda, it's me, Jennifer." She gently stroked the woman's dark hair until her eyes fluttered.

"Jen," she whispered through cracked lips.

"Hush now. I had to make sure you were alright." Tears burned the back of her eyes as she noted the hollow look of Miranda's expression. What she had endured, Jennifer didn't know, but she had a few ideas of the terror dealt at the hands of Mikhail.

"You are in danger here. Leave this evil place," Miranda whispered. "Tell Val that I have caused him enough pain…"

"How noble," Mikhail sneered.

"Tell him to take his women far from here." Miranda's voice failed her.

"No," Mikhail shrieked. "Don't you dare tell him that."

In the blink of an eye, Jennifer was hurled away from Miranda's side. She hit the wall with a metallic crash and slid down into a heap on the slippery floor. Dazed, she struggled to her feet as Mikhail loomed over the defenseless woman bound to the bed.

As he raised his hand to strike Miranda, Jennifer launched herself at his back. She hit him hard, knocking him off balance enough to keep him from striking her friend. Together they fell over the foot of the bed and onto the floor. Over and over they wrestled until she ended up on the bottom, his body pinning hers. Roughly, he shoved between her thighs, pressing his crotch against the apex.

"I love women who fight," he ground out, capturing her flailing arms.

She struggled, fear making her crazed, and she tried to do anything to get away from him. She clawed at his hands but was unable to inflict any damage because he held her wrists too tightly. Whipping her head around, she snapped at him with her teeth. Abruptly he shoved his arm against her windpipe, forcing her head upward to meet his gaze.

"If you bite me, I will tear you to pieces and feed you to my crows," he spoke slowly. He slid his hand downward to roughly clutch at her breast. Jennifer forced her voice to remain steady. "And if you rape me, you will never get your retribution from Val. I will see to it that he takes Shai and Maeve far enough away from you that you will never find them."

He stopped his rough caress. "You are making this so difficult," he growled. He rocked his hips against her. "Hmm...I could change my game plan. Maybe I will let Miranda go if you submit to me, Jennifer. Don't you remember how much fun we had? We could have that again, but you're going to spoil everything, aren't you?"

"*Fun*," she spat at him. "I don't remember anything f-f-fun..." she choked.

He shook his head sadly. "Then you don't remember it as I do. What a pity you cannot remember that night so long ago when..."

"I remember everything from that night. All of it," she snarled.

He rocked his hips against her again and she strangled a cry before it could make itself heard. "We could have that again," he whispered, his fingers digging painfully into her breast.

She glared into his soulless eyes, her breathing harsh. "Hear me now, Mikhail. I will *never* willingly submit to you."

He shrugged, "As if your willingness makes a difference to me. I take what I want and I destroy what I can't have. So be it."

"I don't think Gaby would like to see you in this position, would she?" Jennifer tried to ignore his hand as it tightened painfully. She would definitely have some bruises tomorrow.

Mikhail laughed, "Gaby does as I say, not the other way around. Nevertheless, I should probably keep my mind on business, shouldn't I?" He shifted his hold upward, away from her breast. Tenderly, he stroked the slender line of her throat, his movements methodical. "You need to run back and tell Val that I have his little Miranda. I will accept in exchange for her measly life, a meeting with him. He is to come alone to the *Chapel des Anges Perdu* outside Calais, France, four days from this evening - midnight."

She tensed as he brushed the hair away from the side of her neck. She swallowed audibly as his fingers lightly stroked the base of her throat. "No," she protested, renewing her struggles. A scream began building, as she knew the unthinkable was about to happen as he slowly lowered his head.

"Midnight, dearest Jennifer." His icy lips caressed her throat as a scream was torn, against her will, from her very soul. "Midnight." Pain ripped through her body as Mikhail began to feed.

Chapter 2

"You smell like a whore house."

Conor MacNaughten raised his glass of brandy and saluted his friend. "When you demand my presence at a moment's notice, you take your chances."

Val laughed. "Most mere mortals aren't having sex at noon on a weekday my friend."

"Only if they are lucky," Mac smirked.

"If I had to wait to reach you at a time when you weren't having sex then it would be too late. How do you say, 'Hell would have frozen over first'?" Val smothered his laughter. "It must be tedious knowing that no woman can resist your charms..."

Except one.

Mac frowned. Now where did that thought come from? He forced a smile. "Anything worth doing is worth doing right. I do try to excel in my duty with the ladies and I never let them go home disappointed. It is a moral imperative."

"Interrupted did I?" Val snickered.

"You didn't interrupt me, but the lady didn't get hers." Mac chuckled as he remembered Catherine's enraged face as he left her bed. "Then again, she'd already had four before that one. Just a few minutes more though..."

Val's laughter rang out again. "A true gentleman reveals nothing..."

"Now you wait just a minute! That did *not* come out of your mouth. Valentin, the lady-killer of Paris in the late seventeenth century is mocking me? Val, the man who was laughingly referred to as the gentleman who was *never* unarmed due to the sword he carried in his trousers? I remember the night you and the Armand triplets and I broke that bed in Provence. And then there was the Baroness Von Ravensfeld and her trio of pupils, was it? Though I would wager that what she was teaching them was not what their *mère* had paid for." Mac raised his brandy glass in mock salute. "You were an animal, much to the delight of the ladies."

Val smiled in memory. "Ah yes, Belle, Murielle, Elise and Grunhilde. How could I ever forget them? If I remember correctly, both you and I had problems walking back to the carriage that evening."

"They couldn't walk for a week, though." He smiled fondly at his vampire friend. "That is the best thing about being a revenant. All the women I could want."

Except for her, his mind taunted. He took another drink, willing the voice to go away and leave him in peace.

Val nodded. "Those times are long gone, my friend. Now I have Shai and my wild oats have been sown for good."

Mac swirled the glass of amber liquid slowly, frowning. "While I do know what a gem Shai is, do you not fear that you will grow bored with her?"

Val's bark of laughter brought his gaze up from the glass. "Of course not, Mac. You've known Shai for the past ten years. Is anything even remotely boring about her? That woman excites me more than all the others combined. I only have to look at her and I know that I am in deep and this is fine with me. There never will be another woman for me."

Unbidden, images of Lilith Snowden crowded Mac's mind. Laughing, singing, racing through the *Bois de Boulogne* at 2 A.M., the taste of her lips and the low sounds she made in her throat when she became excited. Almost instantly he became hard. He scowled.

"I see you know what I mean." Val said slowly.

He shoved the images away and ruthlessly attempted to control his wayward emotions. Lilith had left him for another man. He could never forgive, nor forget that slight. One day she'd pay for the pain she had inflicted upon his soul. A pain he would barely admit to himself. He chose to deliberately misunderstand than to tread on the hallowed ground that was his battered heart. "Chatty Cathy is hardly someone I wish to spend the rest of my eternity with," he drawled. "I can barely stand her for a few hours a time. That woman doesn't realize silence is truly golden."

Val let the moment pass by shaking his head and trying to unsuccessfully smother a smile. "You're still as bad as you were in the seventeenth century. Didn't anyone ever tell you that you shouldn't talk about a lady that way?"

"Only if she is a lady - and trust me, Catherine is no lady. She is a well-trodden path." Mac closed his eyes and took a large swallow, enjoying the sharp burn of the aged liquid and the faint blurring of bitter memories better left untouched.

"I didn't ask you here to discuss your love life," Val's voice turned uncharacteristically serious. "I have some news about our illustrious friend Mikhail. He has turned up again and it appears he has kidnapped Miranda from Sinjin's home in Cornwall."

Mac jerked and his eyes flew open. He searched his friend's face, looking for any sign of laughter in his eyes. He saw none. This was no joke. He knew Val's history with the beautiful Miranda of Glencoe. She'd come into Val's life during a time of despair. Vampires that lived for any long period of time sooner or later ran into adjustment problems. The world changed rapidly while the vampires themselves remained static. Mortal friends and acquaintances married, had children and grew old and then they died while vampires watched them like some kind of macabre voyeur. As if the human race were a theatrical play put on for the benefit of vampires. It was enough to drive the strongest of vampires insane and it happened quite frequently. Miranda had saved Val from that fate.

The friendship between them ran deep and spanned centuries. Its only rupture had been the arrival of Shai into Val's life. Miranda had made the mistake of falling in love with her old friend, but when Shai arrived, she'd departed gracefully. While they hadn't spoken in the last ten years, Mac knew that Val missed his friend. Mikhail's action, in Val's eyes, was tantamount to war.

"So what are we going to do?" he asked quietly, setting the glass on the small end table.

Val's dark eyes met his and Mac saw gratitude reflected in their black depths. "According to Jennifer, Mikhail wants to meet with me next week."

He stiffened at the utterance of that loved and hated name. Lilith, Jennifer, two very different names for one deceitful woman. "What does *she* have to do with this?"

"Jennifer confronted Mikhail earlier tonight. She went to his home and demanded to see Miranda."

"She did what?" Startled, he leapt from the chair.

"She went to Mikhail's estate outside Manchester earlier this evening.

She heard from Renault that Gabrielle DesNoir and Mikhail had kidnapped Miranda. For some reason she went there alone to confront him."

Anger raced through his system and along with that a tinge of fear that surprised him. Fear for Jennifer? That was absurd. Mac knew very well how dangerous Mikhail was, but Jennifer had a long-standing relationship with the vampire. While he still didn't know exactly what had gone on between Jennifer and Mikhail a century ago, he knew it was enough for her to choose the vampire over him. Had she been in love with Mikhail? She'd certainly tried to convince him of that, but somehow he hadn't thought so. Her story of undying love for the vampire had never rang true with him. Something niggled at him about the whole affair. It was something he never could put his finger on and Jennifer would never confide to him. Not that it mattered now. She'd made her choices, now she could live with the consequences. He certainly had.

Mac glanced at Val and caught the questions in his gaze. He looked away. "Of all the stupid things..." he began.

"She paid the price," Val inserted quietly. "Berate her if you must, but she has paid the price for her foolishness."

Mac struggled for calm while his mind whirled like a dervish. Even though Jennifer had walked away from him when he had needed her the most, he still had unfinished business with her. Images of Jennifer hurt and bleeding crowded his mind. If Mikhail had hurt her, he would gladly kill the vampire with his bare hands and feed his corpse to the wolves. The strength of his emotions shocked him. "Is she okay?" he ground out.

"She was shaken up but she seemed to be handling it."

He nodded curtly and settled himself on the arm of an overstuffed chair. He glanced mournfully at the abandoned glass of brandy. The fire flickered over the remains of the liquid in the glass, giving it a deep amber glow. If he ever needed a drink in his life, this was the time for it. He didn't reach for it. "Do you suppose Mikhail is coming after Shai?"

"Possibly. Or maybe he is after Maeve. She is the only one that got away from him alive. Jennifer could also be a target, but I doubt it. He let her go this evening." Val shrugged. "Maybe he's after all of us. At this point I don't know. Something must have gone terribly wrong for him to have gotten his hands on Miranda."

"True. Miranda is a clever woman. Mikhail must have tricked her somehow." Mac rose from the chair and reached for the glass that beckoned him. "What is the plan?" He tossed the remains of his brandy into the fire. Brilliant blue flames leapt wildly.

"I sent Maeve to Sinjin's home in northern Scotland. After what happened in Cornwall, she will be completely safe there. I would take Shai also but I have a feeling she wouldn't stay there unless I chained her up. While that is an idea with some merit, she would never forgive me." He shook his head and smiled ruefully. "She is a pistol. I will be keeping her with me for now. Mikhail wants to meet with me at the *Chapel des Anges Perdu* outside Calais four days from now."

"What do you need me to do?"

"See if you can liberate Miranda from Mikhail's house. If something goes wrong, I want to know that at least Miranda is safe."

Mac set his empty glass down on the end table. For the first time in his lengthy life, his taste for the fine brandy had soured. "You need to kill him for once and for all," he said quietly.

Val looked him straight in the eye, his expression haunted. "Truer words have never been spoken, my friend. But the Council of Elders will never stand for it."

"Damn the Council," Mac snarled. "This is the second time in ten years that Mikhail has come after you. Only the Goddess knows how many times he has come after you and others less fortunate before then. It was bad enough when he was killing humans, but now he comes after your women, a vampire and a revenant. If he succeeds, he will never stop the killing regardless of the Council's decision. You and I know this and it is time for it to end."

Val rose from the chair and moved over to where Mac stood. "You are right, but for now my hands are tied until I address the Council."

"When will you speak to the them?"

"I sent a message to Alexandre Saint-Juste earlier this evening. He is the current head of the Council and I hope to hear from him shortly."

"And what will you do if the Council refuses your request?"

"What can I do other than kill Mikhail, regardless of their dictates? He has to be stopped even if I have to relinquish my life to do so." Val shook his head, his expression sad. "How did it come to this? Mikhail has festering wounds that we have never seen, and grows more tragic as the years pass. I found out only recently that Mikhail has lied to me from day one."

"How so?"

"When I met Mikhail in Kiev, I assumed he'd been born there. He spoke the language like a native, he dressed like them and he knew a great many people in the town. I came to find out recently from Jennifer that he is either Irish or Scottish. He's gone to great lengths to hide his background." Val shook his head. "In the beginning I thought we were friends, now I know he lied from the first word."

Mac laid his hand on Val's shoulder. "Mikhail is a lost soul. He was lost when he was human and he's even more lost now. Don't beat yourself up over that which you could never have predicted in the first place. It's almost morning, and we have four days to get their approval and get Miranda out of the house before your meeting with Mikhail."

Val laid a hand on Mac's shoulder and gave it a quick squeeze. "Jennifer has been staying at Fayne's house in Westhumble for the past three months. What will you do about her?"

"I can handle Jennifer," Mac replied. "And I will keep her safe whether she wants me to or not."

"In death, you are even more beautiful than you were in life."

Shai started, her humming halted in mid-warble as the rough voice intruded upon her solitude. She turned away from her small oaken trunk filled with bottles of essential oils, her pursuit of *rose absolute* forgotten as she turned to look at the man who'd stolen her heart on a dark night ten years ago.

Valentin leaned against the doorjamb of the bedroom door watching her with his fathomless dark eyes, his expression grim. His heavy-lidded gaze caused the hollow ache in the center of her chest to expand. For the past ten years she'd adored this man. Lived with him, loved him through the nights, laughed with him, cried with him, and planned to spend eternity with him. And in those years she'd never seen her lover looking as tormented as he did now.

She forced a teasing smile to her lips. "You really know how to flatter a woman."

"Even if you can't sing?" An answering smile lightened his expression. "One should borrow from the masters, my love, not destroy them."

Shai moved toward him, laughter bubbling up in her throat. "Are you trying to say that I can't sing?"

His gaze scorched her skin as he shoved away from his resting place and reached for her. "No my love, you cannot sing. However," he caught the tie of her emerald green silk robe and pulled, "you have other talents in abundance."

A sigh escaped her lips as her robe slid apart, the silk whispering across her skin. Raising her hands, she captured the edges before her bare skin was revealed. "Is Mac gone?"

"Yes." Reluctantly he released the tie and turned away from her. "He left a few hours ago to check up on Jennifer, no doubt." Slowly he walked over to the massive king-sized bed, climbing up onto the dais and settling on the edge of the mattress. His movements were those of an old man, slow and cautious as if he were afraid he might break something.

"He's still in love with her, you know." Shai retied her robe and took up the space in the doorway where Val had stood seconds before.

He laughed as he pulled a jeweled dagger from his waistband and tossed it on the bed. "He doesn't know that. If you asked him right now he would deny it with his dying breath."

"I wonder if he loves the flesh and blood woman that Jennifer is or if he wants her because she left him for Mikhail?" Shai knotted the tie in her hands. "Mac believes that no woman is immune to his charms. Her defection wounded his delicate male ego. I think the fact she refused to consummate their great love all those years ago really burns his butt."

Val shot her a curious glance. "Think so?" He began to unbutton his shirt. "I think you're selling him short."

The sight of her lover's muscular chest drew her from across the room. Shai stepped up onto the dais and brushed his hands away from the buttons. "Do I sell Mac short?" She climbed onto his lap, straddling him as she began to remove his shirt. "I know Mac would travel the world and back for you, but can he open his heart to her? Is he so haunted by the fact he has no memories of his past that he can't trust himself to love anyone? He seems to think that the lack of past memories makes him less of a man for some reason. Men!" She sighed. "Do you think he can love Jennifer the way she needs to be loved?"

"I know Jennifer is an old friend of yours and you're very loyal to her. But, I think you are biased in her favor and that clouds your judgment. Mac is indeed haunted by his lack of a past. He doesn't remember anything prior to the eleventh century, the day Renault found him unconscious at Hadrian's wall, and this eats at him. He doesn't know who made him or why. Who or what his family was, none of it." He dropped his hands to stroke her knees.

"Until he figures this out or decides he can live with the lost memories, he will never be the man Jennifer needs." Shai shook her head. "He will constantly run in circles only to find himself tied up in knots..."

"Why didn't they sleep together back then?" Val interrupted.

Shai shivered as his hands stroked up her thighs, gently nudging the silk of her robe apart. She longed to give into the pull of desire that swept through her at his touch. But they were having a conversation, weren't they? She cleared her throat before continuing, "Jennifer told me that a lady of her time simply did not indulge in promiscuous sex. It was too dangerous. Even though she is an immortal, her upbringing stuck with her, I guess."

He snorted, "I know many ladies of the era who did not subscribe to that theory."

She smiled, "I'll bet you did. And you made it your life's mission to ferret those women out, didn't you?" She sighed as his strong thumbs began a slow ascent up the inside of her thighs. "I know that both of them were terribly hurt over what happened. My question is whether or not Mac can forgive her or if he will make her pay for an eternity. There are a lot of things that went on there that he doesn't know about."

His movements stopped. "Like what?"

Shai shook her head. "I promised Jen I would never tell. I just hope they can work something out before they get hurt again. Any idiot can see they need to be together."

"Is that so?" Val abandoned her thighs and slid his arms around her waist, tugging her closer. "That remains to be seen. Right now we have bigger problems."

She looked up into his dark eyes. She couldn't help but see the pain buried there before he pulled her into a tight hug. Val and Miranda had a long relationship that she knew very little about. On some level of her soul she was jealous of the beautiful vampire. But she couldn't be jealous for long. If it weren't for Miranda, Val would have never lived to be as old as he was. She was the one who saved him in the dark times, and helped him to adjust to the rapidly changing world around him. It was

Miranda she had to thank for the love of her life being whole and healthy and holding her now.

Shai slid her arms around his neck and returned the embrace. "So what's the plan?"

"I just heard back from the Council of Elders. I've been granted a hearing tomorrow evening. I will present my plea for the execution then."

"What kind of a chance do you have?" She pulled back to look him in the eye. "Do you think they'll grant the request?"

Val's expression was bleak and her heart gave a twinge. "A plea for execution hasn't been granted in over four hundred years." His grip tightened on her waist. "It doesn't look good."

Shai shook her head slowly, her throat constricting. "What happens if they deny your request? What happens if they allow Mikhail to go free?"

"Then I kill him anyway. It is the only way I can guarantee your and Maeve's safety."

Tears burned at her eyes and she blinked furiously, she dug her fingers deep into his shoulders as if she could bind him to her, thus guaranteeing his safety. "And what happens if you kill Mikhail anyway?"

His dark eyes bore into hers. "If I go against the Council, they'll put me to death."

A keening wail caught in Shai's throat and she tore away from him. She struggled to her feet as fear ravaged her soul. Stumbling over her long robe, she swerved toward the door. She barely felt the strong hands that grabbed her by the shoulders until she was pulled back into the embrace of her lover. For a second she struggled, a cry burst forth from her lips that would have shattered a mortal's eardrums. A delicate glass vase burst, sending a shower of water and roses onto a mahogany table and the carpeting below. Sobbing, she fell limp against Val's broad chest. She loved him more than life itself; she couldn't lose him now.

"I won't let this happen," she sobbed. "I won't allow Mikhail's actions to take you away from me."

"Beloved, nothing is set in stone," he whispered in her ear. "We still have a chance to do this the right way. Please have faith in me that I will do everything in my power to protect those I love."

"I do have faith in your abilities to protect us," she protested, turning in his arms to face him, "but who will protect you?"

He smiled, pressing a soft kiss to her damp cheek. "That is my Shai, always looking out for everyone else. I am an Elder, one of the oldest and strongest vampires on the planet."

"So is Mikhail," she argued.

"Yes, but he doesn't have you. With you in my corner I can take on the Devil himself and win."

Shai leaned her forehead against his chest, savoring the feel of his strong arms around her. Would the Council take Val away from her? Would they destroy her future and leave her alone for an eternity? She had no faith in this nameless, faceless Council, and from what she'd heard over the years, her lack of faith was warranted. It could happen - they could destroy both Val and Mikhail, taking her life in the process.

She pulled away and met his gaze. "Make love to me," she whispered.

Admiration lit the darkness of his eyes. "My pleasure."

Shai moved out of his embrace. Tugging on the sash of her robe, she heard his stifled groan as the silk parted, revealing her nudity. As if transfixed, Val reached out, trailing his fingers over her collarbone. He lightly caressed her skin as he followed the edge of the robe down her body, his eyes worshipping her.

"I love you," he whispered.

She smiled. Love blossomed in her chest, pushing the fear and anger away for now. If the fates conspired to take this man away from her, she wanted to love him as fully as she could for the time she had.

She was in pain.

Mac stood outside the isolated house in the countryside surrounding Westhumble. Soon the sun would rise, but for now the darkness was a balm to the anger that churned in his gut. He pressed his palm against the solid oak door and instantly he was hit with a wave of jumbled emotions. He closed his eyes, but, against his wishes, the images invaded his mind. The narrow twisting stairway that led into darkness, Mikhail's laughing visage and Miranda, tortured as she lay bound to the narrow cot.

Exhaling slowly, Mac retrieved his lock pick case from his pocket and extracted a thin wire pick. With the ease of long practice, he crouched down on level with the solid dead-bolt lock and set to work. Within seconds the tumblers clattered then fell silent. Replacing his tool, he tucked the case in his pocket, and opened the door and stepped into the house. The silence and the golden light from a single small lamp wrapped around him like a warm quilt.

Mac quietly shut the door and moved deeper into Jennifer's lair. He'd been to the house on several occasions to visit with Fayne. It was a comfortable house with all the amenities and the latest gadgets. Fayne was a big fan of technology; the more toys the better and he amassed them all. As he walked toward the living room arch, he ignored the comfortable furniture and the exquisite artwork. Instead, he focused on the little touches of the woman he'd loved to distraction over a century ago.

A red silk scarf was tossed carelessly over the back of the gray leather couch. A pair of diamond earrings winked at him from the coffee table while black leather ankle boots lay tumbled beneath it. He walked down the three steps into the sunken living room, moving instinctively toward the oversized fireplace. The bookcases that flanked it were filled to overflowing with an assortment of leather-bound books, battered paperbacks and little knickknacks. A tiny Native American bear fetish frolicked with a porcelain unicorn in a lopsided clay ashtray, while a crystal Lalique angel watched from above. There was neither design nor form to the contents, yet harmony reigned, just like the woman herself.

He found himself reaching for the angel, halting seconds before his fingers brushed the crystal. He dropped his arm and turned away from the bookshelves and the contradictions that they presented to him. Coals glowed in the fireplace as he stepped toward it. On the mantel were a variety of unmatched candlesticks with white candles, and in the center of the mantel were the roses.

One dozen long-stemmed glass roses in a black glass vase. A shaft of pain stabbed him as he stared at the gleaming flowers. He remembered the day so long ago in Germany. It had been raining and they were walking along the deserted streets in Munich. The sun had long been hidden behind the black clouds when they came upon a glass blower hard at work. In the graying before nightfall, they'd watched for hours, fascinated, while he created the delicate blooms. Mac purchased one dozen for the woman he loved.

The woman he loved.

The woman he *had* loved, he corrected. He didn't love her now. He scowled at the offending blooms, wanting to knock them off the mantel to shatter on the stone hearth. While he'd fallen head over heels in love with her over a century ago, had she ever loved him? She'd certainly left him within a blink of an eye and run as quickly as she could to Mikhail. Long buried rage hummed along his skin.

Disgusted, he forced himself away from the mantel, but something in the coals caught his eye. Frowning, he dropped into a crouch and pulled the object from the ashes. A scrap of burgundy cloth had escaped the flames. He frowned. What had Jennifer been burning in the fireplace?

He picked up the poker and shifted through the glowing coals, which yielded a melted lump attached to a scrap of cloth. A button? Why was she burning clothing in the fireplace? He glanced at the ceiling. He needed some answers and the only person who could answer them was probably upstairs sound asleep.

Determined to find those answers, he turned toward the staircase and climbed into the shadowed loft. There he found Jennifer. The glow from several small candles in a variety of thick green glass holders illuminated the room and the woman who lay on the tester bed. She lay on her side, curled into a partial fetal position. Her damp hair was strewn over her pillow and she appeared to be sleeping heavily. Yellow sweat pants, and a gray sweatshirt, and thick white athletic socks covered her generous figure from head to toe. A small pharmacy bottle stood on the bedside table next to a half-filled glass of water.

Picking up the bottle, he frowned as he read the label. Sedatives? He never would have guessed that Jennifer would resort to sedatives, no matter what the situation. Then again, he never would have guessed that she preferred sleeping fully clothed either. She'd struck him as a silk and lace kind of woman. Not that he'd ever seen her in a bedroom before. In their previous relationship, Jennifer was the one who'd always called a halt to their lovemaking before they consummated it, much to his chagrin. It'd seemed then that she was the one woman who could resist his charms and that made her all the more desirable to him. Had she been unable to resist Mikhail?

He scowled at the disturbing thoughts of Mikhail and Jennifer making love. With a low growl, he stalked to the bed and glared down at the sleeping woman. He saw immediately that she was much too pale. Without conscious thought, his raised his arm and lightly brushed the collar of the sweatshirt back to reveal her slim throat. A hiss escaped from his clenched teeth as he saw the bruising that marred her skin.

Mikhail had fed from Jennifer.

But was it consensual or against her will? Leaning closer, he saw the jagged holes in the center of the mottled skin. Vampire bites, when they were welcomed, were smooth and even, with very little bruising. These had definitely been taken by force. Nothing else could account for the size and scope of the injury.

For an unwilling victim it was tantamount to rape.

Fury hit him square in the chest, driving the breath from his body. Staggering away from the bed, he quenched the need to howl at the Goddess and rail against the injustice of the vampire's actions against this woman and his friends. He wanted to destroy everything that'd ever frightened or hurt this woman in her entire life. He wanted to wrap her in cotton batting and keep her warm and safe.

He wanted Mikhail's head on a pike.

Slowly, he sucked in a deep breath of air as he struggled to contain the rage that battled inside him. This rage could be his undoing if he didn't master it immediately. He remained preternaturally still, eyes closed, drawing in deep breaths through his nose and exhaling through his mouth.

Slowly reason returned, and once again he was in control. He opened his eyes and moved toward the bed. As he neared her, the pendant against his flesh began to warm. He paused. Reaching inside his shirt, he pulled the pendant out and over his head. It lay in the palm of his hand, the gold and topaz stone glowing weakly against his skin.

It was the Sun.

Many years before, while in Venice, Jennifer told him how much she loved the sunshine. She felt she'd been born thousands of years too late for she would have made a good sun worshipper in Egypt in the time of Akhenaton. Even though it hadn't been fashionable for a lady of her time, she'd built a small solar onto her house and spent many hours laying in the sunshine. Within a few short weeks she'd acquired a pale golden tan. He'd wanted to kiss every inch of her golden skin to see exactly what she'd uncovered while worshipping the sun. It had been rumored among the *ton* that she'd sunbathed in the nude.

He'd commissioned a Venetian jeweler to create the gold and topaz pendant that was no larger than an American quarter. When it was held up to the flame of a candle, fingers of brilliant golden light would shoot from the pendant in a weak imitation of the sun.

He remembered her glee when he'd presented her with the pendant. Her lips warm and swollen from kisses stolen in the balcony of the *Fenice* theater in Venice, she'd placed the pendant around her neck and announced she would never take it off.

But she lied.

She'd removed it the day she told him she'd chosen Mikhail over him. The day she left him. The day Mac had placed the pendant around his own neck where it had remained until now. A bitter reminder of how dangerous it was to give one's heart to a fickle woman.

He shook his head. So much lost time. The span of lifetimes for mortals, the blink of an eye for immortals, but lost to them both nonetheless. Time that neither he nor Jennifer could reclaim even if they wanted to. He rubbed his finger over the stone before placing it back around his neck. He tucked it beneath his shirt where it rested mere inches from his heart.

A wave of exhaustion tugged at his limbs. It had been only 12 hours since he'd left Catherine's bed, but sleep had been the last thing on his mind. It was almost 36 hours since he had actually slept for any length of time, and he was dead tired. Quietly, he removed his boots and climbed into bed next to Jennifer.

Careful to keep a good distance between them, Mac willed his tired muscles to relax. The next few days would be grueling, and he was best served to rest as he could. Closing his gritty eyes, he slipped into a deep sleep.

Something wasn't right. Jerking awake, he was dismayed to find that in their sleep they'd both moved, and the buffer zone he'd left between them was gone. Jennifer was curled up against his side, her head pillowed on his shoulder and her hand fisted in his shirt. Her unique scent of jasmine and warm woman triggered an immediate reaction below his waist.

Scowling, he untangled her hand from his shirt and deposited her head on her pillow. He rolled onto his side away from her and within minutes she moved again, this time plastering herself against his back. Her firm breasts were flattened against him as his growing erection pressed painfully against his zipper.

He shifted away from her again only to have her grumble in protest and follow him. Sighing, he caught her arm and dragged it around his waist, securing her to his back. It appeared he was in for a miserable nap. He was so aroused it felt like he hadn't had a release in months, rather than just a few hours ago.

He groaned and closed his eyes, ignoring the fact that for the first time in a century, he felt that all was right with the world.

Chapter 3

Someone was in bed with her.

Jennifer's eyes flew open as a large male hand slipped into her panties, cupping her backside while another hand caressed her breast. Sleepy, chocolate-brown eyes gazed deep into hers. Very familiar chocolate-brown eyes.

Eyes she'd dreamed about but was sure she would never see again.

"Mac," she croaked.

He surrounded her. His arms, his legs, his scent, his very maleness wrapped around her like a living blanket. She pushed at his broad chest, trying to put some space between them.

"Mmm," he mumbled, tugging her back until she was plastered against him like cellophane on a piece of hard candy. "Don't move," he purred against her collarbone.

"How did you..." She gasped as he placed a wet, open-mouthed kiss on her throat, his tongue tasting her skin. At once her body responded to his touch. He pressed his rock solid thigh against the apex of her legs and an answering dampness sprang to life. Shivers rippled over her skin as lust hummed through her veins. This man, only this man could reduce her to a quivering mass of needy flesh. Tangling her fingers in his long hair, she tried to pull his mouth away from her skin and marshal her wayward body back in line.

"What are you..." A groan escaped her as Mac tongued the hollow at the base of her throat. A sigh escaped her as she involuntarily pressed the lower half of her body against him.

His hand kneaded her backside, forcing her hips into a sensual dance as his other hand released her breast and skimmed down her belly. Expertly he untied the drawstring on the pants and they loosened. Pushing them down, he slipped his hand between her thighs and plunged into the moist heat that awaited him.

"I don't..." A thin cry was torn from her mouth as his talented fingers found the sensitive bud contained within. Heat suffused her body as his fingers seemed to reach deep inside her soul, plucking on her very heartstrings. Releasing her death grip on his hair, she clutched his broad shoulders. Spreading her thighs wider, she welcomed his weight as he rolled over on top of her, pressing her into the mattress.

"Yes you do, Jennifer," he breathed against her throat. "You need this as badly as I do." He pressed tiny kisses along her jaw. "I can feel it inside of you." His teeth nipped at her earlobe. "Just as I want to be buried deep inside of you." Lightly he kissed her lips, a faint brush of flesh on flesh, a taste of things to come. Jennifer whimpered, wanting much more than a chaste kiss. Needing much more. Now.

She caught his head and pulled his mouth from her flesh. "More," she breathed.

Fixated on his mouth, she missed the flash of male satisfaction in his eyes. Leaning forward, he caught her lower lip between his teeth and tugged tenderly, causing waves of desire to rocket through her. With one last tug he released the flesh. His dark gaze impaled hers. "Yes, more," he breathed before he captured her mouth fully.

He ate at her mouth like a starving man and she reveled in it. With bold strokes he invaded her, caressing the sensitive roof of her mouth before maneuvering into position to wrestle with the slick warmth of her tongue.

A soft moan escaped her as Mac sucked on her tongue. Against her will, she tangled her fingers in his long hair. Clutching at his skull, she returned his kiss ravenously as if she, too, were starving with a hunger that only this man could fill. She clung to him as the sensations rocked through her body. A nameless need overtook her limbs as she drew her knees up to align them with his slim hips. She rocked against his straining zipper, fanning the flames of her desire into a raging inferno.

Gasping, he broke the torrid kiss. Startled, Jennifer opened her eyes and met his hot gaze. The fire of his desire burned brightly within his eyes. She wanted to wallow in his heat until it covered every inch of her flesh and warmed the core of her chilled soul.

He pressed a small kiss on the tip of her nose. "Tell me what you want, Jennifer." He placed a tiny kiss at the corner of her mouth; his tongue teased the seam between her lips. "Tell me you want me," he commanded, pressing a kiss just below the center of her lower lip. He pressed another to her chin. "Tell me you want this." He rocked his hips against the damp apex of her thighs, causing a white-hot blaze of lust to rip through her soul.

"I want you," she breathed, drawing her knees tighter to his hips.

He pressed a kiss to the opposite corner of her mouth. "How much do you want me?" He rocked against her again, this time prolonging the upward movement until a cry was wrenched from her. "How much do you want this?"

"Please," she begged, ignoring the warning that sounded in the back of her mind. She strained desperately for the completion that was just out of her reach. The release that only this man could give her.

Mac shifted and pinned her arms to the mattress. "Did you beg him, too?"

Confused, she looked into his eyes. The tender lover of moments ago was nowhere to be seen. "W-w-what?" she stammered.

"I said, 'Did you beg him too?'"

"What are you talking about?"

His grip on her arms tightened as his mouth curled in disgust. "Did you beg Mikhail to fuck you?"

Jennifer tensed; the pain from his verbal blow was more intense than any physical pain she'd ever endured. She was momentarily blinded as tears flooded her eyes. She furiously blinked them away. She would die before she would cry in front of this man. "Let me go," she ground out.

"Were you as hot and wild beneath him as you are for me right now? I can feel your arousal, Jennifer. Did he get you off? More than once?" he demanded.

Jennifer flinched as each word landed like a blow on her heart. "I said," she choked, "get off me." She held herself deathly still, barely breathing as she stared into the eyes of the man she'd once loved with all of her heart. The same man that was filleting her alive with every word he spoke.

"You're so easy," he spat.

She was relieved when Mac released her. As he rolled off, Jennifer vaulted from the bed. With one hand she grabbed at the wall to keep herself upright as her trembling knees threatened to drop her to the carpeting, while the other clutched at the drawstring on her drooping pants.

"Don't you *ever* touch me again," she whispered shakily.

Mac rose from the bed, his expression angry, remote. "With pleasure."

"Now, leave this house."

He shook his head. "Not so fast. You and I have unfinished business, Jennifer. We'll settle it here and now. Today."

She turned away, refusing to look at him any longer, terrified he would see too much of what was going on inside her. Sunshine beckoned through the blinds and for a moment she wished she were outside, wrapped in its warmth rather than trapped in this dim room with a man who was killing her by degrees. Taking a shallow breath, she struggled to calm herself. Catching sight of the open bathroom door, she eyed her escape route. Blessed solitude. That was what she needed to pull herself together, to regain her equilibrium that currently eluded her. Shaky, she edged toward the door, "I don't think you and I have anything to say to one another."

He stepped directly in front of her, forcing her gaze back to his. "You're so wrong, Jennifer. We have volumes to say to one another." He gestured toward the open doorway. "For now you can make your escape, but you can't hide forever." He turned and picked up his boots. "I'll wait for you downstairs. Don't make the mistake of keeping me waiting for too long, or I will come back up here and drag you out. You aren't going to avoid me this time."

Jennifer sank onto the thick carpeting as Mac walked out the door. His footsteps faded down the steps. She drew her knees to her chest and buried her face against them as sobs threatened to choke her. Fisting her hands against her mouth, she struggled to quiet her anguish. She failed miserably. An animal-like keening broke free as her heart shattered once again.

This time she knew it would kill her.

The morning sun beat down warm and welcome on his shoulders as Mac raised the coffee cup to his mouth and took a deep gulp of the thick black brew. In his mind, if you couldn't stand a spoon up in a cup of joe then it just wasn't worth drinking. Now, if he had a warm beignet from the Café du Monde in New Orleans, then his morning would be complete.

Instead he had a steaming plate of revenge, still hot from the infliction.

He frowned and twisted the delicate gold chain of the Sun around his fingers, surprised at his feelings of shame at what he'd done to Jennifer. It was her heartbreaking sobs that almost undid him. Fayne's house was small and cozy; consequently, every wrenching sob could be heard throughout the house. Finally, in desperation to escape her torment, he'd fled into the sprawling kitchen to brew up a pot of coffee, only to dump half of it on his shirt because his hands trembled from the sounds of her distress.

He scowled at the offending shirt as if it had tossed the coffee on him rather than the other way around. It dangled merrily in the cold breeze as it hung off handrail of the deck, the coffee neatly rinsed out in the kitchen sink.

He still wanted her. Possibly more now than he did over a century ago. Damn her black soul for making him want her all over again.

The taste of her skin resonated in his mouth and not even the thickest, blackest chicory coffee would remove it. The scent of her arousal clung to his skin no matter how many times he tried to wash it away. Her breathy cries still rang in his ears as his arousal continued to gnaw at his zipper. He clenched his fist, the Sun digging into his hand

"Damn her," he whispered. "Damn Mikhail and damn me." He released his fist then looked down to stare at the pendant. Brilliant sunshine gleamed from the heart of the topaz, momentarily blinding him.

Stuffing the pendant into his jeans pocket, he set his coffee cup down with a thump on the deck rail and took a deep, cleansing breath of the icy air.

The winter solstice was approaching and the air was cold against his bare chest where his unzipped jacket didn't cover. He'd always felt the deepest kinship with the winter solstice in particular and he'd never really known why. The fact he couldn't remember much of his life before the 11th century bothered him deeply. Obviously he'd been some kind of tree-hugging pagan but other than that instinctive knowledge, he had no idea where he came from. No country to call his home, no people to call his own. There existed only a yawning emptiness in his psyche where his past should reside. There were no clues to his origins before waking up in a niche of Hadrian's wall with Renault crouched by his side. An inauspicious beginning to be sure.

Over the many years of his life he'd acquired quite a few good memories of the shortest day of the year. When he lived in medieval Europe, Winter Solstice was the eve of massive Yule log hunts and long, dark hours filled with feasting and ale. Many a young lady lost her virginity to him on such a night.

His mouth curled in a slight smile as he remembered one lovely redhead, a bottle of burgundy and an all night lovemaking session that'd left him sated for at least a week. Ana with her lusty curves and talented lips and her cries of *vite, vite!*

Visions of Jennifer hot and wanting in his arms superimposed themselves over Ana's image. His smile faded.

Damn her.

Jennifer smoothed her oversized black sweater down her arms as she watched the man who'd invaded her sanctuary. In all of her years, Conor MacNaughten was still the most devastatingly handsome man she'd ever seen. At just over six feet, Mac lacked the sheer bulk that Val possessed. Instead he was sleek and wiry like a jungle cat, and he was incredibly strong. His usual demeanor was restless, sensual and a touch hedonistic. He had an energy that either drew people in or sent them running.

He had a quick temper and the reflexes to match. He was a man of deep passion and tightly leashed emotions, hidden behind a *laissez-faire* exterior. He felt things very deeply, regardless of how much he tried to hide it. It was one of the many things that she'd found irresistible and it drew her to him as much now as it had a century before.

His worn jeans hugged his backside and accentuated his long legs. His black leather jacket covered his broad shoulders and emphasized his narrow waist. The jacket was unzipped, giving her tantalizing glimpses of his lightly tanned chest. Thick, wavy dark brown hair brushed his shoulders and with the sun hitting the strands, as it was now, an illusion of a golden halo appeared.

Her mouth curved bitterly. This man was no angel; he was lethal, to her at least.

Pain crowded her throat as shame set her cheeks aflame. How could she have acted in such a wanton fashion? She knew exactly how Mac felt about her. She knew it before today and she knew it even more clearly now. She was beneath his contempt. So be it. All she had to do was escape this situation with as much of her dignity and pride intact as possible. Forcing herself to breathe evenly, she fought for calm as she watched the man who'd almost been inside her.

Deep inside her.

Jennifer scowled and squelched that thought. It'd been a century since she'd last set eyes on him. The last thing she needed was for him to reappear and wreak havoc in her life. She knew it was naïve to think that Mac wouldn't hear about the incident with Mikhail. Was that why he was here now?

She pushed that thought away. Conor MacNaughten didn't care enough about her to spit on her if she was on fire. A stab of pain shot through the remains of her heart. He'd loved her once, and she'd destroyed those precious feelings in one fell swoop. His current opinion of her couldn't be clearer if he paid someone to sky-write it.

So why was he here and what did he want?

Jennifer squared her shoulders and smoothed her trim black skirt into place. Lurking in the dining room watching him like some sort of Peeping Tom was not going to get her questions answered. She prided herself on being a grab-the-bull-by-the-horns kind of girl, and now was a good time to test that theory.

She stepped out onto the deck into the brilliant sunshine.

"You really should buy some food," Mac spoke without turning around.

"Why? I don't need much," Jennifer shot back.

"What about when your friends visit?"

"No one ever visits."

Mac glanced over his shoulder, his brow lifted slightly. "No vampires either?"

Jennifer's gaze wavered and then slid away from his. "No. No one is welcome here." The unspoken words *even you* hung in the air.

"Good," Mac said decisively.

Her gaze met his once again. "What is good about that?"

He turned to face her, his expression distant, cold. "I wanted to make sure no one has been sleeping on my side of the bed since I've been gone."

She gaped at him. "You never had a side of the bed," she spluttered.

"Until now." He picked up his coffee mug and took a drink. "I would prefer the left side please, nearest the door."

"Until now, nothing," she raged. "Who in hell do you think you are? You and I are old news and you have no say in who visits my bed. None at all." Jennifer stopped as a sharp wave of dizziness washed over her. She groped for the railing as her knees began to buckle.

Strong hands caught her before she hit the ground and she found herself in Mac's arms. Within seconds she was carried into the house and gently deposited on the gray leather couch.

"You need to eat," he stated baldly. "You've lost too much weight." He grabbed a cream colored afghan from a nearby rocking chair and tucked it over her legs.

Jennifer rubbed her forehead as the dizziness began to dissipate. "I was a cow when you knew me before. Of course I've lost weight. I don't normally get dizzy when I need to eat..."

"You don't normally act as dinner for a sadistic Elder either," Mac pointed out. He settled himself on the couch beside her. "And if you would keep more fresh food around rather than frozen pizza and Pepe's Frozen Burrito Supremes, you would be in better shape physically."

She groaned and allowed her head to drop back on the arm of the couch. "Don't tell me you've turned into a health food nut." She tried to move away from the warm, very masculine thigh pressed against her hip. He was deliberately crowding her against the back of the couch by sitting down on the edge of her skirt, effectively trapping her.

"I'm hardly a health food nut but I do know there is more in the Epicurean world than burritos and frozen pizza bites." A faint smile curved his mouth. "Today we are having bacon and scrambled eggs with toast, since that is all you have available. Would you care to eat in the kitchen or here on the couch?"

At the sight of that smile on those wicked lips, her mouth went dry. She shifted her gaze away as her heart beat a little bit faster. Her eyes skimmed the expanse of naked chest, to the soft worn jeans. *Nope, don't look there; don't even think about it!* She fixed her gaze on the foot of the couch. "Here, please," she mumbled through dry lips.

He caught her chin and forced her gaze to meet his. "I would suggest that you eat every bite. Mikhail appears to have taken a great deal out of you." His voice was gentle.

Tears stung her eyes. How could he be so unbearably brutal one minute and then act as if he almost cared about her the next? What kind of a game was he playing now?

"Thank you," she said, pulling away from his touch.

Mac nodded curtly and rose from the couch. Within fifteen minutes he reappeared, damp shirt intact, with a tray filled with glasses of reconstituted orange juice and two plates heaped with bacon, scrambled eggs and toast. Silently he held out a glass of juice. As Jennifer reached for it, her nerves sang out as he leaned toward her.

Their fingers brushed and a shiver rippled over her skin. Stung, she grabbed the glass and pulled away from him, ignoring his raised brow. She murmured her thanks and lifted the glass to her lips, gulping it thirstily. Mac settled the tray over her knees then removed his glass and plate.

"Why did you confront Mikhail last night?" He asked as he settled himself on the floor on the opposite side of the coffee table.

Jennifer lowered the glass. "I had to make sure Miranda was all right."

"He could have killed you."

"He needed me too much to kill me," Jennifer sighed. "He needed me to report back to Val what was going on. My going over there was a setup from the beginning."

"And you walked right into it?"

"I had no choice," Jennifer set her glass on the tray and began eating the eggs. They were fluffy and spiced with basil and a touch of rosemary. She wanted to groan out loud as she swallowed the first bite. "It's over and done with." She reached for a slice of toast heavily laden with butter and lemon curd, just the way she liked it. Taking a big bite, she tried to chew normally without gulping her food down, surprised at how hungry she was.

"What are you going to do?" He asked quietly.

Jennifer hesitated, a slice of crisp bacon halfway to her mouth. "Well, I don't see there are many choices in the matter. I have to figure out how to get Miranda out of there." Images of the silver room and the terrors within crowded her mind. She shook her head to rid herself of the disturbing images. "And fast."

"Then I guess we'll have to go in and get her," he replied lightly.

She dropped the bacon to her plate. "*We're* not going to do anything. I'm going to take care of this myself."

"You'll never make it."

She glared at Mac. "I..."

"Admit it, Jennifer. Mikhail scares the crap out of you and you can't carry this off on your own. You need help." His tone was sharp, angry.

"And he wouldn't think twice of killing you," she shot back. "Revenant or not, we're both still human and make no mistake, he will kill you."

"Damn it," he snarled. "What in the devil makes you think that I need your protection? I've lived the past thousand years without you dogging my every step and I am still here. I'm more than seven hundred years older than you are. Quit treating me like a schoolboy in short pants. You're the one that needs a keeper. Mikhail could have killed you today."

"He wouldn't have killed me," she ground out. "You don't understand, he needed me to carry the message to Val about Miranda..."

"You cannot be that naïve, Jennifer. Mikhail could've hired a messenger service to deliver his damned message to Val." Mac got to his feet, his lunch half-eaten. "Cut the crap, Jen. There has to be a better reason for you to risk your life than to carry a message to Val."

She swallowed and shook her head in denial. "Miranda is my friend, one of my only friends," she whispered. "I can fix this. I don't want you involved in this mess."

"How can you fix this better than anyone else?" His voice was low, deadly. "What makes you so sure that he won't use you to get back at Val?"

Pain squeezed at her heart as she spoke, "Mikhail is my," the word caught in her throat, "master. He won't hurt me."

The silence was oppressive, relieved only by the faint sound of the wind in the trees. Jennifer braved a glance at Mac, she flinched at the expression on his face. His gaze had gone flat, his face stony.

"Did you know this was going to happen? Did you know Mikhail was going to kidnap Miranda?"

She shook her head. "No. I didn't know until Renault called me. I hadn't spoken to..."

"Pack your things," he broke in. "Enough for three days. We're going to get Miranda out of that hell hole your *master* made for her."

"Mac," she whispered, "I just..."

"I don't want to hear it," he interrupted her again. "Once we have accomplished this I hope you and your *master* rot in hell together. But I tell you this, Jennifer, if you betray me again, I will gladly kill you myself."

The tattered remains of her heart shattered into a million pieces as she nodded mutely. Woodenly, she set her unfinished lunch tray on the coffee table and rose to her feet. Starting toward the steps, Jennifer stopped as his hand curled around her forearm. She stared steadfastly at the knotty pine flooring, refusing to look into his eyes until he caught her chin and forced her head back, his steely gaze clashing with hers.

"Don't bother packing any underwear, you won't need it." Mac smiled, it was a cruel smile that sent shivers down her spine. "When I send you back to your *lover*, it will be my name branded on your lips, not his."

Jennifer wrenched her arm away, heartily tired of fighting men who wanted to overpower her and bend her to their will. Men who wanted to own her and destroy what little soul she had left. "Not without my permission Mac," she ground out. "Never without my permission."

He laughed as she mounted the stairs. "We'll see how long you can last, Jennifer. We'll see."

Chapter 4

London

Jennifer pressed her forehead against the cool glass of the window. Chelsea lay before her under a thick coating of gleaming snow, its lights glittering like a tawdry Victorian necklace. How long had it been since she'd stayed in London for any period of time? She loved this city. It ranked right up there with Paris in her heart. She loved the ambiance of the busy streets and the tiny shops stuffed with wares.

While Monmatre had starving artists out hawking their wares in exchange for a hot meal, bottle of cheap wine or cold hard cash, on the outskirts of London there were thousands of nooks and crannies to get lost in. The verdant green of the distant English countryside and the historic moldering castles pulled at her soul. While removed from London it was hard to mark the passage of time, but when she returned it stared her in the face. With the changes evident in the Tower and other historic sites, it was heart wrenching to remember people and times long past.

Earlier in the evening, the bustle of Christmas shoppers, congested traffic and the pedestrians on the streets created a cacophony of music in her soul in a way that very few things did. Just as the man in the other room reached parts of her heart that she thought had long since been lost to the light. But now at midnight, the streets were quiet and still.

For the past seventeen hours, since she'd awoken to find Mac in her bed, her mind had been running in circles trying to figure out how to extricate Miranda from this mess. She was no closer to answers than she'd been earlier in the day. If anything, she was more confused than ever.

A soft knock interrupted her musing.

"It's open."

The door opened and golden light spilled into the dim bedroom. Mac's broad shoulders filled the doorway, his face in shadow. "I've fixed some food for us. We need to eat and then try and get some rest. Renault will be here around noon."

Jennifer forced herself away from the window. The scene earlier this morning had left her feeling terribly vulnerable and exposed. She would like nothing more than to avoid Mac for another hundred years but that wasn't going to happen, at least not until Miranda was free and they could go their separate ways.

"He's bringing the plans for Mikhail's house?" She marveled at the cool sound of her voice. A bystander would never have known this man had torn her heart out and destroyed it only this afternoon. She moved through the doorway even though Mac didn't move to grant her more room. Her shoulder brushed his chest and she forced herself to not recoil from his touch.

"Yes. He's bringing them and we'll set up our plan of attack. The sooner we get Miranda out of there the better."

And the sooner you will be rid of me. She nodded mutely as she led the way out of the bedroom and down the steps. The sudden warmth and light of the living room caused her to realize how chilled she was after the dim coolness of the bedroom. Mikhail's attack had taken more out of her than she'd thought.

The scent of fresh baked bread and sausages pervaded the room and her stomach growled in answer. A small table covered in fine china and silver-domed plates was set up directly in front of the French doors. The velvet night and the lights of London beckoned her. She slipped into one of the chairs, and latched onto one of the many domed covers and pulled it off. An array of pork and lamb sausages awaited her and she stifled a groan as she inhaled the mingled scents.

Suddenly ravenous, she began scooping fat sausages onto her plate. Croissants, biscuits and scones inhabited a wicker basket covered with a fine linen cloth. Another domed plate contained a selection of bite-sized quiches and tiny, individual egg and cheese soufflés. She popped a cheese and mushroom quiche into her mouth. Her eyes closed and she couldn't prevent the growl of delight as the rich cheddar and chopped portabella mushrooms sang an aria of perfection on her palate.

"Is everything to your liking?" Mac's voice intruded on her concerto of ecstasy.

Jennifer opened her eyes to see his amused, chocolate-brown eyes twinkling at her. She gulped down her quiche and swallowed loudly. "Lovely," she mumbled, suddenly embarrassed. "You didn't cook all this, did you?"

"I can cook, you know," he grinned. "I also have an amazing staff. Hilde left most of this in the freezer with very detailed instructions." He reached for a pitcher of orange juice, filling her champagne glass half full. "You've always had a good appetite."

"I have always been a pig, you mean?" She selected a small spinach and mushroom soufflé and stuffed it into her mouth.

Mac popped the top off the bottle of champagne. "I never said anything of the sort." He topped her orange juice with champagne. His voice lowered a notch. "I enjoy watching a woman who indulges her healthy appetites."

Jennifer stopped in her quiche contemplation to frown at him. "You are not to flirt with me. I'm not one of your light-skirts." She blindly selected several quiches and dropped them on her plate.

Shaking his head, he replaced the bottle back into the ice bucket. "And when have I treated you as such?"

"You just did this morning." *Damn!* She silently cursed her wayward tongue. She would rather have avoided that topic completely. She reached for her glass of mimosa.

"Ahh, I wondered when you would mention this morning."

Jennifer scowled as she watched him heaping food on his plate. Her appetite was suddenly gone while his was, as usual, in overdrive. It really wasn't fair how some people could eat like horses and never gain a pound. "You assumed I would bring it up?" She strove to keep her voice light, unconcerned.

Mac was smiling as he applied his knife to a plump sausage. "You, my darling, are nothing if not predictable. At least when it comes to the subject of you and me."

She downed a healthy drink of her mimosa. "Hmm, I wasn't aware that there was a 'you and me.'"

"There has always been a 'you and me.' You just won't admit it to yourself. If you would accept that, you and I'd be together then we wouldn't have to keep fighting this battle over and over. Of course, things will be very different this time around, I can assure you."

Mac's gaze was hot and she felt the embers of desire ignite in her belly. Jennifer squelched her burgeoning desire and almost dumped her remaining drink in her lap with her trembling hand. "I think you presume a great deal, Mr. MacNaughten," she strove for a haughty tone and failed.

"I presume nothing, Ms. Beaumont," he spoke in an oddly quiet voice. Gone was the laughing teasing man she'd remembered from so many years ago, this serious, soft-spoken man was a stranger to her. "I'm simply informing you of my intentions."

She couldn't pry her gaze from his. Her words locking in her throat, threatening to choke her. She'd loved this man for the better part of the past century, and she still feared him at times. She certainly feared for him as Mikhail could kill him in a heartbeat and would take great pleasure in doing so. The only way to keep Mac safe was to ignore the attraction between them as she had so long ago. Mac alive and hating her was preferable to a world without Mac in it.

"I don't want a relationship with you, Mac. And I don't feel the same way you do," she whispered, her heart constricting. "And I can't do this again. I simply can't go back there."

Naked emotion flashed in his eyes. Pain? For a split-second Jennifer thought her words scored a direct hit before his eyes turned cool once again.

"I don't remember telling you anything about how I feel. I don't love you, don't delude yourself into thinking so. However, I do desire you and I will have you. I know what you feel for me, it's written on your face. Look me in the eye and say it, Jennifer," he urged. "Look me in the eye and tell me you don't want me."

She swallowed painfully. Careful to keep her face expressionless, she replied, "I don't want you and I don't love you, Mac," she lied. "I never loved you." Pain streaked through her heart, stealing the breath from her lungs as she looked away. Stumbling to her feet, the champagne glass hit the edge of the plate with a sharp ring as she dropped it to the table. She started to walk away when she was halted by the sudden appearance of a white silk-covered chest. Strong arms curled around her as she tried to move around the obstruction.

"Has anyone ever told you that you are a terrible liar?"

Jennifer sighed and gave into the temptation to lean her head against his chest. She was so tired of fighting both him and Mikhail. What had she done to inspire such depth of emotion in these two? And why was it always the wrong emotions? As a child she couldn't even rouse enough motherly instincts in the woman who bore her to earn even a hug or a word of praise. And now she had two men snarling over her as if she were a meaty bone.

Would someone ever love her just for herself?

"And have I ever told you that you move damnably fast?" she whispered. His heart beat a comforting tattoo in her ear.

He chucked and the vibrations tickled her. "It's the jungle cat in me."

Jennifer couldn't prevent the snort of undignified laughter and pushed away from him. "Alley cat is more like it."

Strong fingers closed around her wrists, his thumbs lazily stroking the tender skin of her inner wrists causing an answering heat to expand in her belly and move languorously through her limbs. "We should finish eating. You'll need your strength for later."

She was torn. This man saw too much in her that she needed to keep private in order to keep her sanity. She wanted to leave his side and mourn his loss again, in private, but he wouldn't let her, yet. Damn her weakness for this man. And damn his ability to see so much of what she tried to keep hidden from him.

"I think I need to go to bed..."

He dipped his head and Jennifer was startled as warm lips caressed the inside of her left wrist. "I promise not to bite," he whispered against her overheated skin.

Shaken, she pulled away from him and walked back to her seat. "I don't think you should make promises you have no intention of keeping," she admonished shakily.

"Methinks the lady doth protest too much." Mac reseated himself across the table and Jennifer envied the easy manner with which he picked up his utensils and began slicing the thick sausages.

"And I still think you presume too much," she replied, picking up a croissant.

He smiled enigmatically and Jennifer had to look away from his knowing eyes, her heart in her throat.

Jennifer was never quite sure what to think about Renault.

It wasn't anything outward she could put her finger on. In reality he wasn't much different than any other revenant she'd known. Except that she wasn't sure that he was a revenant at all. His past was even murkier than Mac's. No one knew where he came from or how old he was. He certainly never volunteered information about himself. She didn't even know if Renault was his first or last name. To her and everyone else, he was simply known as Renault and he'd been around forever, or so it seemed.

Renault was rolling out a large blueprint on the coffee table. Dressed in burgundy leather pants that clung to every inch of his tightly muscled legs, black boots and a sinful black velvet vest that showed off his broad chest and thickly roped arms, he looked intimidating, menacing and sexy as hell. His thick black hair looked impossibly silky in the light of the room. More like the thick rich hair of a cat than that of a man. It fell like watered silk to the middle of his broad back. Today he wore it pulled back with a silver barrette carved in an intricate Celtic design.

While Renault was disturbingly handsome and shockingly sexual, he didn't hold a candle to Mac in her eyes. Jennifer stifled a sigh. Maybe if Renault did attract her and she had a hot and heavy affair with him, she could finally banish Mac from her life.

She glanced over to Mac seated on the couch. Then again, maybe not.

Dressed in worn blue jeans that were almost faded to white and a gray cashmere V-neck sweater, he looked mouthwateringly handsome. His thick brown hair was brushed back from his face and his hot chocolate eyes that seared her soul when he looked at her were now fixed on the blueprints.

He emitted a low whistle as Renault finished unrolling the sheet of paper. "This is quite the house. When did Mikhail build this monstrosity?"

"It is thirty-two thousand square feet. He bought the original manse about seven years ago and remodeled it. Three years ago it was heralded as one of the greatest restorations of the century on the front of *Architectural Digest*." Renault kneeled by the coffee table, his movements curiously elegant, almost animal in their grace.

Jennifer rubbed at the gnawing ache behind her breastbone. Something was terribly wrong. Was it Miranda? She couldn't tell for sure but something in the air wasn't quite right. Menace lurked in the city beyond their windows and she could feel it out there, waiting for her. Waiting for them.

She forced herself away from the fireplace. She headed toward the armchair opposite where Mac sat. Strong fingers captured her wrist, halting her progress and pulled her around the coffee table and down onto the couch beside Mac, her thigh brushing his. Tensing, she started to move away as his strong arm encircled her shoulder, tucking her against his warm side. She glanced over at him and he wasn't even looking in her direction. He was already memorizing the blueprints. Lazily his hand began stroking small circles on her shoulder, an answering warmth sprang to life.

"I'm not exactly a reader of *Architectural Digest*," Mac's tone was dry.

"I didn't know you could read at all," Renault replied blandly.

Jennifer grinned at Renault, liking him more each second. "He likes the shiny pictures," she teased. "He thinks they're real pretty." Returning her attention to the blueprint, she leaned forward, effectively slipping out from under Mac's arm. "The doorway to the basement isn't on this blueprint." She pointed to the right of the wide curved staircase. "It's here, right under the staircase. "

Renault shrugged. "That isn't too surprising. This house was remodeled from the remains of a fifteenth century fortress. It isn't beyond the realm of thought that Mikhail would keep the dungeons intact."

Mac leaned forward, his shoulder brushing Jennifer's and she forced herself to not flinch from his touch. "Is there a blueprint of the dungeons?" The faint scent of sandalwood and warm male curled around her, setting her senses spinning.

"There is a blueprint of the basement." Renault produced another sheet that showed a large basement roughly the size of the house. No walls or rooms were marked on the diagram.

Jennifer looked at the dimensions on the basement and shook her head. "No. This isn't deep enough to be where Miranda is. These dimensions are roughly fourteen feet below the house. I was at a minimum, twenty-five feet below this depth. There has to be a subbasement under this one. There were at least thirty-five steps spiraling down and they're very steep. This basement isn't nearly deep enough for that many steps."

Renault frowned. "It isn't hard to get blueprints altered for the right price." He pointed. "The entrance to this subbasement is on that side?" He leaned forward and scanned the main floor plan again. "Any kind of alarm system on the house?"

"It is an Excalibur system but I can get the code to disarm it." Jennifer tensed as Mac's hand brushed her waist.

"Good," Renault nodded. "Any pressure pads on the floor or electronic eyes?"

She shook her head. "The foyer flooring is marble and there are no electronic eyes. Mikhail thinks his reputation alone will keep out any mortals. He's just arrogant to assume that any immortals will keep their distance."

Mac nodded. "How about ten A.M. tomorrow morning? I want to make sure Mikhail and his she-devil are sound asleep when we arrive."

"Mikhail can walk around in the daytime. What if he isn't in his little coffin dreaming his bloody dreams?" Renault began rolling the floor plans up neatly.

"He can but that's rare. He usually keeps a standard sleep schedule," Jennifer replied. She felt Mac stiffen beside her.

"Good," Renault rolled up the plans and slipped them back into a hollow tube. "I will see you tomorrow then and we will rescue the fair Miranda from this madman." He rose gracefully to his feet.

Jennifer escaped her seat. Moving over to Renault she placed her hand on his sinewy forearm. At once she felt the muscles ripple in a very catlike movement beneath his golden skin. "Thank you, and please be careful," she whispered. She was struck with the strangest urge to stroke and pet that warm skin and see if he would purr for her.

Renault's golden eyes gleamed for a split second and Jennifer thought he would say something. With an abrupt nod he turned away and reached for his leather jacket. A sudden chill rippled over her body. Wrapping her arms around herself, she watched Mac walk him toward the back door that led to the garage on the ground floor.

Could they get Miranda out alive? Fear snaked around her heart as despair formed an ache low in her throat. It blossomed, threatening to choke her. Tears stung her eyes as she stumbled toward the French doors and threw them open. The icy wind penetrated her clothing as tears began running down her cheeks. Stifling the urge to howl out her agony, she stuffed her fist into her mouth in a vain attempt to stifle the sobs.

Mac closed the door behind Renault, frustration gnawing in his gut. The thought of leaving Miranda in that hell another minute churned inside him like an acid burning everything it touched. Silently he sent a prayer up for her safekeeping. He'd always had a soft spot for Miranda. She was a good drinking partner, even though she didn't drink and she loved to prowl for willing sexual partners almost as much as he did. Vampire or not, she had a big heart and she was always willing to help anyone, mortal or immortal. She didn't deserve to be a pawn for a lunatic. No one deserved that fate.

He walked back to the living room. "Jen..." he began. The room was empty. Frowning, he started toward the stairs when the faintest of sounds reached his ears. A sound no mortal ears would've detected. He stopped abruptly and turned toward the French doors that now stood wide open.

London was lit up like hundreds of strings of gaudy Christmas lights and snow was beginning to fall once again. But his eyes weren't on the town laid out before him. They were on the woman who stood in the corner of the snow-covered balcony, sobbing silently into her clenched hands.

Anger burned through his heart as he watched this incredibly strong woman cry. *Damn Mikhail.* Her shoulders shook with the force of her tears; no easily discernable sound escaped her. He reached for her shoulder and she flinched as he touched her. Ignoring her evasive movements, he pulled her into his arms.

The scent of warm woman and jasmine reached him as he tugged her close. She remained stiff as a board against him as he slowly stroked her back in long, sweeping movements. Sliding one hand under her thick hair to the tender skin of her neck, he rubbed small circles in the knotted muscles, willing her to relax and lean against him.

Slowly, by degrees, she leaned into him. Her fisted hands moved from her face to encircle his waist. He released the breath he'd not realized he was holding as he felt her clutch at him. Her grip tightened and she moved restlessly as if she were trying to crawl inside his skin, inside his soul.

He pressed a gentle kiss on the top of her head as a muffled moan sounded against his chest. "Let it out, Jen."

A sound of protest escaped and almost instantaneously a sob was torn from her throat as she sagged against him, her knees buckling. Deftly he caught her up behind the knees and swung her into his arms. The light of the living room beckoned but he bypassed it, striding for the stairs and the bedrooms above. His bedroom was dim, lit only by the golden glow of a candle. Darkness was always preferable when an emotional outburst was to be had.

The bed was soft and welcoming as he settled Jennifer onto it. She emitted a broken sob and released him, reaching for a pillow. She pulled her knees into a fetal position as he moved around the bed. Settling himself on the edge he began removing his boots. Behind him he felt her stir.

"What are you doing?" she asked, her voice husky with her tears.

"Getting into bed." He dropped his boot carelessly and reached for his black leather belt.

"Here?" she squeaked.

Mac smothered his grin. "Here." He dropped the belt on top of his shoes and climbed back on the bed.

Jennifer startled him by releasing the pillow and lunging for the edge and freedom. "Oh, no you don't." He caught her by the back of her skirt before she could roll over, preventing her from leaving the king-sized bed. A cry of frustration escaped her as he pulled her back toward the middle. Her arms flailing, she caught him on the chin with one elbow as he tugged her into his arms.

"Oww...now quit!" He wrestled her into a position facing him, then pinned her by trapping her skirt between him and the bed. "You're going to hurt yourself..."

"Let me go and then I'll quit," she raged.

He caught her fist right before it would have plowed into his eye. "I'm afraid that isn't an option." Neatly he trapped her persistent hands by stretching her arms over her head and holding them in place with one hand.

"An option for who?" She grunted, twisting desperately to free either her hands or her body. She managed to work one leg free when the seam of her skirt gave up the battle. He missed her triumphant smile as she brought her knee upward in a quick, jerking motion.

Shifting, Mac narrowly avoided a knee in the groin. He scowled and caught her thigh and threw his legs over both of hers, pinning her to the bed. Looking into her enraged eyes, he smiled. "Isn't this better?"

"Than what?" She was winded and she gasped for breath.

"Than being upright. Laying down is almost always a better position to be in." He pressed a kiss on her forehead and he caught the shivers that vibrated through her body. She was so terribly pale. Dark circles marred the perfection of her lovely face. Mikhail's attack and the stresses that followed had taken much more out of her than she would ever admit. Whether she acknowledged it on a conscious level or not, she needed him. Her body knew it even if she wouldn't admit it to herself.

"I won't let you use me," she snarled.

He smiled at her enraged expression. Stroking the back of his forefinger down her soft cheek, repeating the motion until her expression began to relax and her eyes quit darting around the room as if seeking an escape, or a weapon to use against him. "I won't do anything you don't want to do."

"Then let me go," she whispered. "Please," her voice broke.

Mac knew how much that plea cost her. He released her hands and as she shifted he wrapped his arms around her, cuddling her to his chest, his heart giving an uncomfortable twinge at their perfect fit. For a long a while he held her tense body cradled against his until finally she relaxed into him. "I can't do that, Jennifer. I can't let you go," he murmured.

A sigh sounded from the region of his sweater.

"You're overly tired. You should try and get some sleep."

"You're bossy. Quit treating me like a child."

He chuckled at her petulant tone. Sliding his hand beneath the hem of her ivory sweater, he caressed the warm skin underneath. She shifted as if to move away from his touch, instead she managed to press herself closer. Her knee brushed his burgeoning arousal. "Trust me, darling, I do not think of you as a child."

"Typical male," she growled without heat.

He shifted on the bed until they lay facing one another. Tugging her even closer, he slid his leg higher between hers, taking her by surprise. "That makes you one lucky woman." He caught the burst of heat in her eyes as he lowered his head to the soft skin revealed by the V-neck of her sweater.

"No, that makes you one conceited man," she shot back.

"Is it conceited to be aware of one's talents? I don't think so." He pressed a gentle kiss to the exposed flesh. His tongue snaked out, tasting her.

"Mac," she pressed her hands against his chest as if to stop him.

He brushed aside her sweater and caressed the upper slope of one breast with his forefinger. How would she taste, he wondered. Sweet like spun sugar or spicy like mulled cider? Whichever it was, he could barely wait to find out. He dipped one finger inside the very edge of her bra and she stiffened in his arms.

Whether she knew it or not, she needed this worse than he did. Reluctantly, he stopped caressing her skin and turned his attention to her sweater. The delicate pearl buttons slipped through their holes and he caressed the tender flesh as it was revealed. At the release of the last button, he spread the halves of the sweater to reveal the woman underneath.

Pale skin gleamed in the candlelight and the ruby colored velvet of her bra looked dark and erotic against it. He lazily drew his finger over one peaking tip and smiled into her dazed eyes. "Jennifer, I had no idea you had such stunning taste in lingerie."

Sudden mischief sparkled in her dark eyes. "They were a gift," she feigned a yawn.

Mac neatly undid the clasp and then smiled as panic overwhelmed her and she struggled to cover her full breasts. "Oh really." He repositioned himself on the bed until her breasts were even with his mouth. He pressed a kiss against the underside of one pale mound "A gift" He nipped at the exposed skin. "From whom?"

"You wouldn't know him," she stammered, trying to reach for the elusive scrap of velvet as if to retain her modesty.

"Him, eh?" Her nipple poked through her spread fingers and he gave it a quick lick. A thrill ran through him at her squeak of surprise that she failed to squelch. "What is his name?"

"N-n-name?" she quavered as he renewed his assault on her exposed skin.

"Yes," he breathed against the damp V between her breasts. "Name. I am assuming that your benefactor of lingerie does indeed have a name. I for one would like to send him a thank you note. I really like this velvet number."

"T-t-thank you-u-u note?" Her voice broke as she hastily reached for edges of her retreating bra, exposing herself to him.

"Oh yeah..." he purred as he latched onto her nipple and suckled deeply.

141

Her response was instantaneous. Her body arched, bowing up into his, forcing more of her into his mouth. Desire electrified him, setting every nerve ending in his body on full alert as her hands fisted in his hair, holding him in place against her. He reached for the other nipple as he lavished attention on the one currently in his mouth. He rolled the pearled flesh against the roof of his mouth, teased it with his teeth, all the while retaining a steady pressure that had mewling sounds coming from Jennifer's mouth.

Reluctantly he released the tasty nubbin. Kissing and nipping his way down the valley of her breasts and up the other rise, he attached himself to the other one, suckling it until it was damp and standing at attention. Reaching down, he located the hem of her tattered skirt. Raising it, he clawed his fingers up the inside of her taut silk-clad thigh, wrenching a cry from her.

He easily rolled her onto her back and parted her legs. Bunching her skirt around her waist, he settled his arousal against the summit of her thighs. He rocked his hips against her as he reluctantly let go of her nipple. Spicy, just as he suspected. Picking up a rhythmic rocking motion, his hips ground against hers.

"Oh my God," she breathed, arching beneath him for more of the same.

Mac chuckled against her warm skin. He kissed the tender skin of her throat, eliciting a purr. "Oh my Goddess..." he corrected.

"W-w-what?" she stammered.

He raised himself onto his elbows to gaze into her lust-dazed eyes. "Goddess." He dropped a kiss onto her chin. "It is 'Oh my Goddess,' not God." He trailed kisses along her jaw line.

"Really?" she smiled "Please explain."

"Well, as a matter of...Oh my G-g-god..." His train of thought went south to his groin as her thighs tightened on his hips and she mimicked his rolling motions. Jennifer had great thighs. It came from all the horseback riding she used to do. And if he had it his way, those luscious thighs were soon to be thrown over his shoulders.

"What were you saying?" An amused voice pulled his attention from his groin back to the woman beneath him.

Mac smiled into her beautiful eyes, her expression self-satisfied, aroused. "I said, I will have you begging for mercy..." And he renewed his attack on her exposed flesh. Trailing kisses down her throat, he journeyed into the valley of her breasts and across the soft terrain of her belly. Reaching the band of her skirt, he grasped the elastic. He raised her hips and slid the skirt down her thighs and over her feet, tossing it carelessly behind him.

Reapplying himself to the task, he kissed and stroked the soft skin of her belly and resumed his leisurely journey down her skin. Pausing to tease her belly button, he dipped his tongue into the indentation, wringing a gasp from her. Smiling against her skin, he pressed tiny kisses against her belly, moving ever lower until he reached the narrow velvet band of her panties.

Jennifer tensed beneath his hands as he reached the band of her drawers. He nudged the band down, covering the revealed skin with damp, open-mouthed kisses designed to entice and arouse.

"Mac," she squeaked as his hand intimately cupped her.

"Mmm..." he growled against her skin.

"I think..."

"That right there is your problem." He shifted his body until he was sitting on his heels between her spread thighs. "You think too much," he drew his hand up her thigh to her knee and then down again. From the dilation of her pupils, his stroking was mesmerizing and arousing her at the same time. "You need to quit talking and start feeling. Just let yourself go."

He hooked a finger in the wide lace band at the top of her silk stockings. "I really do like these," he commented. "They're very sexy but they have to go." He rolled them down her thigh, massaging each tender inch of her skin, until her leg fell limp to the bed. Then he switched his attention to her other leg lavishing the same attention upon it until she was silently trembling and completely open and vulnerable before him.

Mac cupped her tenderly, pleased to find the rich ruby velvet damp with her dew. Sliding one finger past the band that circled one leg, he slipped a finger into the prize that awaited him. Lightly he brushed the hard bit of flesh at the center of her being and was rewarded as a strangled cry was wrenched from her. He wanted to see her, all of her, now. He wanted her completely bare beneath him as she came, and he wanted to watch her find fulfillment.

He stripped her of the velvet panties, her passion-filled eyes watching his every move. Raising them to his mouth, he watched her eyes widen as his tongue snaked out to taste her on the rough velvet. Instantly, a shudder racked his body as her salty sweet taste hit him. His erection lunged against the zipper of his jeans and he wondered for a second if the worn denim could contain him for much longer. Wincing, he shifted, trying to find a more comfortable position. There wasn't one, short of burying himself inside her.

A sigh huffed out. The only other way to relieve the discomfort was to strip off his pants and if he did that he would take her here and now. Nothing could stop him if he did. But this time wasn't about him. It was about her, for her and her alone.

Tossing her panties over his shoulder to join the rest of her discarded clothing, he reached down to caress the wiry curls that covered her feminine mound. Her hips shifted forward as he slipped his fingers into the well of honey that awaited him. A cry from Jennifer was hastily muffled as he cautiously inserted one thick finger. A groan escaped him as her body clasped around him, welcoming him and urging him onward. She was as tight as a virgin. When he did bury himself in her, he would be lucky to last more than a few strokes. Pausing in his delicious torture, he rose over her, his fingers still buried in her.

"What do you desire Jennifer?" he whispered, his voice sounded oddly strained and very unlike himself.

Her lust-drugged gaze met his. "You."

"You're mine." He shifted into position so that her spread thighs were draped over his parted ones, leaving her completely opened to his gaze and his touch. "Mine and only mine." Pressing his fingers deeper within her, he stroked her damp flesh with long even strokes as she writhed on the bed, her body arching, forcing his fingers deeper. Within seconds she peaked, her cries and her scent filling the room, her hands clawing at the bed covers as she convulsed around his fingers. He'd never seen anything more beautiful in his life.

As a lover, he knew his ability to please a woman was legendary, and over the long span of his life he had pleased thousands of them. Indeed, he'd made it a life's mission to ruin every woman he touched for any other man who came after. But none of the other women ever meant to him what this one did.

His gazed locked with her stunned one. Slowly he withdrew his hand from her body. Stretching from his cramped position, he settled himself between her thighs bringing his face on level with hers. Lightly he traced her lips with his damp fingers, memorizing their shape, their fullness, as she watched him with sated eyes. She shifted her hips beneath him and his erection surged painfully. He wondered if he was going to have a permanent imprint of a zipper on his manhood.

"Say it," he whispered, gently parting her lips, allowing her a taste of her own arousal. He groaned as her soft, warm tongue touched his fingertip, tasting, caressing. "Say you're mine," he growled.

She reached for his hand and pulled it away from her lips. "I'm yours, Mac," her eyes glittered with unshed tears. "I've always been yours."

Mac couldn't speak, his triumph caught in his throat. Silently he dipped his head to kiss the woman beneath him. Putting into that kiss what he wouldn't dare say to her.

Chapter 5

Shai tensed as she caught sight of Mikhail entering the Council chamber. "What's *he* doing here?" she snarled.

"He's allowed to speak in his own defense," Val said dryly.

"Defense," Shai snapped. Anger vibrated through her body, causing a slight tremor in her hands as she clenched them together. She stared hard at the smiling blond vampire, hatred curdling in her soul, as he shook hands and exchanged greetings with several spectators in the gallery behind her. "He should be drawn and quartered."

She shifted restlessly, the urge to lunge for Mikhail's throat overpowering. The few feet separating them could be easily covered. It would just take...

Val wrapped his long fingers around her wrist. Instantly she stilled and looked up into his midnight blue eyes. An odd melting feeling hit her square in the chest.

"The Council will stand for no such foolishness Shai." His voice was deadly serious. "Hold your peace for now, my bloodthirsty love. We shall see what he has to say for himself." Val kissed her on the tip of her nose. Releasing her wrist, he twined his fingers with hers, gently stroking her skin with his thumb.

She snorted as his calming touch sent ribbons of relaxation through her body. "I don't care what he has to say," she replied stiffly, returning her attention to her surroundings.

Voices in a multitude of languages ebbed and flowed around her. According to Val, the Council chamber had changed very little in the past 800 years. Carved into the heart of Kings Stone deep in the Carpathian Mountains of Romania, the round room resembled a courtroom complete with gallery and balcony seating that was rapidly filling to overflowing. In place of the jury and judge's boxes, there was a dais with five high-backed chairs arranged in a semi-circle. Intricately carved, the mahogany backrests and wide comfortable seats gleamed from years of polish in the candlelight. Numerous sconces filled the room with a golden glow and the scent of melted wax mingled with sandalwood incense.

A soft laugh drew her attention and Shai glanced over at Mikhail as he solicitously helped Gabrielle DesNoir into her seat. For the first time in the years she'd known of her existence, Gaby looked almost normal. Her hair was now a rich mink brown pulled into a soft chignon at the nape of her neck. Her ripe body was clad in a feminine gray suit that disguised her generous curves. Pearls glowed softly at her ears and around her throat. She looked more like an up-and-coming young executive than the mistress of a sadistic killer. It just proved that even the sickest people could look perfectly normal.

Shai looked at Mikhail, and was startled to find his gaze upon her. Forcing the slightest of smiles to her lips, she tipped her head in his direction. She was secretly glad to see Mikhail's astonishment at her overture. His eyes narrowed.

The room quieted as the massive mahogany doors near the dais creaked open. The Council filed into the preternaturally still room. A small woman, dressed simply in an ivory Chanel suit and lustrous pearls almost identical to Gaby's, was the first through the door. With her olive-toned skin and shiny black hair she looked vaguely Greek in descent.

A man dressed completely in white with skin and hair to match followed her closely. An albino vampire? So it would seem. Beside him walked a mortal male child who looked to be about six years old. The Albino's slim hand lay on the child's shoulder, curled possessively over the fine bones. The child was neatly dressed in a black suit and shiny shoes, his dark eyes solemn. With his dark brown hair neatly combed back from his rather narrow face, he looked absurdly healthy in comparison to the dead man he walked alongside.

Shai leaned over and whispered to Val, "What is a human child doing here?"

"Edward, the Albino, is a mute. The child is telepathic, a gifted medium. Edward can speak through the child and communicate with the outside world."

She was aghast. "What about his parents?"

"They sold him to Edward," Val's tone expressed his distaste.

"How long has this been going on?"

"About two years."

She sat back and scowled at the Albino. Her heart gave an odd little twist as she looked at the child. He was physically beautiful but his eyes were ancient in contrast to his childish face.

Another man entered the room, simply dressed in tight black velvet pants and a flowing white silk shirt. His thick ginger-colored hair flowed down his back and his eyes were a most shocking shade of violet. Those otherworldly eyes scanned the assembled crowd, assessing those gathered, and Shai knew that this man did not miss a thing. He assumed his seat, his big body sprawled in the chair as if it were too much effort to sit up.

A tiny woman followed him, with honey blonde hair and cornflower blue eyes. Dressed in a pale pink dress, she looked like an exquisite china doll following the ginger-haired giant. Shai felt Val stiffen as the woman stepped up onto the dais and assumed her seat. She glanced at him curiously but his face was impassive.

The Council Elder, Alexandre Saint-Juste, entered last and furtive whispers broke out from various parts of the room. A black Armani suit fit his tall, broad body to perfection, set off by a white shirt and a tie that matched the cool color of his piercing green eyes. With easy fluid movements, he climbed the dais and took the center chair. He quieted the whispered voices with a single glance. Silence reigned while everyone held their breath in anticipation of his words. No one moved a muscle. Alexandre remained silent as he scanned the room. His gaze lit on every face as if to commit each one to memory before moving on, allowing the tension to build until Shai wanted to scream. Finally he spoke.

"Valentin," his voiced flowed out into the room and swept across her skin like a cool breeze, raising goose bumps. "You have brought forth charges of abduction of a vampire and attempted rape of a revenant against Mikhail. What say you?"

Giving her hand a quick squeeze, Val rose from his seat and took the requisite three steps forward. "I stand by these charges."

Alexandre gave a sharp nod and waved a hand toward the scribe. The somewhat bookish woman seated on the far right side of the room nodded in response and noted the charges in a massive leather tome. Her pen flew furiously across the page. "Mikhail, you have heard the charges levied against you by your master Valentin. What say you?"

Mikhail rose from his seat. Shai struggled to contain the bile that churned in her stomach as the urbane vampire took his three steps forward. Dressed in fine ivory linen trousers and matching jacket with a white silk shirt, he looked like an angel. She knew better.

"I am innocent of these charges." He spoke clearly; ensuring everyone in the packed room heard him.

At his words, frantic whispers broke out behind her. Alexandre's compelling gaze silenced them.

"I find these charges to be slanderous in the extreme..." Mikhail began.

"Silence, Mikhail," Alexandre ordered. "You will have your chance to speak. For now, sit down and observe."

Titters sounded with Alexandre's dismissive tone. She rubbed her hand over her lips to hide her amusement at Mikhail's thunderstruck expression, which abruptly turned to ill-concealed rage.

If looks could kill, Alexandre Saint-Juste would have a hole in him the size of a dinner plate. Shai glanced at the stone-faced Alexandre. His eyes were hooded, his face expressionless. Something interesting was afoot. Quickly, Mikhail recovered his composure and offered the Council an abbreviated bow before he took his seat once again.

"Valentin, please explain the circumstances of these charges," Saint-Juste commanded.

"I received word early yesterday evening that Miranda of Glencoe had been abducted from a friend's home in Cornwall. According to Renault, Miranda was using Damien St. James' home for a few days to do some research. Sinjin wasn't in residence at the time. Renault arrived on the scene as they fled with Miranda in tow. In the house he found signs of a struggle and a used syringe." Val paused as frantic whispers broke out in the gallery.

Alexandre glared at the crowd until they settled into silence. He nodded for Val to continue.

"Jennifer Beaumont heard of this crime and immediately set out for Mikhail's manor house outside Manchester. Upon her arrival she found Mikhail entertaining Ms. DesNoir in the library. She demanded to know what had happened to Miranda, at which point Mikhail admitted to the crime. Jennifer asked that she be allowed to see Miranda upon which time Mikhail led her to the old dungeon of the original manse where Miranda is being held.

"Jennifer stated that Miranda has been horribly abused at Mikhail's hands." Val paused again, this time swallowing audibly. Anger radiated from every tense inch of his body. "It's at this point Mikhail attempted to rape Jennifer; failing that he fed from her against her will."

Voices broke out in the gallery once again causing Alexandre to lunge to his feet. "There will be no more interruptions," he commanded, "or I will expel everyone from this chamber and conduct these proceedings in private."

Shai stifled a grin as the gallery grew still. Vampires were so predictable. Nothing could whip a group of preternatural killers into submission faster than the threat of taking the unfolding drama away from them. They did love their little intrigues.

The head of the Council settled in his seat again and indicated for Val to finish his statement.

Val glanced at the unperturbed Mikhail. "It is my charge that Mikhail and his mistress Gabrielle DesNoir kidnapped Miranda in an attempt to exact retribution for some imagined slight against them, presumably perpetrated by me."

Tears stung Shai's eyes as she watched her lover. He stood strong and solid in his convictions. Love welled within her as she watched his proud profile. He was putting his life and his reputation on the line in order to stop the damage Mikhail was inflicting. She loved him more at the moment than she ever had before. Silence cloaked the room as he finished.

"Do you have any reason to doubt the word of this Renault and Jennifer Beaumont?" Alexandre asked.

"None whatsoever," Val replied.

"Isn't Jennifer Beaumont one of Mikhail's revenants?" The sloe-eyed Grecian looking woman spoke, her accent thick, rendering her words almost unrecognizable.

"Cassiopeia," Val tilted his head in acknowledgement. "Yes she is."

"Is it not possible this could be a case of...how you say...sour grapes?" She shrugged, her black eyes shining in the candlelight. "Mikhail takes the beautiful DesNoir woman as his own and tosses this Jennifer out in the cold...how you say...like yesterday's trash?" Her voice trailed off as she waved her hand as if to dismiss Jennifer's charges.

Shai stiffened, throwing darts at Cassiopeia with her eyes.

Val shook his head, his voice calm. "That's not how it was at all. Jennifer left Mikhail many years ago. She bears him no grudge and she wants nothing to do with him. She has stated on several occasions that

Gabrielle is more than welcome to Mikhail."

"Where is Jennifer, Valentin? Can we not hear this from her own lips?" The tiny blonde woman asked.

"Bliss," Val acknowledged her question with a nod. "She's recovering from her injuries. I thought it best if she remained in a safe place for the time being. She doesn't need the added stress of appearing here."

Cassiopeia shrugged, her voice disdainful. "I say that one who does not appear before us has something to hide from the Council." Her eyes glittered with barely concealed triumph as she stared at Valentin.

Shai scowled. Just how many enemies did her lover have? It seemed like they were always tripping over one or another of them. Then again she knew how infuriating Val could be at times, especially to those who were in the wrong.

Alexandre frowned at Cassiopeia's expression.

Edward tightened his grip on the child's shoulder. The child jerked as if an electric current had run through his body. His voice sounded shrill in the Council room. "I think it will be necessary for the Council to speak to both Jennifer and Renault."

Shai caught the look of distaste that flashed in Alexandre's eyes as he glanced at the Albino. He masked his expression and turned toward Val. "You will arrange this?"

Val nodded reluctantly. "I'll speak with them to see if they are willing to come here to address the Council. However, there is still the immediate issue of Miranda's abduction. I request that the Council force Mikhail to release her at once and that she be requested to appear here and speak for herself."

Alexandre nodded to Mikhail to arise. When Mikhail had taken the three steps forward, Alexandre spoke. "What do you say about this Mikhail? Where is Miranda of Glencoe?"

"Miranda has indeed been a guest of mine for some time," the vampire admitted.

Shai snorted at Mikhail's words, earning herself a glare from Cassiopeia and a warning glance from Val.

"She contacted me some ten years ago when Valentin dumped her, rather callously I might add, for the then-mortal Shai," he waved a hand in her direction and she stiffened. She could feel hundreds of eyes boring into her back. The attention of the Council shifted from Mikhail to her.

She struggled to remain impassive beneath their probing eyes. Some of their looks were curious, some malevolent. Unobtrusively Shai shifted, sitting up straighter. Anger simmered in her blood as the vampire continued.

"Miranda was of course devastated by Valentin's fickleness and his abuse of her tender feelings toward him," Mikhail continued, his expression dutifully sorrowful at the alleged abuse. "And when he dumped her for Shai, after the human pursued him shamelessly, of course," once again he glanced in her direction, his expression mock-disgusted. He faced the Council again. "She had no one to comfort her since Shai had turned the head of her only love."

Val tensed, his left hand curled into a fist. The knuckles whitened then, slowly released. Other than flexing his hand he remained still.

Great, now they think I am a blood-sucking groupie. Her blood reached the boiling point as Mikhail's lies flowed through the room, but she forced herself to remain still as the Council again regarded her with curious eyes. Squarely she met the gaze of the ginger-haired giant, and was startled when he winked at her, his smile amused.

Mikhail shook his head, his hands clasped on his chest as if he were miming a broken heart. "Miranda has entombed herself in the catacombs of the original manse. I have no idea how long she intends to remain there."

Bravo, Mikhail. Shai glared at the vampire. It wasn't unheard of for a vampire to go underground, as it were. It was near to impossible for anyone, even another vampire, to find one who did not want to be found. To violate a vampire's self-imposed exile would be considered an insult and the height of rudeness.

A burst of laughter surprised everyone in the chamber. Slowly the ginger-haired giant rose from his slouched seat on the dais. To everyone's astonishment he clapped his hands slowly, each clap thundering through the room. "Well done, Mikhail, well done."

Shai switched her astonished gaze from the giant to Mikhail. The vampire's eyes were narrowed but his face was otherwise expressionless. "Fayne," he spoke evenly, "Are you accusing me of lying?"

Fayne stopped clapping, his smile unpleasant. "I would never accuse you of anything, Mikhail. However, I would say that your performance here would earn you an Oscar in the mortal world. Such a performance the likes of which I've never seen."

Shai was shocked to see Val twitch with laughter.

A low growl sounded from Mikhail. Surprised, Shai turned to see Gaby leap to her feet. Gaby placed herself in front of Mikhail, her hands on his chest as if to restrain him. Her expression was intent. While she didn't speak a word, her eyes spoke volumes.

"Enough," Alexandre got to his feet, waving Fayne back to his seat. "Sit down immediately," he spoke to Gaby.

Gaby shot Mikhail another warning glance before turning to smile apologetically in Alexandre's direction. Smoothing her immaculate hair, she regained her seat.

Alexandre waited until she sat before speaking again. "Valentin, Mikhail has stated before the Council that Miranda of Glencoe is an invited guest at his home. What say you to this statement?"

"It's a lie," Val's voice was quiet, assured.

Alexandre nodded just once before turning to the enraged Mikhail. "Mikhail, Valentin has stated you have lied before the Council. What say you to this charge?"

Mikhail visibly pulled himself together, still darting angry looks at the amused Fayne. "I have not lied to the Council. Val is lying to protect himself and his whore. They are trying to frame me and slander my good name."

Val's fist clenched again as Alexandre's face turned stony.

"You are on trial here Mikhail, not Val's consort, and you will refrain from impugning her name before the Council."

"And who will refrain from impugning my good name?" Mikhail roared.

"If you had a good name, then we wouldn't be here in the first place," Fayne snickered.

"Now see here..." Cassiopeia objected, rising to her feet.

"Enough!" Alexandre erupted and again the room subsided into stillness. "I will brook no more arguments. Currently we stand at an impasse, gentleman. Mikhail, you stand accused of kidnapping a vampire and the attempted rape of a revenant. Currently these charges are unsubstantiated. Mikhail, it is charged that you must produce the whereabouts of Miranda of Glencoe within the next twenty-four hours. Failure to do so will result in a penalty of one hundred years of exile in the pit. Do you understand?"

Mikhail flinched, rage etched on every inch of his taut body. "I understand completely."

"Furthermore, you will issue a public apology to Valentin's mate, Ms. Jordan, within the next two minutes, do you understand?" Alexandre's voice was cold as ice and Shai shivered, his words lashing out into the silence of the chamber room.

"I will never..." he began.

"You will indeed apologize or you will suffer the consequences." Alexandre's voice grew colder as the temperature plummeted in the room. "I will not brook any refusal on this, Mikhail. Ask for forgiveness or pay the penalty."

The power of the two vampires whipped around the chamber in a silent duel. Shai sat on the edge of her seat, the tension in the room unbearable. Their power blew around the room, causing the candles to flicker wildly as the temperature continued to fall. Fear showed on the small child's face as he stood by Edward's chair. He tried to pull away as if to run from the room but Edward held him firmly in place. Shai bristled as the child flinched under the pressure of his grip, but the Albino held steady, not allowing him to move. Someone cried out in fear at the back of the gallery.

Suddenly it was over and Mikhail staggered as if he'd been dealt a blow to his gut. Shai didn't miss his quick look of fear before he masked his expression with a thin veneer of civility. With a jerky nod in Alexandre's direction, he turned to her, his expression mocking.

"My dear lady," he bowed in her direction, "I tender my apology here before the Council and those assembled. If anything I said here today was untrue, I rescind my words and I beg for your forgiveness. Truly, I hope that I have not offended you."

Shai glanced at Val to find his gaze upon her, anger lingering in their dark depths. A slow smile spread across his face and he winked at her. She looked over Mikhail and gave a sharp nod. At his look of triumph, a feeling of imminent calamity crept over her. Someone would pay for the slight dealt to Mikhail today. She could only hope it would not be Miranda.

Alexandre spoke again, "Mikhail, you will prove beyond a shadow of a doubt that Miranda of Glencoe is unharmed. You will lead both Bliss and

Fayne to her resting-place. Miranda will not be disturbed. They will view her unharmed body and that will be that." His emerald gaze pinned Mikhail. "Do you agree to this?"

Shai saw that Mikhail wanted to object but he held his peace. His gaze was angry as he locked on Fayne. He nodded sharply to acknowledge his acquiescence.

Alexandre turned to Val, "Valentin, you will bring forth both Jennifer Beaumont and Renault before the Council. They will give testimony as to what they saw. Return to this chamber with them at midnight in two days."

Val nodded.

"Council is dismissed until midnight, two days from now." Alexandre stepped from the dais as voices broke out all over the chamber. He disappeared through the doorway with his fellow members of the Council trailing behind him.

Val turned to Shai and her heart ached as she took in his frustrated expression. "I..." she began when Mikhail interrupted her.

"I will win, you know," Mikhail hissed at Val. "No matter what you try to do, Val, I will win yet again."

"There will be no winners here, Mikhail," Val replied, his voice calm. "The Council will decide what is right and wrong in this case."

"The Council," Mikhail spat, "is a fivesome of despots and petty tyrants. They have no real authority over me, and I will deal with them in my own time." The light of insanity glowed in his eyes.

Val turned away, reaching for Shai's hand, but Mikhail grabbed him by the arm, spinning him around to face him. She gasped as Val reached for Mikhail's throat, but a soft voice underlaid with steel stopped them both.

"That's enough." Bliss moved between them, effectively separating them with her tiny body. She didn't come anywhere near either man's shoulders, yet she pressed a hand on each man's chest, holding them apart. "Gather your woman and leave, Mikhail. I'll not hear of any more threats against the Council or you will find even more charges against you."

"This isn't over," he snarled at Val.

"Of course it isn't over," Bliss shot back. "You have much to answer for."

Mikhail shot a rage-filled look at the tiny woman as Gaby grabbed his arm and led him from the chamber. As they vanished into the milling crowd, Bliss turned to Val, her expression just as cold.

"You'd better hope your witnesses are convincing, Valentin. Mikhail won't let this drop if they aren't."

Val looked down at the tiny woman, his gaze warm and his smile slightly mocking. "I am in the right, Bliss."

The woman smiled ruefully and shook her head. "Still the white knight, aren't you, Val? Always trying to slay the demons of the persecuted and the downtrodden. You realize that one day this will be your downfall?"

He shrugged easily. "I cannot go against my grain, Bliss, you know this."

Shai bristled as Bliss sighed, reaching up to lightly caress Val's cheek. "Yes, I do know this."

Shai darted angry looks at Bliss as the other woman turned away and moved toward the Council doorway, her movements as graceful as a ballet dancer. She'd always hated tiny women who moved so gracefully. She always felt like a lumbering cow next to them with her height and her large bone structure.

Val chuckled and tugged Shai into his arms. She relaxed against his broad chest, wrapping her arms around his waist. Safe in the arms of her lover, she watched the tiny woman walking away. Jealousy melted away like snow under the steady sunshine. She felt him press a gentle kiss to her forehead and a sigh escaped her.

"Val," Bliss' voice interrupted them from the Council doorway. "What happens if Mikhail gets away with his supposed crimes?"

Val's chest rumbled beneath Shai's ear. "I will kill him."

"You realize if you kill Mikhail without the blessing of the Council that you, too, will be put to death?" Bliss spoke evenly, her eyes searching his.

He nodded. "Sometimes we have to do what we feel is right regardless of the consequences."

Bliss smiled faintly and shook her head. "Still the white knight..." She turned and slipped through the door.

Shai pulled back and looked up into Val's dark eyes, "What..."

He shook his head, laying a finger across her soft lips. "Let's go home," he whispered.

Reluctantly she nodded. As they moved through the crowds toward the door, she silently dreaded what the next forty-eight hours would bring.

His first thought upon waking was he was glad his erection had finally subsided. It wasn't easy to sleep fully clothed with a hard-on the size of Texas when there was a willing woman nestled against him. Thank the Goddess for his iron restraint or he wouldn't have made it through the night without pulling Jennifer underneath him and taking her the way his body demanded.

His second thought was something was terribly wrong.

Instantly he sat up. Snow fell heavily outside the windows, causing a thick cloud cover to crouch over the city. The candles in the bedroom had long since burned out, and the only light spilled through the hallway door.

Cursing the sheets tangled around his legs, he kicked to free himself when a soft sound reached his ears and he froze. Silence roared in his ears until a soft scrabbling sound sent chills down his spine.

"Jennifer?"

Silence.

He staggered to his feet, stumbling over the tangled sheets as he heard another sound. It sounded suspiciously like a sob. He grabbed a black sweater and pulled it on as he lurched toward the wall switch.

"Jennifer, where are you?" he commanded. He flicked the switch and light flooded the bedroom. She was nowhere in sight. He stuck his head into the bathroom. Empty.

His feet sounded on the polished oak of the hallway as he ran out the bedroom door, the bright lights temporarily robbing him of sight. Blinking furiously, he heard that odd scrabbling sound again, like fingernails scraping on wood.

"Jennifer," he barked. "Answer me."

Silence.

He thundered down the steps, his eyes scanning the open living room as he paused on the landing. His gaze lit on Jennifer, standing against the French doors. The sheer draperies covered her nude body, as she stood flush against the glass, her arms out straight from her shoulders, her head lolling to one side as if her neck were too weak to support it.

"Jennifer?"

Was she sleepwalking? Mac walked down the five remaining steps into the tiny foyer. *Was she sick?* She didn't stir as he moved through the living room toward her. He shoved the drapes to one side, looking her over anxiously for any injuries. He placed his fingers on her shoulders and she flinched, a protest escaping her lips. Even though the room was warm, her skin was painfully cold. The scrabbling sound came again and he glanced at one hand. Her fingernails had gouged deep grooves into the wood, marring the white paint. Now she clung to the wood with all her strength, her arms trembling with exhaustion.

"Jennifer," Mac kept his voice low, soothing. "It's me, Mac. I want you to let go, darling." He encircled one trembling wrist with his hand and stroked her skin, willing her to release her stranglehold. "Please, darling, let go." He continued whispering calming words until she released her death grip on the damaged wood. He clasped an arm around her, drawing her hand to her chest. He repeated the process on her other wrist until she released the wood. As if boneless, she sagged against his chest.

Deftly he swung her up into his arms, and walked over to the couch. He deposited her on the couch and covered her with a blue afghan. She trembled violently beneath the worn wool as chills shook her body. He strode over to the thermostat and cranked it up to eighty degrees. When he heard the furnace kick in, he turned toward the woman on the couch. Her eyes were open but she wasn't seeing him or her surroundings. Her gaze was distant and horrified, locked on a nightmare he couldn't see.

He moved to her side and seated himself on the edge of the couch. "Jen?"

"He's killing her," her voice was dull, lifeless.

He exhaled noisily, relief flooding through him. "Who is killing whom?" he urged, desperate to keep her speaking.

"Mikhail is killing her as we speak," her voice trailed off. Slowly she turned her head toward the east windows, where in a few hours the sun would breach the horizon. Tremors shook her body harder as her chill worsened.

Mac stared out the window, horror dawning in his soul. *He wouldn't...he would.* "Where Jennifer, where is she?" He looked at her still, pale face.

Her eyes grew even more distant. Locking on a scene that only she could see. "She is laid out on a stone slab in the center of a ring of stones.

The stones are bluish in color and there are thirteen of them with a large, flat red stone altar in the middle. I think it is an old pagan circle. The symbols on the stones are Celtic..."

Mac felt the blood run from his face as she described the stone circle. With a sudden flash of insight, he knew where that circle was located even though he had never been there. Something twisted painfully deep within his soul then lay silent and waiting. The circle she described had haunted his dreams for as long as he could remember; it was one of his earliest memories.

And his recurring nightmare.

"Definitely Celtic," she murmured, drawing his attention away from his tortured thoughts.

"Jennifer..."

Jennifer's voice changed, her accent and language distinctly old Scots. "*Ha maister o'nor stane, micht an pooerfae...*" she faltered. "*Hearken ma roup o'yer...*"

Mac froze as the words poured over him. Ancient whispers, long forgotten by mortal men sounded crisply from the depths of his memories. *Hail Master of the north stone, mighty and powerful. Hear the cry of your...* And he knew the words that would follow. He knew them as if they had been carved on his heart. It was a bastardization of an ancient invocation to the Goddess, one used to call the forces of darkness into the light of day. They were the same words he heard in his dreams thousands of times before, but could never make them out with any clarity.

Something slithered along his spine; a memory long forgotten shifted but remained obscured by the fog of time. Something momentous was about to happen. And like a runaway freight train, there was no way that he could stop it. Trepidation slashed at his heart, threatening to steal his breath from his lungs. The room spun dizzily around him as he slid to the floor. Was he about to come face to face with his past?

"She's dying..."

One thing at a time, one thing at a time. Mac concentrated on regulating his breathing until he could restrain the foreboding that had temporarily immobilized him. *What was he so afraid of?* What lurked in his mind that could render him as terrified as a child? He was a man, fully grown. In his past he'd taken down warriors ten times stronger than the men of today. Fear was something to be controlled, not to let rule. Taking a deep cleansing breath, Mac looked at Jennifer's face - tears ran from her eyes and into her hair.

"I know where she is." He forced himself to his feet, relieved when his legs supported his weight. "I'm going to try and save her." He ran into the foyer where his hiking boots stood by the door. Foregoing socks, he shoved his feet into them, lacing them up quickly. He ran back to Jennifer's side; her eyes were closed and her breathing labored. Chills still racked her body but they had slowed in strength.

"Jennifer, you need to hang on." He pressed a kiss to her forehead, torn between leaving her alone and trying to save Miranda.

Her hand pressed lightly against his chest as if she were trying to push him away. "Go," she whispered hoarsely.

Mac captured her hand. He noted the bruises that were forming from her ordeal at the window. He knew the restorative powers of a revenant well; and by the time he returned very little would remain of the injuries. Even after all these years, those powers still impressed him. He pressed a quick kiss to her palm then tenderly covered her arm with the afghan.

After one last glance at her pale face, he grabbed his cell phone and ran for the kitchen. He dialed as he exited through the kitchen and out the back door. By the time he reached the bottom of the narrow steps that led to the garage, he was at a dead run. With his heart in his throat, Mac ran toward the BMW while a voice in his mind chanted, *Too late...Too late...*

A sensual, sleepy voice answered the phone. "Hello?"

"Addy, I need a favor..."

Chapter 6

S.W. Of Inverness, Scotland

Mac grasped the steering wheel in a death grip, his palms slick as his mind scrabbled around in circles. Random thoughts chased themselves to death with no answers being revealed. He wondered if he were finally going insane. Had hundreds of years of nightmares and broken images irrevocably damaged and tortured his mind?

As he turned onto the ancient road that would take him near the circle, a stab of unease caught him between the shoulders. The freezing rain and snow mix cleared for a brief second, and the circle loomed in the distance, perched on its hilltop as if waiting for him.

It looked familiar - too familiar.

How could this be? He'd never visited this part of Scotland before, or had he? He didn't have any memories prior to the day Renault found him one thousand years before in a niche in Hadrian's Wall. Anything before that time was a blank. Until now.

The Land Rover slid on the icy road, jarring him from his thoughts. With a modicum of effort he corrected the spin and raced toward the circle in the distance. Already he feared he was too late. Mentally he thanked his friend Adeline Marshall-Smythe, Addy to her friends, for her assistance in flying him to Inverness in record time. Without her, all would've been lost.

The undercarriage of the four-wheel drive scraped on the overgrown road, but he paid it no mind. It rocked when it hit larger objects and still he accelerated. Clouds shifted at the eastern edge of the landscape and stripes of pink brightened the sky as he drew closer to the circle in the distance.

He'd been here before, no doubt about it. The landscape was as familiar to him as his own face, the swirling snow notwithstanding. His chest grew tight with tension as he crept closer to the stones and the sun continued its inexorable rise.

The heavy tires spun in the thickening slush as he swung around the last curve in the road. With ease of long practice he counter-steered, righting the truck as he sped toward the circle. The sun peaked over the horizon as the engine suddenly stalled.

An oath broke from his lips as the steering locked and the power brakes refused to slow the vehicle. A large gray guardian stone loomed directly ahead. Hitting the stone at this speed would kill him for sure. Mac fumbled for the seatbelt. Unbuckling it, he flung open the door and threw himself out into the swirling snow. Rolling over in the icy grass, he ducked his head for the crash that was sure to follow.

Silence.

He raised his head. The boxy blue Land Rover, nearly enveloped in the rising storm, stood mere inches from the stone. He rolled to his feet, staring in disbelief. There was no way a vehicle that size could've stopped on icy grass in that short a distance, not at the speed he'd been traveling. Unease trickled down his spine. Something was definitely at work here. Something evil. He could feel it breathing down his neck.

A faint cry, like that of a woman, came from above.

"Miranda!" he bellowed, and took off at a run for the hill. The ice and snow-covered grass impeded his journey as he tried to scramble up the steep slope. The long grasses flattened and quickly iced beneath his boots, making it impossible for him to remain upright. Something didn't want him to reach the top. Mikhail? Could vampires control the weather? He'd never heard of one being able to do so.

He paused in his battle with the elements as the hairs on his neck stood up. Someone or something was watching him. He resisted the urge to look around, opting to continue his grueling climb. He took another step and slid backward two more paces.

"Damn it," he snarled, throwing himself flat against the hillside. He clawed his way upward.

A low keening sound reached his ears, causing a growl to erupt from him. Redoubling his efforts, he ignored the icy rain stinging his exposed skin and continued his clawing journey. Rapidly his fingers grew numb as shards of ice and frozen grass jabbed at his hands. The heart-wrenching keening grew in volume as he gained the top. Icy winds whipped around the standing stones, its haunting whistle raising goose bumps on his flesh. His lungs screamed in protest as the sun broke through the thick snow clouds.

"No!" he gasped.

At the same moment, an inhuman wail rose from the center of the circle. The winds, much fiercer here, yanked at his clothing and lashed at his hair as he staggered to his feet in time to see something burst into flames on the altar.

With a war cry that would have impressed his Celtic ancestors, Mac fought against the torrential winds and threw himself through the western arch. He landed on his knees. Instantly he noticed the winds did not broach the inner circle, instead they swirled wildly around the boundaries as if angry to be denied entrance to this sacred place.

He looked up at the altar, the massive red stone rising from the center of the circle as if it had grown there. The altar was ablaze and through the flames he could see the figure of a woman laid out upon a crude wooden cross. Unearthly screams tore from her gaping mouth as she writhed and burned in the relentless sunshine.

He was too late.

Tears scalded his eyes as he lumbered to his feet, suddenly feeling every day of his thousand years weighing upon his shoulders. He approached the head of the altar and placed his hands on either side. The stone felt icy beneath his touch while the heat of the inferno seared his skin. The moment he touched the altar, the roar of the icy winds outside the circle calmed.

"Why?" he hissed. He threw back his head, a cry torn from his throat. "*Mither, whit wey hae ye forsak ye childr?*" The ancient Scots language tripped off his tongue without a single thought. His fists knotted and his eyes flooded with tears. A warm breeze poured over him, caught his words and swirled them up into the sky. His head dropped, his chin against his chest as sobs shook his body.

"Why have you forsaken us?" he whispered, opening his eyes again. He looked up at the small patch of pale blue sky visible in the layer of gray clouds.

Above him, clouds swirled and thickened as a tunnel began to form around the patch of blue sky over the altar. Almost instantly the flames died down and only ashes and bits of charred clothing remained. The icy winds surged outside the circle and a thick, enveloping snow began to fall, obscuring the circle in a blinding white shroud. As he gazed upon the perfect, three-dimensional ashen image of Miranda, a glimmer caught his eye.

Her golden ring gleamed in the weak sunshine. He moved toward where her wrist lay bound to the cross. Her hand was a perfectly formed ashen image, the gold gleamed on her forefinger where she'd worn it for hundreds of years. He glanced at her ashen face, serene in repose, then back to the ring as it glimmered in the light. Hesitantly, he reached for the ring. As his fingers brushed the gold, her hand disintegrated. The ashes swirled about his hand, as if to caress it for one final parting touch, before settling on the wood.

The ring lay nestled in his palm.

A sense of rightness descended upon him as the gold heated at his touch. Not questioning his instincts, he slid the ring onto his finger where it fit perfectly. A warm wind rushed through the circle from above, disturbing the ashes on the altar. Mac stepped back as the wind relentlessly obliterated her image.

The winds grew steadily stronger, concentrating only on the area of the altar. The ashes lifted into the tornadolike funnel that formed. Images danced within the funnel, shadows moved and swayed with the current. They teased his eyes, showing him nothing yet hinting at the images to come. The winds slowed and the funnel opened like a gray cocoon, revealing a ghostly image of Miranda, fully formed and solid as she'd appeared in life.

Her smile was serene, beatific, and her gaze warm as she watched Mac.

His heart stopped as he beheld Miranda, levitating a few yards above the altar. Tears continued to flow unheeded down his cheeks as the warm winds tugged at his hair. "Pal," he whispered, his heart aching with loss.

"Destiny, MacNaughten." Her voice, melodic and soft, was a balm to his soul. "My final gift to you is your destiny. It will save you and those you love..." With a parting smile, she looked up at the patch of blue sky visible at the top of the funnel cloud. The cocoon slowly closed around her and she vanished forever from his sight.

Instantly the winds turned icy cold and the sun faded, leaving swirling black clouds above the circle. Mac grunted as the winds forced him from the altar. Staggering, he crashed into the west portal. As he touched the cold stone, images slammed into his mind with the speed of a runaway freight train. A ring of black robed worshippers chanted in a circle around the altar, the red stone covered in blood. Naked women danced around the stone. A silver knife gleamed under a star-filled sky with a full moon. He saw a stooped figure in an oversized ceremonial robe.

An unearthly moan drew his attention to the center of the circle as the remains of the charred wooden cross began to rise off the ancient altar. It hovered a few feet from the stone when a sudden *crack* rent the air and the cross exploded into hundreds of pieces. Mac dropped to the ground, nose pressed into the snow to avoid being hit by the dangerous shards.

Around him, the world seemed to tip on its axis. Nothing would ever be the same again.

"Git you up, fool," a voice snarled.

He blinked as the crisp grass poked him in the nose. Raising his head, he saw two men haul a robed figure to its feet where it swayed drunkenly. The robe, richly embroidered with gold and blue silk thread, depicted a variety of Celtic symbols that struck a note of longing in Mac's heart.

He knew this person, didn't he? The robe was certainly familiar enough. His mother had made it on his tenth summer...His mother? He didn't have a mother. Slowly he got to his feet, gaping at the scene laid out before him.

The crisp air was rife with the scent of wood smoke from a massive bonfire. The sound of chanting rang in his ears as he glanced around him to see a ring of black robed figures walking in a widdershins circle around the altar. Their monotonous words were lulling, almost comforting in their familiarity. In the center by the altar, a tall man stood clad in a dark robe, the hood obscuring his face. He stood silent as a stone, his arms raised toward the face of the full moon.

Terror blossomed in Mac's chest as he regarded the ghostly scene. He knew with great certainty this was his Uncle Manfred. This man was his dead father's only brother.

And his father's killer.

The knowledge slammed into Mac's head, and he staggered backward into the west stone. *What?* He shook his head, trying to rid himself of the images, but they didn't change. He wanted to move away from the stone but his limbs didn't want to work. His head felt disconnected as if he'd been drugged. His gaze flickered over the scene before locking on his uncle.

The firelight flickered on the golden thread of his uncle's robe as he slowly lowered his arms. He turned toward the two men and the small figure they held upright between them.

"Bring forth my son," he intoned.

The two men herded the unresisting boy toward the altar. Mac glanced at his bare feet as they coerced him over the crisp, frost-covered grass. What time of year was it? Harvest, maybe? He wanted more than anything to struggle against the lethargy that held him against the stone, but his body refused to respond to his urgent summons. A feeling a dread washed over him. He didn't want to see what was about to happen to the child.

"*No*," his mind screamed as the child was presented before the altar. With brisk efficiency the two men whisked the hood back to reveal the head of the child. Mac stared in horror at the perfect child image of himself. The two men stepped back, leaving the fourteen-year-old Mac to face his uncle alone.

Shock rendered Mac immobile as he watched the images of the distant past before him. "*I am not his son*," his mind shrieked as the scene continued to play itself out.

Uncle moved forward, reaching for the tie on child-Mac's black robe. He tugged at the tie until it came free and he whisked the robe off of the child's unresisting body, leaving him naked to the elements. The moon gleamed on the milky white skin that stretched over the child-Mac's emaciated frame. Bruises and festering wounds covered his pale flesh while bones poked at the damaged skin, making him look like a walking skeleton rather than the healthy fourteen-year-old boy he should've been.

He saw his younger self whisper, "Goddess..." His lips barely moved. Anger churned in Mac's gut as he watched the child he'd once been and the man who should have loved and protected him.

His uncle raised a hand and motioned at two smaller robed figures. They came forward, stripping off their robes as they moved, revealing themselves to be women. Careful to keep their gazes averted, they urged the child-Mac up onto the cold stone. Laying him out, they carefully bathed him in warm water scented with rosemary, chamomile and mint as the remaining robed figures began their monotonous chant once again.

The clear night sky glittered above as Mac watched them move their hands over the child's damaged body. Their touch was light, impersonal almost. When they completed the cleansing, they rubbed scented oils into his skin. The scent of bayberry lingered in the air, replacing the scents of the herbs. When they were through oiling him from top to bottom, they stepped away from the stone and left him to his fate, abandoned on the altar.

The chanting stopped and once again the circle was silent except for the crackling of the fire. Uncle stepped into view again, taking the position at the head of the sacrificial stone. Raising his arms over his head, he spoke.

"Master, on this winter's night, accept the offering of this virgin child. Innocent and as pure as the day he was born, he is known as Conor, the Good Son. We offer up his life in service to you," he opened a small pouch at his waist.

"We offer his life in service to you," the circle echoed.

Uncle withdrew a handful of herbs and tossed them onto the child-Mac's frail body. "Accept our gift of this child's life so that we may worship in your name."

"In your name," the circle chanted.

"Accept our gift of this child's flesh so that we may work your will," Uncle intoned.

"Work your will," the circle chanted.

Uncle drew out a silver knife. Terror left a metallic tang in Mac's mouth as he saw the blade gleaming in the moonlight. Even knowing he'd survived the attack did not dispel the fear that held him immobile, pinned against the stone like some sort of scientific specimen. The robed circle began to move again, this time clockwise, the chanting low and sonorous. Time ticked by as his uncle held the knife poised over the tiny, emaciated chest. The worshippers feet and words picked up speed.

Letting out a cry that turned Mac's blood cold, Uncle plunged the knife into the child's chest and then quickly withdrew it. Immediately pain burst through his body as the memory of the knife tearing through his skin returned in full force. He cried out as the child jerked on the altar, a high-pitched cry echoing Mac's. Blood welled from the wound and covered the child's battered chest.

Mac clutched at his own chest, surprised that he was unharmed. Nausea churned in his stomach as the pain from the nonexistent wound blossomed, enveloping him and driving him to his knees.

The worshippers surged toward the altar and dipped their fingers into the child-Mac's lifeblood as it poured from his chest. Hands reverently stroked his dying flesh until they painted him red from head to toe. Sighs of ecstasy from the mouths of the worshippers filled the night as they stroked the dying child and kissed the hem of Uncle's robe. Their cries echoed off the stones as Mac watched his younger self dying on the altar.

An unearthly scream sounded from outside the circle, halting the worshippers in their delirious exhalation. Startled, Mac turned his head toward the sound. Golden eyes gleamed from the darkness outside the ring.

"'Tis the master," someone whispered.

"Nonsense," snarled Uncle. "I am one with the master and I would know of his arrival." Raising his voice. "Who dares to intrude upon our circle here?"

Again the unearthly cry sounded, followed by the rhythmic padding of heavy feet.

Animal feet.

With a sobbing cry, the younger of the bathing women dropped to her knees. A wild keening sound arose as the majority of the worshippers followed suit. They cried out to the darkened sky and their Master to save them from whatever stalked them from outside the circle. The padding feet continued their pacing beyond the reach of the firelight.

Thud, thud, thud, thud.

And then came a breathy panting that sent chills down Mac's spine.

The worshipper's cries rose to an almost deafening volume.

A shriek like that of a strangled woman cut the night and stilled their voices. Through the north doorway a panther entered. Its black hair gleamed in the flickering firelight as it moved with a restless animal grace. Its golden eyes locked on Uncle.

"How dare you desecrate this place," Uncle hissed.

A low growl escaped from the cat.

"I did this for you..." Uncle snapped.

The cat shrieked again, cutting him off. Its muscles bunched beneath its thick coat. The worshippers scrambled to their feet and edged away from Uncle, leaving him alone at the head of the altar. Golden eyes never leaving its quarry, the cat began to pace, back and forth, back and forth, slow and methodical. Its complete attention focused on Uncle.

It seemed like eternity that they stayed this way, each poised as if to strike. Then Uncle moved.

The cat was on him in seconds. The panther placed massive paws on Uncle's shoulders, locking them both in a horrifying dance. Uncle's screams were blood curdling as the cat's claws tore through the robe to the skin beneath. His hood was knocked back and Mac caught of a flash of silvery-golden hair. Blood erupted from the horrendous wounds and his body crashed to the ground on the far side of the altar. The worshippers scattered, their shrieks fading in the rapidly rising winds.

Mac tensed as the cat approached the altar. With a graceful leap the cat landed on the stone, careful not to step on the wounded boy. It sank down, using its big body to cover the child. Placing a massive paw over the wound in the child's chest, he licked the blood from the child-Mac's face. He saw the child stir under the warmth of the big cat's body and its reassuring purr. Periodically the cat lifted a paw to check the wound until it seemed he was satisfied the bleeding had stopped. Rising, the cat pawed at the child, forcing him to move.

Slowly the boy sat up, shaking his head as if dizzy. Child-Mac swung his legs over the edge of the altar and he tried to slide to his feet with the big cat bracing him. But his knobby knees gave way, sending him face-first into the snow.

Snow?

Painfully Mac rolled over, freezing rain pelting him in the face as he beheld the stormy sky of the 20th century. Chills wracked his nude body as he tried to summon the will to rise to his feet. Exhaustion pulled at his limbs as the enormity of his experience washed over him.

My Goddess, I am the son of a Pagan High Priest from the eleventh century.

Familiar golden eyes appeared as Renault bent over him, obscuring his vision of the cloud-laden sky. Strong hands pulled him into a sitting position as Renault dropped into a crouch, supporting Mac against his own body.

"Mac?"

"I know," Mac whispered to his savior from centuries ago. He caught a glimpse of the ancient ceremonial robe as his eyes slid closed. He felt Renault wrap the wool around him and as he slipped into unconsciousness he heard Renault whisper, "It is about time, brother."

Shortly after Mac left, an icy rain began to fall. After eight hours it finally began to slow but the damage had been done.

Jennifer stood by the tall living room window watching the scene below her. Ice coated everything with a clear sheen in the watery afternoon sun. Naked tree branches, their souls revealed to the casual observer, reached toward the leaden sky. Their branches crashed together, clacking their displeasure at the weather.

Miranda was dead.

The ache that settled in her heart told her this. Her best friend was dead. Gone from the face of the earth she'd walked for over a thousand years. How was that possible? After three hundred years of friendship, gallons of tears and millions of laughs, Miranda no longer walked this earth.

For the first time in her life, Jennifer was truly alone.

If her heart hadn't been encased in ice as the world was outside, she thought she would cry. For now, she was too hollowed out to do anything more than stare out into the icy world and wonder if she would ever feel anything again. Would she ever find the courage to love anyone?

An insidious voice whispered in her mind, *What about Mac?*

Panic fluttered in her chest at the thought of Mac. She loved him. She'd never stopped loving him and it was time to admit that, at least, to herself. As long as she lived, she would love Conor MacNaughten. And as long as Mikhail walked this earth she could never have a relationship with Mac. It wasn't safe for them, for Mac. Because of her, Mikhail wanted him dead.

But did Mac even want her anymore? He'd loved her before, she was sure of it. He said that he didn't want her for anything more than sex, but was he lying? He hated what she was and who her master was; would this knowledge end their relationship?

Could she accept him on his terms? Could she find fulfillment in a strictly sexual relationship with Mac? Could she live with only having sex with him without having his heart as involved as hers?

Can you live without it? the voice taunted.

"I have so far," her voice shattered the silence of the room. But did she want to continue this way? Empty and alone? Never knowing the touch of a man of her choosing?

The door to a small house directly across the street opened and a young couple walked out. For a few moments they stood in the doorway and marveled at the layer of ice that coated everything. The man locked the door and, arm in arm, they started their hazardous journey up the street. As they laughed and slid, they clutched each other's arms to remain upright. Pausing at the corner, the dark-haired man bent and within seconds, on the deserted street corner, the young lovers were wrapped in a heated kiss.

She felt like a voyeur as the man slid his hand inside the woman's coat, at his touch the woman jerked then leaned into him. Without warning the man overbalanced and slid on the ice, sending them both into a heap on the icy sidewalk. Their mingled laughter reached Jennifer's ears as she watched the woman who lay cradled in his arms. The woman leaned forward to whisper something to him then she scrambled off his body, leaving him to gape after her. The woman stood a few feet away from the man, her smile was so filled with love that Jennifer's heart ached at the sight of it.

The woman slowly drew up her skirt and shimmied out of her panties. She twirled them on one finger then tossed them at the man, hitting him square in the chest. Astonished, the man scrambled to his feet and lunged for her, pale pink panties clutched in one hand. The woman shrieked with laughter, easily evading him, and slid her way back to the doorway they'd exited only moments before.

As she managed to unlock the door, the man caught her. Spinning her around in his arms, he shouldered the door open and hustled her through it. He pinned her to the wall with a kiss and his big body while he blindly reached behind him trying to find the door to shut it.

Jennifer smiled faintly as the door finally closed. Was that what she wanted? The thought of that kind of intimacy frightened her. She knew she was a coward when it came to relationships. Even if Mac wanted her physically, could she escape the boundaries she had lived with for so long? She yearned to try, to know what it felt like to make love to a man she loved with all her heart and soul. Maybe she could garner enough courage to toss her panties at Mac sometime...

She started as the back door hit the kitchen wall with a crash. Spinning around, she grabbed the fireplace poker, holding it out before her in what she hoped was a threatening stance. Her heart leapt into her throat as Renault filled the doorway, hauling a semi-conscious Mac in his arms.

"Is he..." she faltered, her knees wobbling precariously.

"No, but he needs your help." The big man labored through the living room and up the stairs leading the way into the bedroom, Jennifer right on his heels. "We need to get him warmed up, and fast." Renault settled Mac on the bed.

She eyed the oddly embroidered cape Mac wore. "He didn't leave here wearing that. Where are his clothes?"

"It's a long story," he said shortly.

She averted her eyes as Renault quickly stripped the robe off Mac's unconscious body. She busied herself collecting extra blankets from the top of the closet. When she turned around, Renault had him covered with the bedclothes.

She added the blankets as shivers wracked his body. "What happened to him?"

He shook his head, "That's for him to tell you." With brisk efficiency Renault turned his attention to the tiny fireplace. Within moments he had the fire laid and he applied a flame to the tinder while Jennifer busied herself rubbing Mac's chilled limbs through the layer of blankets. Within minutes the fire was crackling merrily, lending the room cozy warmth against the frozen world outside.

Renault rose from his crouched position in front of the fire. Jennifer could feel his gaze on her. She looked up to meet his haunted golden eyes. "Look after him," he said quietly. "I have to take care of something."

She nodded and looked away, "I..." Her throat constricted as she caught sight of the golden ring on Mac's finger. Slowly she reached down, lacing her fingers with his chilly ones until her ring lay beside Miranda's. How many times had she and Miranda done the exact same thing? Lacing their fingers together so that the rings lay side by side, chanting a silly childish rhyme about friendship. Hundreds of times? Thousands?

"She's gone," she croaked. Grief threatened to steal her voice.

Jennifer felt Renault's hand on her shoulder and he squeezed gently, confirming what she knew in her soul. For a second she thought her heart would stop beating and her lungs would just stop breathing. The world hung still and silent. Then her lungs expanded again. Maybe she would live through this.

"He's had a bad shock. You need to get his body temperature back up and let him rest. He will awaken when he is ready."

172

She turned and looked into his unusual eyes. "Thank you Renault, for bringing him back to me."

With another squeeze, he released her and left the room. Moments later she heard the back door open and close once again.

The crackle of the fire was her companion as she watched the man she loved. His face was deathly pale and still, lacking the animation that usually resided there. A sudden urge to be close to him seized her. Not questioning her instincts, she stood and shed her clothing. Clad in her underclothes, she lifted the covers and slipped into bed beside the man she loved.

At the first touch of his chilled flesh, the breath flew out of her lungs. Resolutely she massaged his cold skin beneath the blankets. Shivers seized his body as she worked her way down each arm. As she rubbed her way down his long legs, the shudders slowly lessened until they finally ceased altogether.

He really was magnificently built. At just over six feet in height, he was long limbed and wonderfully muscled. Jennifer worked her hands across his chest, massaging in long, heavy movements to stimulate blood flow. His chest was hairless and broad and marred by a single, thin scar on the right pectoral. Thick with muscles, and golden from the sun, Mac had a body that was every woman's dream. She wanted nothing more than the right to be cradled against that chest for the next thousand years.

When she finished with a foot rub, Mac was sleeping peacefully. Exhausted, she stretched out beside him. Linking her arm through his, she shifted forward until her lips lightly grazed his shoulder. She breathed in the scent of warm man and sandalwood that was uniquely Mac, and rested her head against his arm.

Weariness pulled at her limbs as his warmth began to seep into her skin, relaxing her. What would she have done if he'd run into Mikhail? She hugged his arm tightly. She couldn't bear to lose him now that she'd found him again. Now if only she could convince him that he needed her as much as she needed him. She closed her eyes, if she could do that, all would be right with her world.

Chapter 7

"So what's the deal with the sunglasses, James Dean?"

Jennifer glared at Mac's broad back as he laughed and swept Shai into a bone-crushing hug. He'd abruptly awakened her four hours earlier, demanding she get up and dressed immediately. It was easy for him to make demands; he'd been awake awhile and was already fully dressed. Oddly dressed at that. The black jeans and dark blue turtleneck were normal but the black sunglasses were an odd touch even for Mac. She'd expected him at any minute to proclaim "I vant to be alone," or "No pictures, no autographs."

Instead, he'd hustled her into some warm clothes and out into the ice-covered world for the dangerous trek to Val's house outside Guildford. It was a two-hour journey under normal circumstances. Due to the ice, it had taken almost three hours. During the drive he'd offered no explanations or answered any questions. Instead, he'd patted her hand, telling her all would be revealed, as if he were some great magician.

Jennifer snorted, kicking the door closed behind her. Something was certainly different about him, something she couldn't put her finger on. His energy was different. Before, Mac had been a rather intimidating physical presence. Unpredictable and wild like an animal, his energy had been predatory, dangerous. Now there was a sense of restraint. The leashed energy he emanated fairly hummed along her skin. What happened and where this change had come from, she had no idea. It was unnerving yet oddly reassuring at the same time.

Shai grabbed her for a quick hug, jolting her out of her reverie. "Darling girl!"

Jennifer smiled at the familiar endearment. The scent of cinnamon enveloped her as she returned the hug. "I've missed you."

She pulled back; a wide grin animated her face. "And I you." Her gaze turned concerned. "Are you okay?"

Jennifer nodded, tears pricking her eyes in the face of her friend's concern. "Yes. How is Val?"

Her friend's expression turned sad. "I've never seen him like this. He's so hurt and so angry right now," she whispered. "I'm afraid that he'll do something rash."

Jennifer linked her arm though Shai's and they walked toward the library door, where Mac had vanished only moments before. "I know. I feel so helpless right now. I just don't know what to do..." her voice trailed off as they entered.

Mac stood in the middle of the room, his gaze concentrated on Val, where he stood before the darkened window. Val looked exhausted, as if he hadn't fed or slept in days. His eyes burned with an unholy light and they were locked on Mac. The tension in the room was palpable as the two men stared at each other, one daring the other to break first and look away. For a few seconds they all stood frozen in time. Shai broke the silence.

"Well, I think that is pretty much enough of that." Shai unlinked her arm from Jennifer's and strode into the room. "Can anyone join in on this pissing contest or is it limited to territorial males only?"

Val visibly relaxed, his gaze never wavering as Shai approached him. Ignoring the fact he was one of the most powerful vampires on the planet and he could kill her with a glance, she stepped directly in front of him, lacing her arms around his waist.

"Anyone care to tell me what is going on here?" Shai asked.

"Ask him," Val nodded toward Mac.

Jennifer moved to Mac's side, laying her hand on his arm. The muscles tensed then relaxed beneath her fingers.

"I did all I could to save her," Mac's voice was pained. His arm trembled faintly beneath her touch. She squeezed it, earning a faint smile.

"I want to hear all of it." Val's voice was raw.

Jennifer resisted the urge to cover her ears. She didn't want to hear about the agony Miranda had suffered. She pulled away, but Mac's arm snaked around her, tugging her into his side. Surprised, she glanced up at his dark sunglasses. She frowned as the dark lenses reflected only her image and nothing of the man behind them. She raised her hand to remove them, but he stopped her, and pressed a tender kiss to her palm. A shiver rippled down her spine. He lay her hand over his heart, its beat steady and reassuring beneath her touch.

"Jennifer woke me around four-thirty this morning. She was in some sort of a trance and she told me Mikhail was killing Miranda. She described the place where he took Miranda and I recognized it. How, I don't know, but I did. So I left Jennifer bundled on the couch and took off to the standing stones." He shook his head. "The weather was so bad. It is almost as if something conspired against me. The closer I came the farther away the circle seemed to be."

Jennifer squeezed his waist in sympathy.

"When I finally drew close to the hill where the stones are located, my Land Rover failed. The electrics, the engine, I was unable to do anything. The vehicle was headed directly at one of the guardian stones at the base of the hill. I had to risk bailing out of the vehicle or crashing into it at forty miles an hour. Miraculously, the Land Rover stopped before it hit. I still don't understand it, it should have hit the stone." He shook himself from his musing.

"I started to climb the hill, but the winds seemed to be trying to prevent me from reaching the top. I had to drop to my knees and claw my way up. I kept praying that the clouds would hold and protect her from the sun," his voice grew hoarse with suppressed emotion. "When I reached the top of the hill, the sun broke through." He pulled away from Jennifer, his movements agitated.

"I was too late," he whispered.

Jennifer reached blindly for a nearby chair and sank bonelessly onto it. Her hands trembled as she wiped away her sudden tears. Through watery eyes she watched Mac approach the fireplace. He placed his hands on the mantel, his hands fisting over the edge of the Carrera marble. Miranda's ring glimmered in the firelight.

"Too late," he whispered again. The room grew still as Mac stared into the fire. The expression on his face tugged at her heart. His torment was there for all to see. Clearly, he was reliving something that she couldn't begin to comprehend. After a few tense minutes he shook his head, removing himself from the past.

"I approached the altar where Miranda was chained to a wooden cross." His voice was flat, emotionless.

"A cross?" Val croaked, his voice rough with emotion.

Mac nodded. "As I approached the altar, the fire burned down, leaving only the ashes." He frowned. "I've never seen anything like it. It was a perfectly formed, three-dimensional image of Miranda chained to the cross - but it was made of ashes."

Jennifer scrabbled for her purse, only to realize she hadn't brought it with her. A hand appeared in front of her face with a handkerchief. With trembling hands she snatched it from Val and wiped streaming eyes.

"I saw her ring, and something told me to take it." Mac continued. "As I touched her finger, her hand disintegrated. Then..."

Silence.

She abandoned her mopping operation and looked at Mac. He stood as still as a stone before the fireplace. Shai moved toward him, laying her hand on his shoulder.

"I can't explain what happened next. I don't understand it yet." His voice was jerky and filled with frustration. He pulled away from Shai and turned to face Jennifer.

Her heart constricted at his look of torment that played across his face. She offered him a watery smile, trying to encourage him to go on.

"I guess I had a vision of my past. I saw who I was and where I came from." In frustration he ran his hands through his hair, causing it to stand on end. "I knew where the standing stones were when Jennifer described them, even though I know I'd never been there. I knew how to get there and I knew what I would find, but I don't know how I knew."

Shai sank down on the couch directly across from Jennifer, her expression stunned. Val moved close to his lover, perching himself on the arm of the couch linking Shai's fingers with his.

"You know where you came from?" he asked.

"I think I do." Mac exhaled noisily. "I know I do. As I took the ring from Miranda, a cloud appeared over the altar, sweeping the ashes up. When the cloud opened, Miranda appeared as alive as ever. She said something about giving me the gift of destiny and it would save those I love. Then she disappeared.

"The next thing I knew, I was lying face down on *autumn* grass. The snow was gone and the grass was covered with frost. Around me was a circle of men in black robes. I, as a young child, was being led to the altar in the center of the stones. I was dressed only in a ceremonial robe."

Jennifer gaped at him. "Like the one you returned in?"

Mac nodded sagely. "It sure looks like the same one. My father's name was Mireen and he was a powerful pagan High Priest in the eleventh century. He was the last of his line and he was training me to take his place. His brother Manfred was a black magician. He was jealous of the power my father possessed. In a fit of rage my uncle killed my father by offering him in sacrifice to the Goddess. He thought if he made a big enough sacrifice, the Goddess would bestow her gifts upon him as she had my father. His plan backfired. Instead, he brought famine down upon his people. Many died. When this happened, Manfred turned his back on the Goddess and embraced the Master of Darkness, whom we called *He Who Shall Remain Unnamed.*

"Upon my father's death, Manfred took my mother and I into his house as servants. We lived in the cellar and I worked in the barns taking care of the horses and livestock. My mother," his voice cracked, "died within a few months of a broken heart. She simply couldn't live without my father."

"How old were you?" Jennifer asked, her heart aching for the parentless child.

"Around eleven summers or so. A few years later, after the harvests had not improved, Manfred decided he needed to make another sacrifice, a bigger sacrifice to the Master. He wanted to sacrifice his own son to show he was willing to suffer in his devotion, but he felt his own son was flawed. His son had a peculiarity, an affliction Manfred viewed as a curse. He felt that offering his son to the Master would be viewed as an insult. He needed someone untouched and pure of heart for this ultimate sacrifice."

"You?" Shai whispered hoarsely.

"Manfred banished his own son from the house that summer in preparation for this great event. He decided the close of the pagan year, harvest, was the best time to make his offering. So, on a cold autumn night they gathered at the standing stones. They drugged me and hauled me out there. After they chanted and invoked the Master, they tossed me onto the altar."

From his closed expression Jennifer knew there was much more to it than that. But she didn't want to push him now. She could feel his tension and confusion even from a few feet away.

"What happened?" she asked.

"My uncle tried to kill me, to sacrifice me to his dark God." Mac spat the words. His expression tightened, his pain plain to see.

Jennifer could stand it no more. She rose from the chair and approached him. Sliding her arms around his waist, she released the breath she'd been holding as his arms came around her, holding her tightly as if he never wanted to let go. "That's where the scar came from isn't it? The one on your chest?" Her voice was muffled against his shirt.

She felt him nod.

"How did you survive?" Shai asked. "How did you escape?"

"Someone arrived at the right moment and saved me. He killed my uncle and saved my life."

Jennifer raised her head to look at him; her reflection stared back from his black glasses. "Who? Who saved you?"

Mac raised a hand and pulled the sunglasses from his face. Those gorgeous, hot chocolate-colored eyes were now liberally streaked with gold, glowing warmly as he stared down at her. Her breath caught in her throat as the power of those catlike eyes poured over her, into her, warming her from the inside out. Deep in those eyes, so different and yet the same, was knowledge beyond her wildest dreams.

They were also familiar.

"Renault?" she quavered.

Mac nodded, his gaze never leaving her face. "Renault is my uncle's son, my cousin. He was known as Niall then and I was to be sacrificed in his place. He saved my life."

"Your name," Shai croaked. "Your name means 'son of the good one.'"

Mac nodded. "I knew that long ago but I never really knew what it meant. I assume Renault gave me the name, as it wasn't my name as a child. My father was a good man, and a kind one." He shook his head sadly. "Such a waste of lives."

"I'm glad you found your destiny, Mac." Jennifer said fiercely, tightening her arm around his waist. "I know how much it haunted you." Those golden-brown eyes swept over her face, warming her. "I'm also glad I found my destiny." He leaned forward, his lips grazing her ear. "And I'm thankful I found you again."

Jennifer froze, her senses going into full alert. She pulled back, staring into those mysterious eyes, and lost another piece of her heart to him. "I..."

"Shush." he placed a warm fingertip over her lips. "Not now." He pressed a light kiss to her forehead before he released her.

Shaken, she lurched over to the end of the couch and sank down onto it. Was her deepest wish about to come true? Could Mac really love her? Knowing what Mikhail's reaction would be, could she risk letting him love her?

"I don't understand how Mikhail thinks he can get away with this," Shai said. "He has to know the council will come after him."

"I don't think he cares," Val answered. "He wants to taunt the Council into coming after him as he wants me to come after him." Val eyed Mac warily as if he were unable to decide how much had changed in his old friend. "I think it might be time for a meeting."

Mac nodded. "I agree. It is time for this to end. Shall we send word to Mikhail to meet us tomorrow evening at the *Chapel des Anges Perdu*?"

Jennifer frowned at the *"we"* in his statement.

Mac turned as if he knew of her unspoken resistance. "It is my fight too," he said quietly.

"So macho," she snapped, fear making her words sharper than she intended. "I'm going, also. Mikhail is unfortunately my master and I have some stake in this."

Shai frowned. "What happens if you kill Mikhail, Val? What will happen to Jennifer and Maeve?"

Val looked at Jennifer, his expression speculative. "I don't honestly know what will happen. I don't know anything will happen to them."

Mac stared at Jennifer also. "So we don't know what happens to a revenant when their master is killed? Do you know of any vampires who had revenants when they were killed?"

Val shook his head. "Miranda is the first vampire killed in hundreds of years. Contrary to Bram Stoker, we are a relatively peaceful bunch."

"What about vampire lore? Is there anything in the lore that might give us a clue?" Mac's gaze remained fixed on Jennifer.

"I'll have to contact Sinjin," Val replied. "He's done extensive research on vampires and our humble beginnings. He might have the answers we need."

Mac nodded. "Then I think we are done here." He held out his hand and Jennifer's heart leapt into her throat. Hesitantly, she placed her hand in his and allowed him to help her up. "We need to get back to London. I want to catch Renault in the morning."

Val rose to his feet, his expression solemn. "I ask for your forgiveness with regards to my actions earlier. I should never have doubted you would do everything in your power to save Miranda."

Mac's expression was equally grave. He held out his free hand. "Shake my hand, *brither*, and all will be forgotten."

Val smiled at the use of the Scots language. "Did the language come back to you also?" he asked as he shook Mac's hand.

"Parts of it. It's the language I grew up with," Mac grinned. "And it feels great to know that fact."

Jennifer rose from her seat and followed the other three as they walked through the library and into the main hall approaching the front door. So much had changed in the past hour and she couldn't get a handle on it. She felt stunned, numb and anxious all at the same time.

The night air chilled her skin as she stepped into the darkness with her man beside her. Val halted her progress and pulled her into a swift hug. "Have a care, Jennifer. All will work out," he whispered to her.

Her smile felt wobbly. "Promise me. Promise me that no matter what happens, you will do everything in your power to keep him safe."

Val's smile was kind. "I promise."

She released him. Mac stood by the car, and warmth spread through her as she met his heated gaze. He held out his hand once again. "Let's go home."

Something shifted inside as she heard those words. Nodding mutely, she walked down the steps to the man who waited for her.

Chapter 8

Chelsea, London

"Wake up, sleepyhead."

Jennifer stirred. Her reclined position in the front seat of the BMW looked incredibly uncomfortable. Just how did she get her neck into that position?

"Mmm," she mumbled.

"I love a woman who articulates." Mac grinned as she settled into a more accessible position. Leaning forward, he pressed a light kiss to her cheekbone. He inhaled the scent of warm woman and jasmine, a mix uniquely Jennifer's. Brushing his lips down her cheek, he blazed a trail to her jaw, lingering to kiss the exposed skin of her neck. Her pulse fluttered beneath his lips. He snaked his tongue out to steal a taste then nipped at her skin, pulling a reaction from her.

"What..." She shifted, moving away from him.

Enthralled, he watched as she slowly roused. Her eyelids fluttered. Then she stretched the full stretch of a sated, sleepy cat. First, she raised her arms and arched her back, pulling her jacket and sweater away from the top of her black skirt, leaving her soft belly vulnerable to his gaze. Her thighs whispered together as she moved sinuously. Her stocking-clad toes pointed as the stretch worked its way down her body. His groin tightened at the innate sensuality of her movements.

Fastening his gaze on the expanse of exposed skin, he leaned forward and pressed a damp, open-mouthed kiss on her belly. The air whooshed out of her lungs as his lips touched her.

He nipped at the tender flesh eliciting a squeal from her. Fingers tangled in his hair and gently tugged as if to pull him away from his tasty morsel. Then he blew a raspberry on her belly.

Shrieks of laughter exploded from Jennifer as the raspberry sounded loudly in the silence of the car. He trailed his fingers up her side as she twisted, abandoning her grip on his hair. Shrieking, she tried to evade his questing fingers.

"That tickles," she yelled, arching wildly as if to throw him off her.

Mac chuckled against her skin, gracing her with another opened mouth kiss, this one just above her belly button. His hand nudged at the bottom of her sweater before slipping underneath to explore uncharted territory. Pressing kisses up her stomach, he pushed the sweater out of the way until he reached her black lace bra.

"I do love your lingerie," he breathed against her skin.

Jennifer giggled and he delighted in the sound. This woman didn't laugh nearly enough. It was up to him to see to it that she laughed a great deal more in the future.

"Shai bought these for my birthday. We went to a lingerie party together."

He eyed the scanty black lace and the creamy mounds it covered. "Val is a lucky man." Flicking open the front clasp, her breasts spilled forth. "Not as lucky as I am, though."

Jennifer cried out as his lips coaxed the tip of her breast into a pearl. Her fingers tangled in his hair as he tasted the warm woman beneath him. He shifted to reach more of her tender skin and groaned in frustration as he banged his knee on the steering wheel.

"We have to get out of this car." He pulled back from her and the temptation she presented.

She watched him with hazy eyes. "Where do you want us to go?" she shifted, bringing one foot up to rub his thigh, a sensual smile curving her lips.

"My bed." Mac ground out, his voice hoarse. He grabbed her foot, dipped his head and nipped at the instep before raising his eyes to meet hers again. "I want you beneath me, over me, surrounding me, now."

Her eyes widened. She swallowed convulsively. "Okay," she croaked. She licked her lips and Mac could barely contain a groan. Didn't she know what she did to him?

Jennifer shivered as Mac threw open the car door and a cold gust of air whipped into the car. He grabbed her around the waist and helped her over the console.

"My shoes." She reached for them on the passenger side floor but he scooped her up into his arms instead. "Wait..."

"No time," he rumbled.

Kicking the car door shut, he started for the front door. His boots crunched in the snow as she wrapped her arms around his neck and relaxed against his chest. When was the last time someone treated her so tenderly?

Not since the last time Mac was in your life.

Sad, but true. No one had ever treated her as this man had. By rights he should hate her for who she was and what she'd done to him. But she wouldn't question the fact that the Goddess had deemed she receive a second chance. She'd grab it and hold onto it with both hands. She pressed a gentle kiss to his neck. He smelled of snow, leather and man. Encouraged by the growl he emitted when her lips touched his flesh, she nipped at his skin, excited by the taste and proximity of him.

"Have mercy, woman." He spanked her smartly on the backside.

A bark of laughter escaped her as he bounded up the steps to the front door. He released his hold on her legs as if to put her down on the snowy cement. No way she was going to put her stockinged feet in the snow! Agilely, she wound her legs around his and clung like a limpet to his broad frame and licked his throat instead.

"You are playing with fire, little girl," he growled.

Jennifer pulled back and gave him what she hoped was a sexy smile. "Promise?"

His breath hitched. "Do I ever."

The door swung open and he stumbled in, hampered by her twining legs. She laughed when she almost ended up on the marble floor of the tiny foyer. Images of the couple across the street doing almost this very same thing flashed through her mind. Joy expanded in her heart. He slammed the door behind him, plunging them into darkness relieved only by the glow of a small lamp at the top of the steps.

Jennifer sank into a molasses pit of desire, pulled deep into the sensual darkness. She trembled as he braced her against the wide oak door, pressing the ridge of his arousal against the apex of her thighs. Dear Goddess but she wanted him. With every fiber of her being she wanted this man to possess her. She wanted him with a need so ferocious it could no longer be denied.

Mac's breathing was urgent as he leaned heavily into her, pressing his erection into the softness of her body. He removed her jacket, shifting her away from the door long enough to slide the garment out from behind her, and dropped it to the floor. His fingers tangled in her long hair, pulling her head back to accept the deep thrust of his tongue into her mouth.

She whimpered into his mouth, wiggling restlessly against him in a vain effort to appease the growing ache between her thighs. She ached for him to fill the emptiness inside her. The same emptiness that was rapidly growing damp with her need.

Hastily she shoved his jacket from his shoulders, wanting to feel his bare skin beneath her hands. The leather hit the tiles with a slap as she raced her hands beneath his sweater. Warm male skin, slick with sweat, awaited her. She kneaded and stroked the thick pads of muscle that rippled beneath her touch. Her fingers found flat male nipples as a groan burst from his throat. Greedily she swallowed his cry as she sucked hard on his tongue.

Loathe to break their torrid kiss but needing to feel more of him, Jennifer moved away. Mac gasped for air, his body raging against her as she tore the turtleneck off of him, tossing it into the darkness. She licked her swollen lips, tasting the essence of Mac before pulling his head back down to hers for round two of their sensual battle. He gave in immediately, his mouth hard as it nipped at hers. Her head reeled at the sensations he aroused and she clung to him to keep from floating away. He was her anchor in a world gone dark with desire.

She sighed as he slid his hands beneath her sweater, cupping her breasts against his big palms. He kneaded them, his callused thumbs running over their taut tips, setting off another explosion that caused a moan to break from her lips. As if Mac understood what she needed, he broke the kiss, this time pulling her sweater off over her head. He tossed it carelessly over his shoulder. She wriggled out of her unclasped bra, dropping it to the floor.

With her breasts bared to his touch, he slid one arm underneath her buttocks, lifting her higher. His mouth unerringly found one pointed nipple as it grazed his chin. Greedily he attached to it, suckling hard on the pearled tip. She cried out as the new sensation raced through her, pooling at the apex of her thighs. She arched against him as if to drag him closer or throw him off her body, she didn't know which. He responded by pulling her tighter against him, grinding his erection against her. The erotic rocking motion set off a chain reaction. A high keening cry broke from her lips as the tension spiraled tighter, coiling low in her belly. As his left hand plucked at the erect peak of her breast, ecstasy flooded through her.

She clutched at Mac's broad shoulders as she convulsed against him, cries escaping her lips as the miracle washed over her in rolling waves. Her breath raged in her lungs and her head fell to his shoulder as residual tremors seized her. She clung limply to the man who held her so gently cradled against his chest.

"That was the most beautiful thing I have ever seen," Mac murmured against her damp shoulder.

Jennifer roused herself to chuckle. "I don't see how you can see anything in here."

"I see everything," he replied in a solemn voice.

Jennifer forced her head from his shoulder and looked into the blur that was his face. The face she loved so dearly. In the darkness his eyes glowed with an inner light, with wisdom she couldn't begin to fathom. She wanted to be close to that light, that wisdom, and most of all, the man. She wanted to climb into his skin and remain there, safe and surrounded by his soul.

Her throat constricted. "Make love with me," she whispered.

"With pleasure." Mac pushed off from the door and headed for the steps. She was bemused when he didn't climb them. Instead, he sat her on the edge of the first landing, bringing her gaze even with his. The light from the lamp above illuminated his beloved face.

"What about the bedroom?" she asked.

"Too far away, we'll never make it." He branded the damp skin of her throat with a hot, open-mouthed kiss.

Jennifer purred as she felt the muscles ripple beneath his skin. That she could make this big strong man lose control was a very heady thought, indeed. She wanted to sing with the sheer power of it. She stroked his back - muscles contracted beneath her touch as her hands caressed him.

He shoved her skirt up and she wiggled, lifting herself to shift it up around her waist. The cool air tingled on her exposed skin and the gleaming wood of the landing was chilly against her backside.

"Where are your drawers?" he rasped.

"I didn't wear any."

A low growl erupted from Mac as he seized her by the back of the knees. She delighted in his strong grasp. He pulled her thighs apart, pushing himself between them once again.

Her head fell back and a low moan escaped her as his zipper brushed against the core of her desire. Abruptly his hands left her and she swayed dizzily. She braced herself by placing her hand on the landing to keep from falling backward.

She watched him in the pale lamplight as he fumbled with his jeans. Smiling, she halted his movements by sliding her hands over his erection, cupping him. His hands fell away and she watched his eyes dilate with lust. The feeling of power leapt within her as she squeezed gently, eliciting a moan from him. He gave an involuntary thrust against her palm.

"If you keep doing that, this will be over really quick," he groaned.

Jennifer laughed, a soft throaty chuckle. "And the problem with that is..."

His gaze claimed hers. "I want to be inside you when I come."

Her mouth went dry. With that erotic image in her mind, desire blossomed, leaving her breathless. She wanted that more than anything else in the world. She wanted this man buried deep inside her. She wanted to cradle him with her body, her soul, and she wanted it now.

With hands that shook, she finally managed to unzip his jeans and his engorged flesh sprang free. He really was magnificent. And so big. She had no idea the male anatomy could be this big. She slid her hand around his steely length and the air hissed from his lungs. Would it fit? Gently she stroked him from the engorged head to the root, marveling at his size and the feel of him in her hands. Would it hurt? The silk-over-steel feel of him transfixed her as she stroked. A bead of fluid escaped from the blunt tip.

"I think you'd better stop now," he hissed through gritted teeth.

She grinned, reluctant to relinquish her new toy. "And I was just having fun." With one last stroke she slid her hands up his hard belly, encircling his nipples with her fingertips. She lightly pinched one and he jerked beneath her touch.

"I'll show you fun," he growled.

He shifted, pressing the blunt tip of his erection against her damp folds. "I want to come inside you, now," he growled. Sliding his hand between her thighs, he caressed the damp flesh with long slow strokes until she writhed in his arms. He slipped a finger into her honeyed flesh, sinking into her. Jennifer shuddered at his touch, instinctively drawing her knees up to take him deeper. Desire threatened to engulf her. She shifted her hips tentatively, wanting more but not quite knowing what to do.

"That's my girl," he encouraged. "Just like that." Tenderly he explored her damp flesh, coaxing and teasing, preparing her for his entry.

A moan escaped her as his thumb brushed the sensitive nub at the top of her sex. She wound her arms around his neck, drawing him closer to her as the world tilted wildly beneath his knowledgeable hands. His slow strokes grew more rhythmic and her hips rocked in response, her inner muscles subtly clasping his finger as she answered his mating call.

Suddenly impatient, Mac removed his fingers and replaced them with the broad head of his erection. Jennifer tensed as he began to enter her. Her entire being focused on the growing pressure between her thighs as he pushed deeper. A twinge of pain had her trying to shift away from the tension. He laced an arm around her waist, holding her in place. His hands gently stroked her damp skin.

"Sssh, *ma hirt*," he whispered against her throat. "You can take me. Just relax a bit, *jo*." As he spoke he rocked his hips, slow tentative movements, sliding in mere millimeters with each shift.

She moaned, straining in his arms. She arched against him, trying to accept his invasion easier. He slipped a hand between her thighs. Finding that sensitive nub, he gently stroked it in a tight figure eight pattern. Soft moans were wrenched from her as he dazzled her flesh and her hips moved in response. With each movement he slid in a little further until she felt she would burst.

Jennifer clung to him, plastered against him like moss on a tree, afraid to move. He was so huge she felt she might tear at any second. Surely no more would fit inside her. He slid his hands down the outside of her thighs. Catching her beneath each knee, he drew her legs up higher. The tiny shift in position allowed him to bury himself up to the root. Her breath caught in her throat as his erection brushed that sensitive nub, sending chills over her body.

Looking deep into those mysterious eyes, she saw tenderness glimmering in their depth. Something inside of her relaxed and broke free; rapture blossomed in her soul. She smiled, tightening her thighs around his waist, trusting him not to hurt her. He shifted positions again, moving against her. A soft cry was wrung from her. Gripping her waist, he began to thrust.

Fire rippled through her body and pooled between her legs. She closed her eyes, concentrating on the sensations that rocketed through her blood. Strong hands held her steady as he hammered into her, each thrust taking her higher than the last. Her nails dug into his shoulders as he forced her body into taking a second orgasm.

She screamed with the force of her release, her body arching against his. He continued to move, slow rippling movements of his hips that prolonged her ecstasy. It flowed through her again and again, rolling over her in slow waves. She never wanted this feeling to end. Slowly she drifted back to earth, clinging damply to Mac.

"Good?"

"Yes..."

She'd barely caught her breath when he began thrusting in earnest. Within seconds another cry was wrenched from her lips as a harsh groan exploded from him. With his head thrown back and his face contorted, she held him tightly as he came deep within her.

It was the most beautiful thing she'd ever seen.

Someone was petting her.

Jennifer frowned. Skilled hands stroked down her side, cupped her hipbone then began the leisurely journey upward. A purr escaped her lips as that magical hand paused to massage her shoulder. Warm lips touched her arm.

"Time to wake up, sleepyhead," Mac's voice sounded in her ear.

She opened her eyes to see her lover standing over her with a tray in one hand. "What is it with you and waking me up?" she grumbled, fumbling for the sheet to cover her nudity.

"I don't want you to spend your whole life sleeping," he grinned.

Her heart gave a little twist at the sight of his smile. She glanced away, "It isn't like I don't have all of eternity..."

"Exactly. You have all the time in the world to sleep." He set the tray on the bed. "But for now we have to talk."

Jennifer scooted away from him, clutching the sheet over her bare breasts as he climbed onto the bed. She eyed his unbuttoned blue jeans. "I need something to wear." The last thing she wanted to do now was talk!

The events of the last few days had left her feeling too raw, exposed. Topped with their spectacular lovemaking, she wasn't sure she could form a coherent sentence at this point. She needed time and distance to pull herself together.

"You look perfect just the way you are." Mac grinned at her, reaching for a croissant. "If you insist, please avail yourself of any of the clothing in the closet."

Jennifer glared at him as he lavishly buttered the croissant then added a dash of cinnamon. Eyeing the expanse of polished wood floor between the bed and the closet, a devilish idea came to her. Waiting until Mac filled his mouth with the pastry, she defiantly threw back the sheet. Rising from the bed, she sauntered over to the closet, aware of the complete stillness of the man behind her. Feigning a yawn, she stretched sinuously, arching her body before reaching for the door handle.

"That will get you tossed back into bed," Mac growled.

She grinned to herself. "As if you could stop eating long enough. Besides, I thought you wanted to talk," she shot back. She selected a white silk dress shirt. She slid it over her shoulders and turned back toward the bed. He watched her with hot eyes, and a ribbon of desire unfurled low in her belly.

"I do."

His gaze scorched her skin as she buttoned the shirt, pausing to ensure each button was secure before moving to the next one. By the time she finished dressing, Mac's croissant was crushed in his hand.

"Well then." She added a slight twist to her walk as she meandered across the room. "Maybe I can change your mind?" She climbed onto the bed on her hands and knees, delighting in the way Mac watched her every move. She crawled between him and the tray, causing the crockery to rattle, and insinuated herself on his lap. His burgeoning erection poked her in the hip. "I certainly think I can," she purred, squirming against his heat.

Looping her arms around his neck, she pulled his head down for a kiss. Just before his lips touched hers, he said, "We still need to talk."

Jennifer hesitated. She really didn't want to talk but it seemed important to him. She released him, and started to climb off his lap but he restrained her, holding her in place against him.

"You can stay right here."

She snuggled against him as her heart gave another silly flop. "You may feed me," she commanded.

"Oh, really," Mac chuckled. He dropped his mangled croissant on the tray and selected another. He liberally spread it with lemon curd, just the way she liked it. "Your wish is my command."

She grinned and took a bite of the offered pastry. "What do you want to talk about?" she mumbled around her mouthful.

"Mikhail."

She stilled, swallowing loudly. "Why do you want to speak of him?"

"I don't want to speak of him at all, Jennifer. But we need to speak of him. You need to speak of what happened and I need to know."

She didn't miss the pain in his voice as he spoke. Wearily, she closed her eyes and leaned into his warmth. So much lost time. So many lives had been shattered by Mikhail's treachery. Did she have the strength to tell him her story?

"I was so lost when I first met Mikhail." Her voice was low. The beating of Mac's heart was reassuring against her ear. "I was twenty-four years old. My mother had been sick for many years, bedridden. She said I was such a comfort to her and she begged my father to not marry me off until she was gone. My father was the Viscount Lynnford, a lowly second son but heir to the Whitehall Estate in southern England. My father's grandmother left everything to him. She took pity on him, I guess."

She felt Mac nod. "You're royalty," he stated. "Lady Lilith?"

She shook her head. "My name wasn't Lilith then. It was Margaret. After I finally escaped Mikhail I changed it to Lilith."

He began stroking her hair, the movement calming. "You don't look like a Margaret."

Jennifer chuckled. "I never felt like a Margaret, not even when I was one. I was always the odd child, I guess. My two sisters were married off to wealthy husbands and my brother married the daughter of a duke. I think he got her pregnant, actually. It was a real shotgun wedding, as it were. My father was depending upon his children's marriages to elevate his status in life. All of the marriages were good matches, for him at least.

"When my mother died, my father almost immediately betrothed me to Marshall Whiting, Duke of Waverly. He'd two prior wives and a passel of rather unpleasant children. I felt like I was being sold into another form of bondage. My mother's illness had kept me by her sickbed for almost eight years and now - when I had a chance to spread my wings a bit he sold me to the highest bidder."

Jennifer heard the bitterness that laced her words. Even after 300 years the coldness of her father was a hard pill to swallow. "Whiting was a cruel man. He took a whip to his youngest son for spilling ink on a rug. He almost killed him. His wives had died under somewhat suspicious circumstances. One committed suicide while the other died from a supposed carriage accident. Several of the Whiting servants claimed he threw her down the steps then took elaborate measures to cover up his crime. Regardless of what happened, I knew I couldn't marry him."

Mac's arms tightened around her but he said nothing.

"I was in the habit of going riding at dusk. Silly and dangerous I know, but I did it anyway. Shortly after the betrothal I slipped out for my usual ride. My father, fearing I would do something to circumvent the betrothal, hired a guard to watch over me. He was a large man but somewhat stupid. It was easy to lose him, as he was rather enamored of the port. I loved to ride at night. All I would do is ride the lane between Whitehall and my neighbor's home of Charlbourough Hall. It was about four miles, I would imagine. It was then I met Mikhail."

Mac tensed, the stroking stopped.

"He wasn't like he is now. He was charming. Dashing really, and he said everything I wanted to hear. Afterwards we met a few times in secret. I decided, foolishly enough, I was in love with him. I know now he was toying with me. I was so lost and was desperately looking for a way out. I would have done anything to escape." Jennifer sighed. "I was a stupid and naïve little cow and he recognized that. He offered to run away and marry me and I took him up on it." She stopped, remembering both the terror she'd felt at leaving the only home that she'd ever known and the relief at knowing she had thwarted her father's plans.

The stroking resumed, startling her from her thoughts.

"Things went awry rather quickly. Back then Mikhail didn't have the ability to walk around in the daytime. Instead of taking me to Gretna Green, he took me to his home in Ireland. It was there that I began to figure out that he wasn't human. Even when I confronted him he wasn't angry. He offered me immortality. I think he fooled himself into thinking he loved me, too. Or maybe he really did love me as much as Mikhail could love anyone. I think he truly wanted to spend his life with me."

Jennifer shook her head sadly. "I called him a monster and told him I would never submit to him. I told him I would kill myself first. He locked me up in a tower of the house." She laughed. "Just like a bad fairy tale. The poor princess locked in the tower, awaiting rescue by a prince that would never come. He left me there for almost a year. He would come to me every week or so and try and badger me into accepting him. I refused."

Her voice wobbled. "I was so tired, so tired. I just wanted it to end. I wanted some peace and I didn't care how I got it. He came to me one night. When he entered the chamber he left the door open to taunt me with freedom close enough I could taste it. I could leave if I would submit to him. He wanted me to come to him of my own free will. I can't tell you how many times I almost gave into him. That night I was so desperate. When he came in I maneuvered him away from the door. When he was distracted I just ran. I tried to throw myself down the steps of the tower. I prayed it would kill me."

Mac paused in his movement; tears sprang to her eyes as he pressed a kiss to the top of her head. For the first time in three hundred years, she wanted to sob her heart out for the lost woman she'd been. Instead, she ruthlessly marshaled her wayward emotions under iron control. Her one legacy from her father, other than her dark hair, was her iron will.

When she had her emotions under control, she spoke again, marveling at the cool tone of her voice. "I had no idea vampires could move in the blink of an eye and I never stood a chance. He stopped me from throwing myself down the stairs. He railed at me for hours on end and all I could do was weep at his feet like a broken child." Loathing crept into her voice.

"He left me that night. I was so empty. I lay down on the bed and prayed to die. I refused all food and water. Mikhail knew I was going to end it one way or another. He finally ran out of patience. After a few days without water I was fading fast. I was dying and he knew it. He was in such a rage. I have never seen him so angry. That was the night he made me immortal."

Mac tensed. "Against your will?"

"Yes, but he never touched me sexually that night. He unlocked the tower door and I stayed with him for almost five years because I didn't know what else to do. I had nowhere to go and I was in shock. I guess it took me a while to realize the ramifications of what he had forced upon me." Jennifer sighed. "Then I met Miranda. Mikhail had left the manse for a few weeks and Miranda arrived unannounced. I'd never met another vampire - I didn't even know if another one existed. Until that time Mikhail had kept me pretty well secluded. When someone would come by I would hide in the tower until they left.

"Miranda stayed with me for a few weeks. She taught me a great deal and I will always be grateful to her for saving me from my own ignorance. She taught me about the possibilities my life held, and about what it meant to be immortal. I knew then I had to leave Mikhail. I had to see what I could do for myself. I was going to leave before he got back but he arrived early. He was angry and he stopped me from leaving him. It was that night he begged me to submit to him sexually. He told me he loved me." Jennifer shook her head. "I was so lost and I just wanted to be free to figure out what I wanted. I refused him and he raped me."

Mac tightened his hold. She slipped her arm around his waist and clung to him, drawing strength from his nearness. After a few moments she spoke again.

"Miranda returned that night with Val. She didn't know Mikhail had returned. She came back to try and convince me to leave with her. Instead they found me unconscious and a bit worse for wear. According to Miranda, Val, as Mikhail's master, demanded Mikhail relinquish me to his charge. Mikhail refused and Val had to fight him. Mikhail was beaten badly and they took me away with them that night.

"I remained with them for the next twenty years or so, acting as their gatekeeper while they slept in the daytime. They taught me so many things. They've been alive for so long and they've had so many wondrous adventures. My family refused contact with me - and one by one they died off. I was alone in the world except for Val and Miranda."

"So you were the first person Val took from Mikhail?"

Jennifer nodded. "Yes, Val saved me. I left Miranda and Val after those twenty years. I guess it took some time for the fear to lessen enough so I could function on my own. I spent many years in Italy, Paris, Germany and Spain. I never heard word one from Mikhail though I have no doubt he kept tabs on me. During those years I still spent a lot of time with Val and Miranda. They would visit me or I would visit them."

She laughed. "I heard many tales of the outrageous MacNaughten and his bevy of beautiful ladies. Your exploits were legendary, my friend."

Mac chuckled. "Is that so?"

"Oh yes, very much so. When I finally met you in the eighteen-nineties, I was quite on my guard." Jennifer sighed and cuddled closer. "You were so charming and so sure of yourself. You were the first man, besides Val, who actually listened to what I was saying rather than eyeing my chest."

"I was doing that, too." He gave her a quick squeeze.

"Yes, but you genuinely love women, everything about them. I knew you were trying to hide your innate goodness beneath those rakehell stories but I could see through it. I so adored you from the first moment I saw you."

Mac pressed a kiss to her forehead and remained silent.

"I needed someone like you so badly. I didn't know if you would stay with me or not but I knew you had to be the first one I would allow to breech my defenses. I was so lonely." She sighed. "We'd been flirting around with each other for a while before Mikhail heard about us. I guess that he felt as long as I didn't show any interest in any man, he might still win me back. Later, after the night at the opera, the night you gave me the pendant of the Sun, Mikhail came to me. He demanded that either I leave you or he would kill you. I was so scared; I knew then that I would lose you no matter what I chose to do. I decided that not having you would be easier to bear than if you were dead. Alive and hating me was preferable to losing you to death. I wouldn't have been able to live with that.

"So, the next day I told you I loved Mikhail and I was going back to him. It was the hardest thing I ever had to do," she whispered. "I stayed with him for a few months, out of fear mainly. I wasn't sure he would truly honor his word and leave you alone. Val told me later he never knew anything about you and me until you got drunk and spilled your guts. Once again he and Miranda rode to my rescue. They took me out of Mikhail's house while he was away. I never saw or heard from him again until a few days ago."

Mac cleared his throat. "It took a lot of courage for you to go to his house."

"It was for Miranda. I would've done anything for her. She saved me many times over and in the end I couldn't do a thing to save her." Jennifer sighed.

He hugged her tightly. "I know Miranda suffered in her last days on earth, Jennifer. But when I last saw her, there was happiness on her face."

"It's so hard to believe that," Jennifer whispered against his chest.

"Believe it." He reached into his pocket and retrieved the Sun. Gently, he placed it around her neck where it lay nestled between her breasts where it should have been for the past one hundred years.

"I'll never take it off. This time I mean it." She pulled back and looked him straight in the eye. "Does it matter...that I was with Mikhail?" Her voice was hesitant, frightened. She gnawed at her lip.

He gazed down tenderly at the woman he loved more than life itself, etching each beloved feature on his heart before he spoke. "Things happen to us in our lives that are beyond our control. They don't taint us in any way. They make us who we are. Like steel strengthened by fire, people are the same way. No *jo*, it doesn't matter to me." The relief on her face angered him. *Damn Mikhail...*

"Of course, there is the little matter of all the women you've been with..."

Mac watched the mischievous look come into her eye. "Oh yeah?"

"Umm..." Jennifer stretched, pressing her silk covered breasts against him. "I think I need to thank them," she purred, looping her arms about his neck.

"Oh really? For what?" His gaze fastened on her mouth. He could taste her already.

"Practice makes perfect," she sighed, pressing her lips against his.

Mac laughed, breaking the kiss. "You think I am perfect?"

Jennifer laughed. "I was talking about your sexual prowess, not your personality. That needs work."

His grin grew bigger. "You think I was perfect in bed?"

She sighed. "Well, not quite. I think you might be a little rusty. However, with a little practice..." she squealed as Mac flipped her off his lap and pinned her to the bed.

"I'll show you perfect..."

Chapter 9

Jennifer lifted her head from the pillow when she heard the front door shut. Was Mac back already? She glanced at the clock. Only a half-hour had passed since he'd left the house. Did he forget something? She yawned, rolling over onto her stomach. The Sun jabbed her breastbone. She shifted the pendant out of the way then stretched her arms, rolling her shoulders to work out the kinks.

She was completely sated. Even moving was too much effort. And she couldn't seem to wipe the grin off her face. She grabbed Mac's pillow and buried her face in the soft cotton. The pillow muffled her laughter as joy sang through her veins.

Making love with Mac exceeded all of her deepest fantasies, and invented a few, too. She inhaled the scent of the man who'd made her dreams come true in the darkest hours of the night. Languor drifted through her body and she sighed again, shifting to bury her head farther into the pillow.

Footsteps sounded on the stairs.

A grinned tugged at her lips as she popped her head out of the pillow. Reaching back, she moved the sheet down until only a corner covered her backside. Maybe she could entice him back into bed...

The footsteps reached the top landing as she arranged herself on the pillow again, facing away from the open doorway.

One step...two...

She held her breath.

They stopped in the doorway.

Silence.

"Did you forget something?" she called, bending one knee, she waved her foot in the air.

Silence.

"Mac?"

A creak of leather.

"Why are..." she rolled over. Shock made her blood run cold.

A giant stood in the doorway watching her, and huge was the only word to describe him. He filled the doorway from top to bottom and side to side. Dressed completely in black, his head was as bald as a cue ball and a gold earring glinted in his ear. His features were coarse, his nose crooked as if it had been broken on several occasions. His narrow black eyes bore into hers.

Jennifer snatched the sheet and covered herself. "Who are you?" she demanded, hoping her fear didn't show.

A grin appeared on the man's face. As it grew, the trickle of fear down her spine turned into a torrent. "A friend sent me to pick you up." His voice was surprisingly cultured for one so rough looking. The man ducked through the doorway, gently closing the door behind him. "He desires a visit with you, as his honored guest, of course." He bent and picked up the shirt Mac had pulled off her willing body only an hour before. "Put it on," he tossed it on the bed.

"I'm not going anywhere with you," Jennifer scrambled to the far side of the bed, fumbling with the sheet.

"Actually, you are." He held his hands out. "We can do this the easy way or the hard way. It's your choice, Ms. Beaumont."

She eyed the man's meaty hands. While he probably couldn't kill her unless he actually beheaded her (a revenant was virtually impossible to kill), he could inflict serious pain. She stopped retreating. Maybe she should try taking the offense? Summoning a cool tone she ordered imperiously, "Please wait by the door while I dress."

The man paused, then tipped his head slightly. Still holding his hands out to show he was harmless, he backed away to lean against the door. His gaze was insolent as he watched her tug the sheet back into place.

"Turn around, I need to dress," she ordered.

"I don't think so, Ms. Beaumont. You might have a weapon hidden somewhere." He smirked, his eyes scraping over her sheet-clad figure. "You don't have anything I haven't seen already." He glanced at his watch. "You have three minutes."

Jennifer stiffened. Had this beast somehow watched her and Mac make love? She glanced out the window. The house sat on a slight rise and the window overlooked the narrow street and onto the roof of the house where the lovers lived. She felt violated and something shriveled inside. She would never feel safe again.

"Two and a half minutes, Ms. Beaumont."

She glared at him and sniffed imperiously, presenting him with her back. She reached over and snatched up the shirt. She struggled into it while trying to keep the sheet in place. As she buttoned it up, she looked around the room furtively for a weapon of some kind.

Unfortunately for her, Mac was more of a lover than a fighter. She scowled - hadn't he been a highlander a few centuries ago? She glanced at the crossed swords that hung over the bed. No chance of getting to those very quickly. It appeared the twentieth century had relaxed Mac's guard.

Her hand closed over the delicate chain of the Sun. Wrapping her fingers around the pendant she yanked, snapping the chain. Making a great show of tossing the sheet onto the bed she dropped the Sun on Mac's pillow. She turned toward the closet when a glint caught her eye.

On a small table near the window, an ornate *athame* glinted in the sunshine. She walked to the closet bringing her closer to the table. She opened the closet door and made a show of looking for a pair of sweat pants. She gauged the distance between the closet door and the table. One good leap and maybe she'd reach the ceremonial knife.

Locating some sweat pants in the top of the closet, she pulled them down. Holding them out in front of her, she stepped into them with one leg. Raising the other leg, she deliberately overbalanced, causing her to stumble toward the table.

"Go for it, Ms. Beaumont. While I like hurting women, I don't think you will enjoy it nearly as much."

She tensed, her leg half in and half out of the pant leg. Slowly she straightened, pulling the pants on and tying the drawstring. "I have no idea what you are talking about," she said in a cool tone. The *athame* was only two feet away and her palms grew sweaty.

"You're a terrible liar, Ms. Beaumont."

Jennifer laughed sharply. "Where have I heard that before?'

She bent over to adjust the long pant legs then lunged for the table. Her hand closed on the worn leather handle as three hundred pounds of man hit her broadside. The table exploded under their combined weight, sending them both crashing to the floor. The air whooshed out of her lungs as his shoulder dug into her diaphragm. Gasping for air, she clutched the *athame* as she wriggled beneath him, desperate for oxygen and freedom. Too quickly, the shortage of air caused spots to dance before her eyes. Her grip weakened.

Without any effort, he knocked the ceremonial knife from her hand. He tossed her onto her back as easily as he would a child. She lay face up on the floor with him sitting across her torso. He bound her hands with some duct tape he produced from a pocket of his leather jacket.

"You bastard," she wheezed. "You won't get away with this."

"We'll see about that." He smiled; it was an evil smile of intent. He retrieved the *athame* and dangled it before her eyes. "I did ask you to accompany me, and I was very nice about it. But no, you had to make me hurt you. I think you need to pay the price for this little indiscretion." He licked his lips. "Seeing you are a revenant, it isn't as if I can actually kill you, now can I?"

Jennifer stilled as she caught sight of the anticipation in his gaze. *He was enjoying this.* She fought for calm and won by a thread. "Your employer won't like it if you bring him damaged goods."

He shrugged. "You'll heal. Your kind always does." He reached over and grabbed the trailing edge of the sheet she'd discarded on the bed. Brushing the collar away from her throat, he waved the blade, making sure she watched him as he lowered it to press the tip against her skin. The *athame* was ice cold and she jerked in response, a desperate moan caught in her throat. The weight of the man held her in place. She couldn't budge an inch. She whimpered as the tip pierced her skin.

He leaned forward, his breath hot on her face. "Did I ever tell you I love to make women scream..."

Pain blazed a trail through her as the blade sliced through her skin. A wail was torn from the fabric of her soul, causing the man to jerk his face away from her. For a second, time stood still.

Blessed silence.

Dimly, she heard the explosion as the windows imploded. Jennifer didn't feel the shards of glass raining down on her. Her attention was focused on the pain that raged from the injury. Stretching down her neck and across her collarbone, blood pumped from the wound in time with her heartbeat.

Cursing, the giant eyed her. "Witch," he snarled.

She hissed between clenched teeth, "You don't know the half of it."

He snatched the sheet and dampened it with her blood. Dropping the stained sheet to the floor, ruthlessly he yanked her to her feet and tossed her onto the edge of the bed.

The first wave of pain was receding as he taped her ankles together. He tied them tightly, cutting off the circulation and bruising her skin. Jennifer winced and cupped her hands over her shoulder to staunch the flow. Loss of blood was making her dizzy. She concentrated on taking deep, even breaths until the black spots began to fade.

He yanked on the tape around her ankles, checking his work. His rough movements drew her shirt up, exposing her stomach. Revulsion crawled across her skin as the giant stopped and looked at her.

He stood and wrenched her to her feet. "Don't worry Ms. Beaumont, I like little boys."

Revulsion crawled over her skin. Summoning the dregs of her energy, she spat in his face. "Bastard." She sucked in a deep breath as his face darkened with rage. He drew his hand back and clenched a fist, aiming for her face.

Pain blasted through her jaw as the darkness embraced her.

The edge of the Sun cut into Mac's palm as he eyed the destruction of his bedroom. Rage hummed in his blood as his gaze passed over the blood-soaked sheet again. Vaguely he heard the buzz of voices in the street as the emergency people and his neighbors milled around in bewilderment. Every window within 50 yards of his home had been shattered.

Only he knew what the cause was.

A deadly calm descended as he reached for the phone, glass crunching beneath his feet. He dialed and when the voice on the other end answered, he spoke.

"He's taken Jennifer and I'm going after him. This time he's a dead man. Are you in?"

MacNaughten clenched his fists, his patience rapidly reaching an end. "Where are they, Gabrielle?"

Gabrielle DesNoir licked her lips, her gaze moving restlessly over him. She looked at him as if he was a dish of crème brulée and she a starving woman. She licked her lips before she spoke. "I haven't seen Jennifer since she invaded our home a few days ago. As for Mikhail, he didn't tell me where he was going, only that he had business with an animal or some such nonsense."

"Liar."

Her eyes flashed annoyance before she averted them. "Now really, Conor, how rude," she purred. She shifted in her chair, her ruby silk dressing gown gaping to reveal the inner curve of her abundant breasts. "What have I ever done to you, *grand homme,* that I would deserve such treatment?"

Mac's lips twitched at her quasi-endearment. "I sincerely doubt I hurt you, Gaby." He picked up a bottle of champagne that stood unopened in an ice bucket. With the ease of long practice, he popped the cork, poured some into a waiting flute and lifted the glass in a mock salute. "Have you ever thought that maybe it isn't what you have done? But rather the company you keep?"

She laughed. "I know you and Mik have had your differences, but I really think it is time to let this animosity go." She shrugged and her robe slipped off her shoulder. "Boys will be boys."

He took a long swallow of the champagne in order to give his temper time to cool. "You'll have to forgive me if I don't think of murder as a schoolyard prank," he replied.

"Surely you don't think Mik had anything to do with that dreadful incident?" Gaby fluttered her eyes innocently. "He truly was crushed when he heard about dear Miranda. He considered her a good friend; it was a great personal loss to him. They'd known each other for years, you know. He told me once that Miranda had retained the most humane soul he'd ever seen in a vampire."

He stared down at the flute, the taste of the expensive vintage sour in his mouth. "Do you still retain any humanity at all, Gaby?"

She slid to her feet. Her walk was easy, predatory. "What a question. Of course I retain a great deal of my humanity." Her hands moved to the sash of her robe. With a practiced flick of her wrist she opened it, revealing her perfectly sculpted body. Her pale skin shone like marble in the firelight. Large breasts with their erect brownish nipples stood at attention, her torso slimmed into a tiny waist and narrow hips. Her small thatch of neatly trimmed pubic hair was as blonde as the hair on her head.

He cast a bored glance at her overblown charms. "Well that answers one question," he mocked.

Her eyes narrowed then smoothed again, a smile playing on her lips. "I have a lovely idea..."

Her robe slipped off her other shoulder just before she reached him. Leaning close, she pressed her ripe body against his. Linking her arms around his neck, she whispered, "Why don't we just forget about Mik and Jennifer. We can go upstairs and I'll show you delights the likes of which you have never seen before..."

Mac shuddered as the chill of her skin seeped through his shirt. He set his flute down on the corner of the desk. "While that is a tempting offer," he reached for her linked hands and disengaged them from his neck, "I'm afraid I must decline." He stepped back. "I will ask you again. Where are they?"

She sighed. "I really don't know what you are talking about..."

He grabbed her by the shoulders and gave her a shake, hard enough to make her teeth snap together. "You and I both know Mikhail has taken Jennifer." He released her, resisting the urge to wipe the feeling of her cold skin from his hands. "If you retain even the slightest bit of humanity as you so claim, you will tell me where they are."

"Like I give a *damn* about your *putain*," Gaby snarled. "She's done nothing but make Mikhail miserable. Flaunting herself and your great love affair. I hope he kills her slowly, painfully. I hope he makes her pay for everything she has ever done to him."

He watched rage twist the lovely face before him. Gaby and Mikhail were one of a kind: power-hungry, vengeful and quite mad. Continuing the conversation would be fruitless. He would get nothing more from her. He looked her straight in the eye. "I will kill him. And if you get in my way, I will destroy you also."

She laughed. "You might try, Conor. But you won't succeed. Mik is stronger than you will ever dream. You're only a revenant." She picked up her robe and drew it on. "You know, I might be able to spare your life in return for a little something."

He watched her sway over to the desk. She seated herself on the edge, the robe gaping to reveal her long limbs. "And that would be?"

"Maeve. Bring her to me."

He shook his head. "Your price is too steep. I will not trade my life for that of an innocent."

"You'll lose, Conor. Mik will destroy Jennifer, Val...all of you will

perish and not in a tidy way. Your only chance is to save yourself and..."
Her words ended in a squeak, her expression changing from rage to horror.

"Is that so?" Val walked into the room, stopping beside Mac. "I wouldn't be so rash in planning your victory dance, Gabrielle." His tone was deceptively lazy.

She covered her shock with a sneer. "Val, shouldn't you be at home with your little slut?"

"You're so predictable. You realize I can kill you with one finger," he replied evenly. Mac caught the glint in his eye.

"You wouldn't hurt a lady. You are far too *civilized*," she fairly spat the word.

"Only if there is a lady present," Val smiled mockingly.

"Oh, but there is." Shai fairly danced into the room. "Only one of us is a lady, though." She gave Val a flirtatious smile and kissed Mac on the cheek. "Hello, darling boy!"

She glanced at Gaby then back to Mac. "I really can't say I appreciate your taste in companions, Mac." She turned toward Gaby. "Now, you and I are going to have a little chat."

Gaby scowled at Shai. "I want all of you out of here."

Shai made a rude sound like that of a game show buzzer. "Wrong answer, Gabs. Now, I believe the current question is: where did Mikhail take Jennifer? You have ten seconds to answer. Please remember to phrase your answer like a question. Failure to do so will result in disqualification."

"Like you can hurt me, Shai," Gaby smirked. "I am years older and much..."

A shriek erupted as Shai's fist shot out and hit Gaby square in the nose. Blood splattered the front of her robe. Shai shook her head mock-sorrowfully. "Hurts, doesn't it? It really isn't a bad injury, but *man* does a broken nose hurt. It is like a bomb exploding in your nose and the pain is just ghastly. That kind of injury makes it so hard to think of anything other than the pain. Not to mention it is so hard to breathe." She glanced at Val, her eyes gleaming with mischief. "Do vampires need to breathe, honey?"

"No, not really," Val replied. He crossed his arms over his chest and propped himself against the arm of a chair.

"I didn't think so." Shai looked at Gaby again. "Aren't you lucky?"

Gaby shrieked again and cupped her hands over her nose as blood poured down her face. She staggered toward the fireplace. "You bitch," she sobbed.

"Like I've never heard that before." Shai rolled her eyes and looked at Val. "I don't know, judge, ten more seconds?"

Val nodded imperceptibly.

Shai turned her attention back to the sobbing vampire. "Second chance, Gabs. Please answer the question."

"I am going to slaughter you," Gaby raged.

Val winced and whispered to Mac, "Watch this."

"Wrong answer number two," Shai shook her head. In a blur of movement she caught Gaby in the chest with a backspin kick. Knocking the vampire off balance, Shai caught her behind the knee and knocked her flat on her back. She grinned at Val. "How am I doin', honey?"

"Very good, love. Let me know if you need any help." Val spoke to Mac. "Kung Fu. She loves the stuff. She spends lots of time watching Jackie Chan movies."

Mac watched in disbelief as Shai dropped onto Gaby's body, eliciting a *woof* from the bloody vampire. Gaby, her arms pinned around her waist, thrashed wildly, teeth bared to bite.

Shai waved her finger at her victim. "Now Gabs, if you bite me I am pulling your teeth out. Then where would you be? A vampire with no teeth is like a sundae without hot fudge. What is the point of that, I ask you?"

Gaby gave another shriek of rage and tried to buck Shai off.

"Whoa horsey..." She winked at Val. "Darling, if this hound from hell does bite me, will I need tetanus or rabies shots?"

Val pretended to consider the situation. "Both possibly. You might want to be careful as I hear the shots are quite painful."

Shai nodded, satisfied with the answer. She turned her attention back to Gaby. "So, where were we? Oh yes," Shai shifted, driving her knee into Gaby's side. "Speak. And I warn you, one more wrong answer and I tear your throat out."

Mac caught the look of rage in Gaby's eyes. "You know," he said to Val, "Shai is a dead woman when Gaby gets up."

Val shook his head. "You underestimate Shai. Gaby won't be getting up anytime soon." He winced at the sound of flesh on flesh. "Are you okay, love?" he called to Shai.

"Just spiffy," Shai shot back.

"Were you ever able to find Renault?" Val asked Mac.

"No, it's as if he has vanished off the face of the earth. No one can find him." Mac watched in horrid fascination as Shai broke one of Gaby's fingers. "She's vicious. Where was she during the Middle Ages?"

Val grinned. "She's mine. Go find your own."

Mac held his hands up. "I couldn't handle her. She is a little too wicked for even my taste."

Howls burst forth from Gaby and both men turned their attention to the women just as Shai twisted Gaby's earlobe hard. "The circle. He took her to the circle," Gaby shrieked.

Shai released Gaby's earlobe. "Finally, a winner." Mac watched as she made a fist and sent it crashing into Gaby's jaw, knocking her out cold. "No bonus round for her."

"You were brilliant, darling," Val clapped as Shai got to her feet.

"Hmm, she really wasn't a very good contestant, though. No stamina." She dusted her hands off. "One has to wonder how she got past the preliminary judges."

Mac snorted with laughter. "Thank you for your help, Shai. I couldn't have done that to a woman, even if it was Gaby."

Shai chuckled. "I always suspected you were a gentleman."

Val shook his head. "I am not touching *that* with a ten-foot pole."

Shai nudged Mac in the ribs. "Don't let him lie to you, Mac. He doesn't have a ten-foot pole, or if he does I've never found it and trust me I've looked..."

Val spanked her hard on the backside and she squealed. "Behave, young lady. The sun will be rising shortly and we need to get you someplace safe."

Shai scowled. "How long until I can walk around in the daylight?"

Val took her arm and led her out of the room. "How does the year Three Thousand sound?"

Chapter 10

The light was waning.

Jennifer cast another worried glance at the lantern hanging on the wall well over her head. The flame was definitely shrinking. That one small flame was the only thing keeping her from being alone in the dark with *them*.

Jennifer glanced across the narrow, dank chamber at the rows of hollowed out niches lining the wall. Human remains were neatly laid out, one body per niche, dozens of them stacked up like so many books on a shelf. Granted, they were only bones and scraps of cloth at this point, and they'd been down here for hundreds of years, but they were human remains nonetheless. She shuddered.

She hated dead things.

Vampires were dead, but she didn't hate them. One of them maybe, no, one of them definitely. A nervous giggle escaped her. She placed a hand over her wildly fluttering heart. She was in danger of becoming hysterical. Jennifer took a deep breath.

Calm, calm...I can do this...I can survive this...

The walls of the catacomb were damp and slimy in spots and the bone chilling cold gnawed at her skin. She shivered, drawing her knees closer to her body for warmth. The lamp flickered and she glanced at it nervously. The flame was definitely dying.

She hated the dark.

She'd always hated the dark. Even as a child it was the one thing that could paralyze her with fear and send her running for the nearest lighted room. When her father learned of her near-crippling fear of the dark, he'd used it against her as Mikhail was doing now.

Jennifer moved cautiously. The dirt floor beneath her was cold and damp. She winced as her foot hit something slimy. Drawing her foot closer to her body, she shifted cautiously, the ache in her shoulder overriding the one in her jaw. The scurry of tiny feet sounded in one dim corner. She shuddered.

Rats.

She hated them too.

She took a deep breath of the dank, fetid air. It tasted of death. Her death? She leaned her head back against the stone wall. She wasn't afraid to die. For many years she'd wanted to die rather than go on with Mikhail relentlessly haunting her every step. Now that Mac was back in her life, for one brief shining moment she'd hoped all would work out. She was a fool.

It still could.

Tears burned the backs of her eyes. All she could do was hope, and pray. Jennifer didn't consider herself a particularly religious person, but Mac certainly seemed to believe in his Goddess. Anything would be help at this point.

She clasped her grubby hands together and closed her eyes. "Goddess," her voice cracked and she cleared her throat. "Goddess, you don't know me but my name is Jennifer. I'm a good friend of Conor MacNaughten's. I was hoping you might be able to help me out here." She paused as a rustle sounded, followed by scrabbling toenails. Swallowing, she continued. "I really want you to keep my friends safe. And if you could help me get out of here..."

A faint hissing sound had Jennifer's eyes popping open just in time to see the light fading.

"No," she whispered.

Darkness fell.

She froze, blinking rapidly as if she could bring the light back by doing so. It was still dark. Jennifer wrapped her arms around her knees as a broken whimper escaped her. The crumbling rock of the wall dug into her spine as she pressed into it. For one split second she thought she could make herself small enough that she could simply vanish into the rock itself.

Something brushed her foot and a shriek escaped her lips. The darkness crowded her, stealing her breath and causing her heart to thud wildly. She lurched to her feet and stumbled along the wall. Waving her hands in front of her, a rapid keening was torn from her throat. Cobwebs brushed her cheek with their deadly caress. She lurched away from them and stumbled along the wall. She finally found the sanctuary she was searching for. Crouching down, she wedged herself in the corner, feeling only marginally safer until she heard the approach of scurrying feet.

She dug her nails into her palms in a futile effort to still the screams that clawed at her throat. A rat scampered behind her head on a small ledge; it's long wiry tail struck her cheek as its plump body brushed against her hair.

That was all it took.

Her terror was unleashed, and the catacombs reverberated with her screams.

"They're here."

Mac's voice was flat, emotionless as he climbed out of the car. Val looked out the window to the snow-covered countryside around them; trepidation pulled at his limbs. As he exited the car he caught the faint scent of blood on the icy breeze. He stilled. He could feel Mikhail nearby, and others were with him.

Fayne slammed his car door, the noise obscenely loud in the stillness. "What's that?"

Val scanned the weatherworn guardian stones before them when a flutter of white caught his eye. Frowning, he walked over to the center stone. Pinned under a rock was a white silk shirt stained with blood. "What the devil..." he hissed.

Mac's hand reached the silk before Val's did. "It's mine." Mac pulled the shirt from the rock. "Jennifer was wearing it last night." He spread the silk out. Drawn on the back in what was undoubtedly blood, was a ragged circle complete with altar.

Val saw Mac's expression tighten and his lips thin. Power hummed along his skin and Val had to stop himself from stepping away from it. Vampires were inordinately sensitive to the power of others. Some power was narcotic, addictive, leaving the vampire craving more. While other power was dangerous to vampires, even deadly in some circumstances. He wasn't quite sure which kind of energy Mac was emanating and he was somewhat hesitant to find out.

"It's the circle." Mac spoke, fingering the silk.

Val didn't miss the shudder that whipped through Mac's body as his finger touched the blood.

"She'll be okay Mac," Fayne said. "She has to be."

Alexandre stepped forward, his expression in shadows as he gazed up at the circle perched on its hilltop. "They're waiting for us."

Val clapped a hand on Mac's shoulder; a jolt of raw energy ran through his body at the touch. He quickly released his old friend. For the first time in hundreds of years he felt a tinge of fear as they started up the hill.

They were approaching.

Mikhail could barely contain his excitement. So many years of planning and preparation had taken place, all leading to this moment, his moment in the sun. He glanced over at the altar where Jennifer lay unconscious. In her full-length white dress, she looked like an angel, or a bride. He laughed at the imagery. She'd been meticulously bathed and groomed to remove any trace of *him*. And her visit to the catacombs had left her a bit worse for the wear. The dress would cover a multitude of sins, though. It was a simple white silk sheath, sleeveless and scooped neck. The lace overdress was high necked and long sleeved, covering her from her neck to her toes. Intricate beading and delicate embroidery at the neck, sleeves and across the bodice relieved the severity of the style and gave it a wedding dress air.

Her long dark hair was curled and lay loose on her shoulders in thick ropes of living silk. A coronet of lavender roses and white silk ribbons adorned her head and the altar was also covered in roses. It was his monument to his love, his Margaret, his Lilith, Jennifer.

His beautiful, fiery Jennifer.

Of course her little excursion into the depths of the catacombs had irrevocably changed her. Not physically of course - physically she was perfection as always. Mentally, she was not the same woman. Hours in the cloying darkness had broken her spirit and shattered her soul. A mere shadow of her former self.

That would teach her for defying him.

He turned away from the fetching sight and looked through the west stone portal. He frowned as he caught sight of Alexandre Saint-Juste and Fayne as they started their climb up the hill. His lip curled at the intrusion of Fayne. No matter, let them all come. He turned and his gaze swept the circle and the people gathered there for him. They were here to share in this day of triumph, his day of retribution.

He looked back at the four men advancing up the hill.

Let them all come, let them all die.

Mac stopped as Alexandre stuck his hand out, halting their progress. Both Alexandre and Val stood still, their vampire senses scanning the area around them. Even the crows that had been heralding their arrival were silent now. The light breeze made a mournful sound as it tugged at his cape. Something wasn't right here.

"Cassiopeia," Fayne spoke quietly. His head was lifted as if he were scenting the wind itself.

"And Edward," Alexandre added.

"That isn't terribly surprising," Val commented. "Both of them have been challenging your reign from day one."

Mac saw Alexandre's gaze narrow, his mouth attain a grim line. The foursome resumed their climb up the hill. If Cassiopeia and Edward willingly entered the circle with Mikhail, this meant they'd turned against the Council. Their punishment would be death.

A cloud passed over the sun, stealing the light. He suppressed a shiver. Many would die for their actions today. Mac resumed the climb, his friends falling in line behind him. He would fight to the death for Jennifer and he would do it gladly. Should he die here today, it would be the will of the Goddess, not the will of Mikhail.

As they passed through the west portal, Mac thought they'd stumbled into a garden party from hell.

A small group of vampires were lined up neatly in rows before the altar, hiding it from his view. They all wore pale colors of white, ecru or ivory. Mikhail stood at the head of the group looking devilish in black from head to toe.

"Welcome my friends," Mikhail tipped his head slightly. "May I offer you some refreshment?" He gestured to someone behind him and two men came forward carrying a battered human between them. Unceremoniously, they dumped him at Alexandre's feet.

Mac knew who it was before he hit the ground.

Renault.

A low growl erupted from Fayne. He started forward and Val restrained him.

"Of course, he wouldn't be terribly tasty for you Mac. Perhaps I have something else that will do as well?" Mikhail smiled. The crowd parted to reveal the altar and the woman who lay upon it. "Now doesn't she look just delicious?"

Mac's heart leapt into his throat as he beheld the woman he loved. She looked unharmed, possibly asleep and incredibly fragile in her white gown.

Cassiopeia stepped out from behind the altar, her eyes glaring at Alexandre. "Let's get on with this," she snapped impatiently.

Mikhail smiled indulgently at her. "Patience, my dear, patience."

"Do you choose to be here of your own free will, Cassiopeia?" Alexandre asked.

"Well, of course I do, you strutting fool. Did you think I wanted to live under your ancient laws of chivalry forever?" she snapped. "Your misguided sense of honor and duty will be the end of us. It is time for new blood, a new rule."

"And I also choose to be here," a childish voice shrilled. Edward stood with his hand on the child's shoulder. "It's time for changes in our clan," the child piped.

Mac caught the look of distaste on Val's face as he looked at Edward.

Mikhail grinned. "Did you honestly think I would coerce these people into attending me?" He shook his head. "How little you think of me."

"What do you want, Mikhail?" Val's voice was smooth, low. "Do you want to fight me? Do you want to make me pay for the wrongs I've supposedly perpetrated against you in the past?" He held his hands out. "Here I am."

Cassiopeia laughed. "Oh, you funny little man. Is that what you think this is? Do you think Mikhail would have orchestrated this magnificent coup just to exact revenge upon you?"

"According to Jennifer, Mikhail wants to exact retribution from me," Val replied evenly.

"You think too narrowly," the child spoke. "Look at the big picture."

Mac watched the faces of the gathered. Something else was at play here, something bigger than a few imagined slights against Mikhail.

"I told Jennifer only part of the story," Mikhail waved his hand airily. "I do want retribution from you Val, make no mistake about that. What I want is retribution from all four of you." He looked at Fayne. "I didn't expect you to be here, so I consider your presence to be an extra added bonus, as it were."

"Lucky me," Fayne muttered.

Mikhail's gaze locked the Alexandre's. "I invoke the law of seven."
Silence.

Mac held his breath. The wind picked up slightly, its cry mournful as it cut around the stones. A single red rose fell from the altar like a drop of blood.

"You know not what you do," Val ground out.

"Of course I do," Mikhail smiled, a manic light in his eye. "I'm challenging Alexandre for the head of the Council. In killing him I will assume control of the Council as Elder. I'll rule over all the preternatural creatures. Vampires. Revenants. Shape-shifters. And soon I will rule the witches, too. All of them."

"You're insane," Fayne ground out.

"Oh, my pretty kitty-kitty. Your kind I will love most of all." Mikhail crooned. "From what I understand, were-cats, such as yourself, can perform all night long. Is that right? This kind of entertainment would fetch a great deal of money on the black market. Sexual slaves are in high demand among the glitterati."

A low growl burst from Fayne.

Mikhail laughed delightedly. "Come on, kitty-kitty. Shall I find a ball of string for you to play with? Maybe a nice juicy mouse or a bit of catnip?"

The growl grew deeper, more feral. His fists clenched and Renault twitched, a low moan escaping him.

"Enough," Alexandre thundered. "You have invoked the law of seven thus challenging me to a duel to the death. So be it."

Mikhail scowled at having his game interrupted.

"What about Jennifer?" Mac stepped forward.

"What about her? She's mine and you aren't getting her back." Mikhail shrugged. "She is my revenant, to do with as I please. As you can see, I have dressed her to be my bride. Tonight I will make her mine." His eyes glittered.

"Wrong. Your ownership of her was terminated almost three hundred years ago when Miranda and I took possession of her." Val answered. "She's mine."

Mikhail glared at Val. "No more. I am her master. It is up to me to decide her fate."

As the men argued, Mac scanned the circle. Something his father taught him niggled in the back of his brain. What was it? Something about the origins of the circle and those who dwell in it.

"Who cares about the whore?" Cassiopeia was saying.

His father's voice drifted into his mind. *"The threefold law and the laws of light shall always prevail upon the sacred ground of the standing stones. For it has been blessed by the Goddess herself."*

And what was the threefold law? His mind scrambled for an answer. *Whatever you put out into the universe will come back to you threefold. This is a holy place. A holy place blessed by the Goddess...blessed by the Goddess...*

His eyes closed as the voices around him receded. Stillness spread through his mind and invaded his body. The law of light was to harm none and to only do good works for the world. His eyes opened, fixing on Mikhail. His presence here in the circle was an affront to the Goddess. How dare he invade this place, sacred for thousands of years, with his darkness, his corruption.

Uncle desecrated this holy place first.

Anger blossomed in his soul. His father was a good man, a holy man. Murdered by his brother in this place, on that very altar. He turned toward where Jennifer lay on her bed of roses. His Jennifer, the love of his life. He frowned. Why this place? Why would Mikhail bring them to this place? What could this place possibly mean to the vampire? He knew without a doubt that it hadn't been chance that they ended up here.

"Why?" Mac spoke. "Why did you come here? Why did you bring us to this place?"

Mikhail turned to him, a chilling smile graced his face. "You haven't figured it out yet, have you?"

Something shifted, like a curtain to the past it opened and images tumbled forth. His father laughing, grabbing his son and hugging him tightly. His mother, shaking her head as she let the hem out in his cape yet again. Images of his father lying dead on the altar, his brother standing over him.

His uncle.

Images superimposed themselves, blending into one. His uncle, his father.

Mikhail.

His father's brother, his uncle.

"You. You killed my father." Mac's voice was flat.

Mikhail laughed. "Your father was a bumbling fool. I saved him and his people from himself and his ignorance."

Horror closed Mac's throat, his breathing strangled as he beheld the man who murdered his father and destroyed his mother. "My father was a good man," he choked, "a kind man..."

"Your father was a fool. But, he was a fool with powers. So I took them, and you. I took everything and I left you nothing. I took his knowledge, I took his woman, and I tried to take his son." He kicked at Renault's leg. "If it wasn't for this fool I would have succeeded. Renault, child of my loins." He laughed harshly. "An abomination to the Master. A were-cat." He spat. "I could not have sacrificed him in service to the Master. That left you. The son of my dear departed brother. Untouched, the holy son of a holy man. The only living offspring of a Pagan high priest. The ultimate sacrifice."

"And it went awry."

"Oh yes, it went awry. After I came to, the villagers had risen against me. They sold me into slavery. My *master* then traveled to Kiev." He glanced in Val's direction. "It was Val's intervention that saved me, made me a god." He laughed harshly. "I'll rule forever."

Mac shook his head. "You forgot one thing."

"I forgot nothing," Mikhail smirked.

Mac walked to the head of the altar, parting the gathered vampires seamlessly. He looked down upon the serene face of the woman he loved. "You forgot me."

"You," Mikhail laughed. "As if you can do anything to stop me."

Lightly Mac brushed his finger across Jennifer's cheek. Her skin was as cold as ice. She wasn't dead. He could feel her spirit inside her. Cowed, wounded, but not dead.

He stepped back from the altar. Raising his arms, he spoke. "I, Conor MacNaughten, invoke the threefold law and the law of light upon this circle."

Mikhail smirked and Cassiopeia tittered behind him.

"What is he doing?" the child chirped.

"This should be a good floor show," Mikhail laughed. "Before I kill him."

Mac ignored the words around him. He closed his eyes, concentrating on the light that grew within. He intoned in the ancient Scots language

"*Guardians of the North stone, Ancient keeper of the earth, I call upon you to attend me here.*" Beneath his feet the ground gave a faint tremor.

Mac opened his eyes as Mikhail burst into laughter. He began clapping his hands as mutterings broke out among the vampires.

"*Guardians of the East stone, ancient keeper of the air, I call upon you to attend me here.*"

A low wind sprang up ruffling clothing and tossing hair. Clouds began to gather above the circle. Mikhail stopped clapping.

"*Guardians of the South stone, ancient keeper of the fire, I call upon you to attend me here.*"

A crack of lightning rent the sky, striking one of the ancient oaks. The wood splintered as it burst into flame, the scent of ozone and wood smoke permeated the air. The wind grew to a low howl as several of the lesser vampires scrambled to seek shelter against the east stones.

"Stop that," Mikhail snapped.

"*Guardians of the West stone, ancient keeper of the water, I call upon you to attend me here.*"

A clap of thunder rent the air as fat snowflakes began to fall outside the circle. Val, Alexandre and Fayne grabbed the limp body of Renault and carried him to the west entrance. They settled him on the ground in the shelter of the massive stones. The rest of the vampires huddled against the South stone, leaving Mikhail alone at the foot of the altar.

"*Goddess, wondrous lady of the moon, mistress of the night. Mother, maiden, crone, oh wise one, ruler of the elemental realm, I call upon your power now. Cast your power unto this circle.*" The wind increased to a shriek and Mac had to yell to be heard.

"*Mother Goddess, hear the words of your servant MacNaughten. Here, in your sacred circle, I invoke the threefold law and the law of light.*"

A crack of lightning rent the air causing the earth to tremble beneath their feet and Mac's eyes popped open. He tipped his head back as the ferocious power tore through him, darkness danced before his eyes.

Val watched in astonishment as several of Mikhail's followers were literally thrown from the circle as Mac called to the guardians. The wind tore at their clothing and tossed them down the icy hill, their shrieks fading in the rising storm. Val glanced at the remaining vampires as they clung to the stones. Cassiopeia and Edward were huddled by the south stone, looks of abject horror on their faces. The child clung to the Albino's leg, sobbing wildly.

Mikhail stood at the foot of the altar, his hands clenched to the red stone, his eyes darting looks of rage at Mac, his lips curled into a feral snarl.

"I ask that you look into the hearts of those gathered here," Mac bellowed, power rolling off him in waves. *"Expel from this magickal place all who seek to covert your laws."*

A bolt of lightning rent the sky, striking the lintel of the east stone. Wild cries arose from several of the vampires as those who stood nearest the stones burst into flames. Panicked, the surviving vampires dispersed. Some ran for Mikhail while others ran outside the stone circle and down the hill.

Cassiopeia and Edward looked at each other uneasily.

"I will destroy you," Mikhail cried. He shook off the vampires that clung to his legs. "I will destroy you and all your kind."

Mac lowered his head and impaled Mikhail with his gaze. Val caught his breath, shock clutched at his heart. Mac's eyes were completely golden now and they glowed eerily. The sight of those glowing golden eyes gave even Mikhail a pause.

"You," Mac thundered, "have corrupted this sacred place and those who dwelled in it. You have perverted the power of the Goddess to do evil and you see not what you do. You do not see the crime you have perpetrated in this, the holiest of places." He lifted his eyes to the heavens and the black clouds that circled in the sky. "I ask that you use me, Goddess, as your weapon against evil. Drive this darkness from the circle of light and restore harmony here."

The dark clouds parted and a beam of brilliant sunshine shone down on the altar illuminating Mac and Jennifer. Mac flung his arms out to his side, and the wind caught the old wool of his cape, parting the folds.

The Sun glowed on Mac's bare chest and the pendant seemed to expand before Val's eyes. As if it were gathering energy, absorbing the power of the sun and the man who wore it. A golden glow surrounded Mac, expanding to include Jennifer. Mac suddenly jerked as a narrow beam of light blasted from the pendant, hitting Mikhail in the face.

Wild screams erupted as the vampire staggered back from the brilliant light. Clasping his hands over his face, he fell to the ground, writhing in agony. The remaining vampires scrambled away from him, running for the south portal and their freedom.

As the Albino clawed the child from his leg, Cassiopeia lurched to her feet. She ran to Mikhail's side as he shrieked and clawed at his face. The stench of burnt flesh filled the air. She grabbed one of Mikhail's arms and the Albino grabbed the other and they began to drag him from the circle.

Val got to his feet, intending to go after them when Alexandre grabbed his arm. He pointed to the altar.

The massive red stone trembled as if it were under some great pressure from the inside. Grabbing Alexandre's arm, the two men fought the rising wind in their journey to the altar. Jennifer's eyes were still closed, her hair ruffled and her coronet askew. Alexandre pulled her into his arms, careful to avoid the brilliant beam of light that still emanated from the stone around Mac's neck.

They struggled against the rising wind to the west stone as Fayne appeared with the child in his arms. Val and Alexandre placed Jennifer on the ground beside Renault, between the stones to protect her from the wind.

An ear-shattering crack rent the air as Mac's body gave a violent jerk. The light from the pendant hit the altar as he fell backward to the ground. The altar cracked down the center, exposing the raw insides. A thick red liquid ran from the cracks and spilled to the ground. The noxious scent of tainted blood filled the air as it pooled around the shattered rock.

"We have to get out of here," Alexandre shouted above the wind. "If we stay here, we die."

Val nodded. "Take them down. I will get Mac."

Alexandre nodded. Val helped him to his feet. Alexandre tossed Jennifer over one shoulder and took the child from Fayne. Val saw them off down the hill before helping Fayne grab Renault and heave him over one shoulder. Fayne started down the hill as Val turned to get Mac.

He lay unmoving a few yards from the destroyed altar. The pooling blood already surrounded his boots and was rapidly advancing toward his legs as if to devour him. Val ducked into the rising wind and struggled to his friend's side. Grabbing his hands, he dragged him toward the west portal and freedom.

The winds made it impossible for Val to make any good progress. By the time he reached the west stone, he was panting and Mac hadn't stirred. Gritting his teeth, he pulled Mac out of the circle as the winds increased. It was as if something did not want him to remove Mac from this place.

Frustrated, Val cried out, "If you truly are the Goddess and this is your chosen one, help me to save him." A gust of warm air, familiar and comforting wrapped around him. Infused with the scent of jasmine and something spicy, his breath caught in his throat.

Miranda?

The hillside gave out from underneath him and he and Mac fell. He wrapped his arms around the unconscious man, trying to save him from serious injury as they rolled down the hill. When they came to a stop at the bottom, Alexandre and Fayne were waiting for them. The wind was much calmer and only a light snow fell.

Shaken, he allowed Fayne to pull Mac from his battered arms.

"You came down that hill like a bat out of hell." Alexandre grinned. "Are you all right, my friend?"

Val nodded shakily. "Yeah, I think so. I thought for a minute we were dead."

"I thought so too. I looked up and saw you struggling then a flash of white light appeared and you fell down the hill." Alexandre shook his head. "I could have sworn I saw Miranda in that light."

Val grinned, his heart lightened. "I think you did, my friend. I think you did."

Epilogue

Four Months later

Jennifer wasn't the same woman she was before her kidnapping.

Mac paused in the doorway to watch the woman who'd stolen his heart. She stood at the corner of the deck, tossing breadcrumbs over the edge to the birds. A rainbow of colors moved over the grass as the birds squabbled over the bits and gulped them down greedily.

His heart leapt as he caught sight of the faint smile that flickered across her face. Mikhail had scarred her, and for a while, he'd thought irrevocably. She claimed she didn't remember anything from her abduction after being taken from the bedroom. But the shadows that lingered in her eyes told him that maybe she remembered something and it wasn't pleasant.

Little things about her had changed. She was terrified of storms. Where before she would've raced outside to embrace the fury of nature's wrath, thunder now sent her into a panic that would have her climbing into the closet for protection. She refused to go to bed in the nude. No matter how many times he undressed her and they made love, she would dress before she went to sleep. And she was always armed, even in the shower.

How long until she would feel safe again?

How long until they all felt safe?

Only when Mikhail is dead.

"What are you thinking?" Jennifer's voice broke into his thoughts.

He beheld her lovely face. "I was thinking how beautiful you are." He chuckled when she blushed. "And I was wondering where the pizza guy is. I'm starved."

"I don't know if I can spend all of eternity with a man who doesn't eat meat on his pizza." Her smile teased him.

He pushed away from the doorframe and snorted with laughter. "Well, that won't stop you from eating more than your share." He walked across the deck and pulled her into his arms. "Last week I had to fight you off to save my share. I'd have starved to death if I didn't."

Jennifer rolled her eyes. "Oh puh-leeze." She poked at his belly. "You have enough to live on for a while."

Mac looked down at his flat stomach. "I resent that remark, young lady. I have the body of a man one-tenth my age."

"You should give it back as he's probably looking for it by now." She snickered.

Mac grabbed her by the waist and spun her around against the deck rail. Before she could draw breath he pressed his body into hers, slipping a leg between her thighs. "Are you laughing at me?"

Jennifer grinned, trailing fingers down the ridges of his belly. "With all of my heart."

He blew a smacking kiss on her collarbone. She squealed and jerked in surprise, knocking the bag of crumbs off the railing to the grass below.

"Look what you made me do," she laughed.

He didn't spare the mess a glance. "The birds will clean it up." He rocked gently against her body, catching the spark of desire that leapt to life in the depths of her eyes. "All the little vampires are asleep in their coffins. What shall we do for the afternoon?"

Jennifer giggled, "Shai and Val do *not* sleep in coffins. They sleep in a bed like normal people do."

"Mmm," Mac lowered his head and kissed the shadowed valley between her breasts, losing himself in the scent of her skin. A faint crack of thunder had her tensing in his arms. He raised his head to see her gaze locked on the distant storm clouds. Pain pierced his heart at the expression of fear that streaked across her face. He caught her chin, turning her to him. "*Jo*, I'm sorry Mikhail hurt you. I kick myself everyday for leaving you alone that morning."

She shook her head. "I'm not going to lie to you. Mikhail did hurt me that day, and others too. I want to see him suffer for it. In the end he gave me you, and for that I will always be grateful to him."

Touched, Mac tucked her against his chest. "I do fear for the future, Jen. Mikhail is wounded. From what Val told me, he was possibly blinded. Mikhail is a wanted man and he is being pursued by many of the preternaturals. There is no telling what he will do."

Jennifer shivered. "What do you think will happen? He has invoked the law of seven, a direct challenge to the authority of the Council. What will happen to Alexandre?"

"If Mikhail can challenge Alexandre and win, he can take control of the Council regardless of his past actions. He will head the governing powers of the preternaturals including you and I. There are many out there who believe Alexandre's time of iron law is no more. They want freedom to create more creatures at will."

"Alexandre wants what is best for us all," she objected. "The last thing we need is a massive influx of new vampires running around."

"He is a fair man, and a hard man. On himself and others. All we can do now is wait until Mikhail resurfaces and until then, we have to try and keep everyone safe and accounted for. Especially Maeve."

"Poor Maeve, she's been through so much. What will happen to Fayne and Renault?"

"Fayne has taken in the Albino's child." Mac chuckled. "I don't think he ever thought he would be a father at this late date."

"The child is a mortal?"

"Yes. He was sorely abused at the hands of Edward. Fayne said the child has some rather unusual psychic gifts. The Albino used him as an interpreter, since he was mute. As for Renault, no one has seen him since he left here a few months ago. Bliss says that if he doesn't reappear within a few months she will go after him."

Jennifer shook her head. "So many ruined lives, all for what?"

"Power, prestige, the ability to govern those weaker." Mac kissed her throat. "Men have killed for less."

"Mikhail doesn't realize this but he is the weakest of them all." Jennifer's fingers tangled in his hair. "What about you, my high priest, what shall you do?"

He kissed the tender skin of her inner breast, eliciting a sigh. "I think I shall study the old ways and make love to my woman."

Jennifer chuckled. "Your woman?"

He smiled and nipped at her skin, his nose brushing the Sun. "My wench? My old lady, my..."

"I am no one's *wench*." She laughed and punched him lightly on the shoulder. "Don't you forget that."

"So what should I call you?" He pulled back to look her in the eye.

"How about Jennifer?" She grinned.

"How about Love Goddess?"

"I like the Goddess part..."

"How about heart of my heart?"

She stilled. "Sounds good to me," she rasped.

"Stay with me, Jennifer. Let me love you for eternity."

She shook her head and his heart nearly stopped. "You have that backward," she choked out, tears flooding her eyes. "Let me love you for an eternity, Mac. I love you so much it hurts right here," she placed her hand in the center of her chest.

Relief flooded through him and he pulled Jennifer against him. "I knew that even if you didn't." He kissed her forehead. "So, tell me something, does this mean you want to be on top?"

About the Author

J. C. Wilder lives in Westerville, Ohio where she's owned by a Japanese Akita named Severena and a really obnoxious Jack Russell Terrier named Copper Penny. She spends the majority of her time dusting her 6,000 books and staring at her blank computer screen in complete terror.

After six years working for CompuServe Inc., she's working as a Business Analyst for the State of Ohio. When not writing, she devotes much of her time to studying the medicinal uses of herbs and essential oils and howling at the moon.

You can write to her at wilder@jcwilder.com.

Books by J. C. Wilder

The Shadow Dweller Series: Volume 2

And in electronic format:

One With the Hunger
Retribution
Shameless
Redemption

and coming soon ... *Sins of the Flesh*

Available at www.LTDBooks.com